THE COWBOY TAKES A BRIDE

THE WYOMING MATCHMAKER SERIES
BOOK ONE

KRISTI ROSE

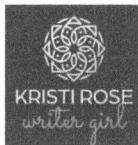

Vintage Housewife Books

PO BOX 842

Ridgefield, Wa 98642

www.kristirose.net

Publisher's Note: This is a work of fiction. Names, characters, places, and incidents are a product of the author's imagination. Locales and public names are sometimes used for atmospheric purposes. Any resemblance to actual people, living or dead, or to businesses, companies, events, institutions, or locales is completely coincidental.

Book Layout © 2017 Vellum

Cover Design © 2023 The Killion Group

Edited by: CDM Editing

The Cowboy Takes A Bride/ Kristi Rose. _-- 1st edition Special Edition with images_

ACKNOWLEDGMENTS

There is no possible way I could put a book together with the support, patience, and guidance of a host of people.

My family: For tolerating my irrational fear of bears and understanding why I don't want to sleep near the wall of a tent. And also sleep by the bear spray. Eryn Scott, G.L. Snodgrass, Frankie Love, editor- Paige Christian, my friends Chris Wood, Ryan Nix, and author Katie O'Connor who answered ranching question. Piper Davenport who fielded all my horse questions. Any error is mine and not theirs.

I have some amazing beta readers who deserve more than the eternal thanks I offer them: Melissa, Joni, and Darlene.

Thanks for all the words of encouragement. This 'making - your-dreams-come-true' stuff is hard but you all make is fun THANKS!!

XOXOXO

Kristi

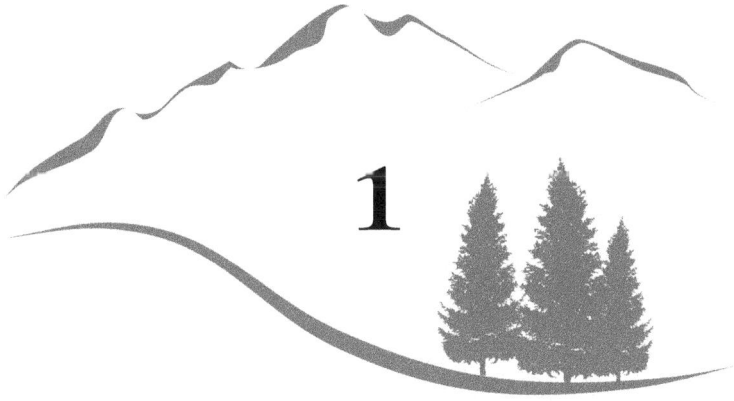

1

When old man Brady brushed up against her, using the contact as an opportunity to slide his hand around her thigh to cup her butt, Meredith Hanover was positive one of two things would happen.

She was either going to vomit the petit fours and hors d'oeuvres of tonight's charity event all over his tux or knee him in the groin.

Maybe both.

Oh, how she wished she could do *something*. Meredith swallowed hard, forcing back the bile that had risen, and stepped away, scanning the room for her father. If she made a scene, if she insulted the man Father hoped would soon merge his bank with Father's brokerage company, there would be hell to pay.

Why couldn't he have left her alone? She'd selected a quiet corner by a plant as her cover and was attempting to enjoy the profiteroles, her dessert plate thankfully hiding a brochure that someone—she couldn't recall who—had thrust at her at the dessert table. Inside the folded paper contained the outline of the next charity and likely her next obligation. Tonight's charity event not even over and already someone was planning another. It wasn't about doing good; it was about looking good. Looking important and being seen. She could hear their requests in her head. She really must be on the board they'd said. They couldn't do it without her. Yet, they'd done just as well before she got involved.

The brochure had been the instigator for the initial flashes of a headache.

Then Brady had infiltrated her hidey-hole spot and pinched her rear.

Behind her right eye, a sharp stabbing pain began to pulse.

She should have stayed in the open. He'd have never been so bold had she not been behind the potted plant.

She thrust her dish at Beady-eyed Brady. "I'm not feeling well."

He took the dish and leered. "I can take you to my home. Your father would approve."

Meredith covered her mouth and spun on her heels. Her goal was to reach the nearest ladies room as quickly as she could without breaking into a run.

Were there other people in the world that hated their lives as much as she did?

For what had to be the millionth time, she wished her life were different. She craved a miracle that would change everything.

If given the chance at one wish, Meredith was certain most people would ask for three more wishes. Not Meredith, she would be content with the one. That was all she needed to change her life. One simple wish. The trick came in how she would word said request.

There would be no asking for freedom. It wasn't specific enough. Asking for freedom from her father was likely too vague as well.

No, she would have to be right on point. She'd have to ask for a new life in a certain town with a great job. Maybe running a bookstore or being a teacher. She did have her degree in education, after all. Though, if that didn't work, she'd clean houses or work with animals, having always loved horses. Anything had to be better than what she did. Eavesdropping for her father was not an occupation or a purposeful life.

While managing to avoid all eye contact, Meredith wove through the crowd, circumventing her father, her focus on the ladies' room. Her teeth clenched together with hopes of holding back both the headache and nausea, she pushed the door open then slipped through the narrow opening, anxious for the door to close behind her. Blissfully, she noted the room was empty. Afraid she might still be sick, Meredith locked herself in a stall and waited, hoping the quiet would help her headache recede.

One wish. That's all she needed.

Meredith knew there'd be some nuance she'd forget to consider with that one wish. A distinction small enough it would easily be overlooked but significant enough she would end up with her "freedom," but living a life just as unfulfilling, uneventful, and sadly as heartbreaking as her current one.

Therefore, she concluded, even if she found a genie in a bottle, her life would not improve, and wishing things would change was never going to be enough. Action would be required on her part. It was up to her to take back her freedom.

How did the saying go? Freedom doesn't come free. Apparently not in any situation. Was she willing to pay the price? Looking from the outside, her life appeared cushy. After all, she was a resident of Victors Club, one of the richest suburbs outside Dallas-Fort Worth. Nothing said "winner" more than a postal code that deemed it so. Oh, and the three-quarter-of-a-million dollar starter homes. Her father's home, a brick two-story

McMansion with a chauffeur, a cook, and a housekeeper was a dream for most people. Who wouldn't want that?

All these people around her, but no one to really talk with. All the money to make life enjoyable, but the marble and steel decor of her father's home made her feel cold and breakable. All those advantages, but none for her. She was only permitted to go and do as much as her father's leash would allow. Sure, he thought she had everything. Pretty dresses and fancy shoes to wear to charity events. What more could she want?

What more indeed. Simply contemplating her life made the pain behind her eyes flare.

She braced her hand against the stall wall, not caring if her forced yoga breathing sounded odd or out of place. Giving into the oncoming headache would be far worse. These events did this to her every time. Bad Breath Brady made them come on quicker.

It was hard to make conversation and "keep her ears open" like her father demanded when she was doing everything in her power to not lie on the floor, cover her eyes with her arm, and fade to black. That was the best way to deal with a painful onslaught poorly named a benign migraine. It should be called "sledgehammer headache" or "slow death."

Her hand shook when she raised her arm to cover her eyes. The paper she'd forgotten she was holding drew her attention when it flapped and crinkled.

She peeked at it from under her arm.

Youth Village of Dallas. A local orphanage and treatment center for kids. It was an admirable charity in all aspects. Who didn't want to help parentless children? Who didn't want to give them clothes and toys they would not normally receive?

Meredith Hanover, that was who.

Oh, sure, she wanted to help, just as much as the rest of them. She was not even remotely that black-hearted. She rather liked the idea of being present when the kids got their gifts. That would be far lovelier than these sterile, extravagant money-wasting banquets. She'd done her share last year, her first year with the charity. She'd done so well she'd exceeded the established goal by an additional eighty thousand dollars. Her colleagues, a term she used loosely since they were her mother's friends, had closed the event with a stunning gala and awarded Meredith Woman of the Year. Something her mother had also achieved during her short life before her unexpected death. Meredith had come away from the event with additional pressure from her father, her first migraine, and never seeing the face of one kid who would benefit.

Crumbling the paper, Meredith dropped it in the toilet and flushed.

"I'm an awful person," she mumbled, rubbing her temples, and squinting as she watched the crumbled ball swirl around the bowl before disappearing.

"I highly doubt that," said the person in the stall next to her.

Meredith hadn't heard anyone come into the ladies' room. She knew she should apologize but said instead, "It's true."

Ducking her head to rest against the cold metal of the stall, she closed her eyes once more and gave a fruitless effort to mentally bat away the pain. The headache was in full bloom.

"I've known you a long time, Meredith Hanover, and being a horrible person is never a phrase that's associated with your name. Ever. Quite the opposite, actually."

Meredith tried to place the voice, but as the throbbing increased, her awareness decreased. "That's because I have you all fooled. The thought of helping orphaned children has sent me to the restroom hiding." Never mind Brady's wandering hands.

"Funny, it did the same to me as well. Perhaps it's because we, in our own way, are orphans ourselves."

Curiosity getting the best of her, Meredith slid along the wall of the stall until she came to the door and turned the latch, releasing it. Stepping back, she let it slowly swing open while she lifted her arm to shade her eyes. She searched the room for the woman who was speaking.

"Migraine?"

The lights dimmed, she assumed by the other woman in the room, and Meredith took in her first steady breath of relief. "Yes."

"Come sit."

She felt a hand gently take her elbow and guide her to a plush bench in the waiting room of the ladies' restroom. Because, even here, at the Museum of Fine Art, women needed a place to gossip privately. Many deals were made while lipstick was being reapplied and hair resprayed.

"Thank you." She leaned back against the bench and slowly moved her arm to her side. The lack of direct light was a relief of the highest degree. The only thing that would be better would be to fall into bed and sleep it off.

Through squinty eyes, she stared up at her benefactress. "Sabrina Holloway?" She knew of the woman more than she knew the actual person, though her mom had spoken kindly of her since they'd served on many boards together.

Sabrina eased down next to her. "It's been a while since our paths crossed. These days I think the only event we chair together is the fundraiser for the Veteran's home."

"That had been my mom's favorite." Meredith forced herself to think of something other than her mother or else she'd likely break down in tears. With pain akin to that of the migraine, each trip down memory lane was powerfully heavy with remorse and laced with what-ifs. But was the grass ever greener? Entertaining those fantasies was an awful endeavor that left her feeling more alone and hopeless than usual. She'd rather push back the sun than journey down the what-if path.

"Of all the vets, those old, cranky world-war vets are my

favorite as well. I could give every last charity up but that one."
Sabrina sighed. "It's harder seeing the young guys come in. And
with no families."

"Heartbreaking even." She leaned her head against the wall,
her eyes closed. "Do you ever get tired of it all Sabrina?"

"All the time. But I take a vacation or try something new—a
hobby if you will—and reset. There are worse activities one can
be engaged in."

Meredith lifted one lid a smidge. "I'm not sure there is. At
least for me there isn't. Making constant pleasantries is
wearing."

"You need to get away." Sabrina sat next to her and held out
her hand, palm up, presenting two small capsules. "Take these."
She held a cup of water in her other hand.

"Will they put me out of my misery?" Meredith mumbled
before scooping up the pills.

"Temporarily, I hope. You really should think of taking some
time away."

Meredith's nod was subtle, as motion tended to make her
stomach roll. "The last time I got away was...eight years ago."
Man, she sounded pathetic. But it was hard to sound anything
else when admitting the last time your family went on vacation
was the trip when your mother died.

"Ah." Sabrina didn't need to offer anything further. She
knew. Everyone knew really. Her mother was greatly missed.
Meredith was a shallow replacement for a woman so beloved. It
wasn't that she hadn't tried, but had her father not demanded
she participate in every single charity situation imaginable that
he felt would benefit him, had he not forced her into her mother's social shoes, she might have found happiness in the work.
But when every aspect of a person's life was controlled by
another, Meredith was certain pleasure couldn't be found. At
least she'd never come across it.

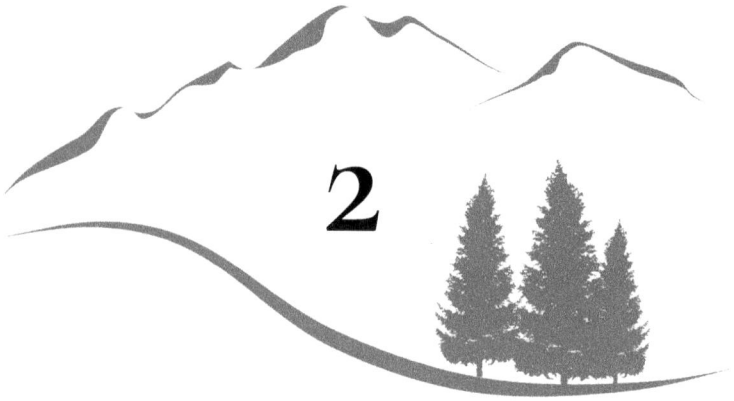

2

Sabrina Holloway knew how to read people. After all, she learned from an expert. Her daddy was a man whose easy manner and laid-back approach belied his scrutiny of others. It made him an envied poker player, not one to lose often, and when he did, they wondered if it was intentional. His honed skills gave him the foresight of impending trouble and the ability to see when she was about to tailspin into a personal crisis as she often did back then, as teens were prone to do.

Thankfully, he passed that trait onto her.

And what she was reading from the tall yet slight woman was not that she had a headache—any moron could ascertain that by Meredith's actions alone—but something far more heartbreaking. Meredith was what? Six...no, eight years younger than Sabrina and looked nothing like a wealthy twenty-four-year-old single woman in a modern world. Instead she had the presence of a matron, a spinster, to use the antiquated word. Meredith's mother, Rebecca, a woman Sabrina had often looked to for fashion and diplomacy guidance, had dressed tastefully but still showcased her wealth and beauty. Meredith's midnight blue evening gown, cut to accentuate the assets of any woman was worn plain. Almost matronly. Her neckline, the only skin showing other than her arms, was bare. Not one jewel glistened drawing the eye to her. A rarity among the Texas uber-rich where cleavage, big hair, and large gems were the norm and a measuring tool for status. Sabrina herself was sporting ten-carat teardrop earrings and had called them "these old things" more than once tonight.

No, the slump of Meredith's shoulders and the defeated curve to her spine as she sat forward spoke volumes, hinted to a story that was about more than headaches. Sabrina searched for possible reasons to explain the Meredith that sat before her. Was it more than the loss of her mother? "You're like her, you know. Your mother."

Meredith's eyes glistened. "It seems as if she's been gone forever."

"I feel the same way about my father. He passed a few years before your mother."

"I'm sorry," Meredith whispered.

Sabrina nodded. "Life without him still feels wrong. I suppose I'm still adjusting to my new normal."

Following a derisive snort, Meredith said, "If this is the new normal, no thanks. I can't bear to live like this much longer." But her own words broke her, and the unshed tears released and coursed down her face.

Turning toward Meredith, Sabrina wrapped her arm around her and held her close. She certainly was in need of some kindness and love. "Oh, honey. What could be so awful that can't be fixed? I can't imagine your momma would be happy to hear you talk like that."

Eyes large, Meredith said, "My life is awful. What small number of friends I do have is starting to dwindle. They're all getting married and having babies, and I'm here being a tool for my father's business gains. A means for him to gather information."

"I don't mean to sound callous, but have you told him no?" Sabrina was certain she knew what the answer would be, but she needed to hear it from Meredith. There were two kinds of people. Those that let life happen to them, and those that made a life. Her instincts told her which one Meredith was, but she needed to be sure.

"Honestly, I've stopped. The more I refuse, the tighter he tries to control me. He's taken away any source of money other than one credit card. I tried to get a job a few years back, right after graduating college, but he called the superintendent of the school district. I'm a teacher—well, I would be if my father allowed me to work. Anyway, he called his poker buddy, and I've been essentially blackballed from this district and some of the outliers." Meredith's breathing was ragged.

Sabrina rubbed her back. "What does he want from you?"

"I stopped asking that question as well. He used to say it was to keep me safe, but now he either glares at me or ignores me. After momma died, I thought it meant he was scared to lose me, too, but if that's the case, then his fear has gone so far off the rails, I have no idea the direction in which normal resides."

"So you have no money or a way out." This was the telling moment for Sabrina. Now she would know if her services would be needed or not.

Meredith pulled away slightly, her gaze darting around the room before returning her focus on something over Sabrina's shoulder.

Sabrina knew to wait, her only action to hand Meredith a tissue. Answers to questions were revealed if there was an opportunity, and talking or pushing Meredith into the moment was not how it was done.

"I have a plan," she said a few moments later.

"Plans are marvelous. When they come together."

"I won't live like this much longer," Meredith said with determination, then clutched her head. The force of her words likely had increased the pounding in her head.

Meredith was made of sterner stuff, probably from carving out something of a life while under the authoritarian thumb of her father.

"If I can help in any manner, please let me know." Sabrina handed Meredith a plain white business card made from textured cardstock. The word HOPE was embossed in silver on the card, the light making it sparkle. Meredith ran her thumb over it. Below, in navy blue lettering were the only other words on the card: Sabrina's name and phone number.

Meredith flipped it over a few times before looking back at Sabrina. "Hope?"

Sabrina pulled her arm from around the girl's shoulder so she could face her. "Yes, I give people the prospect of an alternative. Hopefully one that brings them happiness and love."

Meredith folded the tissue over her fingers. "How so?"

This is where things got tricky for Sabrina. "I'm a matchmaker." Yes, that much was true. But the rest would be told in due course.

"And you think setting me up on blind dates will solve my problem? I can barely get away from the house to shop at a bookstore. How am I to go on a date? Meet him at something like this? No. I want a different life for sure, but I don't see how dating is going to make that happen. Truthfully, I don't see men in my future anytime soon. I want freedom. When I start over—" She clasped a hand over her mouth, the white card still in her hand.

"Don't worry. I won't say anything. You plan to start over how? Where can you run where your father won't find you? You'll need a new identity."

Meredith shredded the tissue. "I know," she whispered.

"Has it come to that?"

Meredith nodded. "I believe so. Getting away is something I think about all the time."

"How are you saving the money? A new identity isn't cheap."

"I know." Meredith raised her Jimmy Choo-clad foot and lifted the skirt of her dress.

"Clever," Sabrina said. Meredith was selling her clothes and shoes. "Consignment shops?"

"Yes, my father thinks I've been donating to the Junior League charity auctions and such. I use those engagements to my advantage."

"Brilliant. Like your mother. I hope it's working."

"It's slow, but with the wedding season coming up, I hope by fall I will have enough funds." Though she said it as if it was exciting news, her face spoke of the fear she was feeling and likely, Sabrina surmised, afraid to acknowledge.

"Can you make it to fall? I'm guessing those migraines will only get worse with time if something doesn't change soon."

"I have to make it until autumn. What other choice do I have?"

Sabrina tapped her nail to the card Meredith was holding. "I'm not saying I'm the right choice. I'm saying I can give you an alternative. You see, I'm not setting people up on dates. I'm essentially, for lack of a better, more contemporary term, a mail-order bride service." She held up her hand at Meredith's gasp, hoping to stop any disagreement. "Every date a person goes on is an attempt to find their life partner. I help speed that process up. I can offer you a new life, Meredith. A new life as yourself and not some identity you bought online. How do you propose to work? Are you buying a new education as well? What will you do if your father catches you?"

Meredith let her head fall back against the cushion. "How does trading a controlling father for a potentially controlling husband give me freedom?" She massaged her temples. "It doesn't."

"Running, hiding, changing your name? That gives you freedom?" Sabrina was not challenging Meredith's plan, only hoping to help her reason through it, so she kept any skepticism from her tone.

A single tear slid down Meredith's face.

"If you've thought this through entirely, this running, I'm here to help you any way I can. I may even know someone who can help get you the new identity. But I can offer you an alternative. A real life. A husband that will protect you. Give you safety and security. Someone you can be yourself with. Create a life together that you want. All this can be done without your father knowing anything. You could escape him." Each time Sabrina gambled on someone, she was aware of what was at stake. If Meredith told the wrong person, say her father, he could make life difficult for Sabrina. Possibly affect her standing within the community she'd grown up in, and that was something Sabrina would rather avoid. Being a matchmaker required anonymity since many of her clients were running from something. Her company wasn't illegal by any means, and she had a success rate of ninety-five percent. That was better than any of those online services. But all it took was one naysayer—a heretic to bring down her business.

"Escape him yet take on an entirely new problem." Meredith snorted her derision.

"This would be on *your* terms. It's an option. You have my card. Should you change your mind, please call." With that, Sabrina stood. She clasped her hands before her and stared down at Meredith's pretty, tear-stained face. Sabrina owed it to Rebecca, Meredith's mother. Rebecca had always been nice to her and had been one of the few people to go above the standard condolences when Sabrina's father had died. She'd come by often and called to check on Sabrina.

"Picture what you want from life, Meredith. Who you want to be. Ask yourself if you are ready to give up Meredith Hanover." Sabrina wiped a lone tear from Meredith's cheek. "Good luck, honey." Then she walked away.

3

The sun-kissed and snow-capped mountains reaching into the bright blue Wyoming sky was a vision Jace Shepard never tired of. Sitting on the top of the fence, he wrapped his ankles through the wooden slats, brought his hands to rest on his upper thighs, and paused to take it all in.

The view left him breathless. Every time.

The six years he'd spent away at college and interning with the beef industry had been the longest of his life. This ranch, this landscape, and its lifestyle were in his blood. It made up the very fibers of his core. He would never leave if he didn't have to. Heck, he planned on being buried here like all his ancestors who were the original homesteaders and had claimed the land by parking their wagons.

Now the deluded ideas of a crazy old man were threatening to take it all away.

It was true that Jace lived and breathed the ranch. No point arguing that. That was why part of him understood where his father was coming from when he told Jace to square away his personal life. A man liked to leave an imprint somewhere along the journey of his life, and Jace was no different. Like his father and his grandfather, he'd always imagined his mark would be in passing down the family business to his son or daughter. A tradition and lifestyle he was proud of.

But—from the words of his single-minded father—time was getting away, and he was right. Hell, his thirties had snuck up on him, and the prospect of settling down was starting to look slim. The odds of finding the old grizzly he suspected was hunting his herd and convincing him to hunt elsewhere look more probable.

Jace snorted as he thought about *that* conversation at the dinner table.

Keep the gun close by, dear. There's a grizzly hunting these parts lately.

Not much of an enticement to be sure.

Jace was no fool. He knew living in remote Wyoming would require certain compromises on anyone's behalf. Winters could be rough, days without power. It was an isolated existence. Sometimes he went long stretches without seeing others. All reasons why finding a wife was darn near impossible, and the few times he had managed to match up with someone, the remoteness killed whatever interest they had in him. Even the local girls couldn't bear the isolation, or those that could, had already been snatched up. It took a special person to be a rancher's wife. It wasn't all big cars and large diamonds as TV liked to portray.

Settle down with a wife, or Pop's would give Jace's controlling share of the ranch to some nitwit cousin—who, last time Jace checked, was obsessed with Pokemon Go. All because Pops wanted Jace and his sister, Willow, to have lives beyond Three Peaks Ranch, and his father was stubborn enough to stick to his threats. Lucky for Willow, she had plenty of time.

"Hey, man." Tucker Williams came up beside Jace and leaned over the fence, one foot resting on the lower bar. "If it's all right with you, I'm gonna split and see Mandy before she heads out to her book club."

Jace glanced at his childhood friend. They'd found more trouble than was healthy for kids, but together had managed to survive, and the process cemented a lifelong friendship. "Yeah, sure man. Have a good night." Jace bumped Tuck's fist. "Tell Mandy to have fun with her book friends."

Tuck rolled his eyes. "Did I tell you she wants me to read the books too, so we can discuss them? Like she doesn't get enough chatting in at her club."

Jace snorted. Tuck discussing a book was as far-fetched as picturing bear negotiations.

"She also said that Cassidy Martin is still single if you want her to set you two up." Tuck ducked his head, likely hiding a smile.

Jace shook his head. "She scares me. Always has, ever since she clocked your brother on the playground in third grade. I haven't seen a right hook with that accuracy since. Tell Mandy thanks but no thanks."

"Listen, I know it ain't my business, but I heard what your Pops said the last time he was here. About getting a wife. And uh... Heck, man, this is awkward." Tuck kicked the fence. "You want any help with finding one, I might be able to assist. I got a couple girl cousins in Bozeman that aren't hard to look at." Tuck wiped at his face and looked away at the mountain before them.

Jace didn't know what to say. He knew his friend preferred not to get involved with affairs of the heart, so to make such an offer was a true test to the depth of his friendship.

"What makes you think I'm gonna give in to the demands of a crazy old man?" Jace tried to joke, but they both knew he'd do just about anything his Pops asked him to do, even if he hadn't threatened his share of the ranch. Knowing that his father's days were limited, his body deteriorating from ALS, only made Jace that much more eager to please. If Pops needed Jace settled before he died, then so be it.

"Your Pops has been good to me. After mine passed, yours stepped in. If he had told me he wanted to see me get settled and happy before he passed, I'd have run out and taken as many wives and adopted as many kids as it took to make him happy. Regardless of the law."

Jace laughed. Yeah, he felt the same way. In fact, it's all he'd been thinking about in the four weeks since his dad made the request.

I need to know you're happy before I go. Nothing has filled my life as completely as your mom, you, and your sister. I want that for you. You understand what I'm saying, son? Why I'm doing this?

But how does one concoct a wife from thin air? If he went into town and down the list of single girls, more than half would be too young, a third too old, and the rest like Cassidy Martin were not the sort of girl he pictured himself with for the entirety of his life.

Or even for the bit of time his father had left. Getting a temporary bride would require a special someone who would be willing to let go when the time was right.

Though "borrowing" a wife temporarily was likely the best plan, Jace worried it might be borrowing too many problems. "I'm taking care of it, Tuck. But thanks for being so willing to sacrifice your cousins." Jace leaned forward and rested his chin on his palm.

"That's all right. Let me know if I can help."

Jace grunted. "You better get home to your pretty wife."

"Yeah, she gets upset when we don't get some time together. I guess she knows the schedule's about to get hectic so she's trying to get in what she can." Tuck shrugged. "You know how they are."

"Then you better get along." Truth was Jace didn't know how

"they" were. His last serious girlfriend was during his internship. She'd taken one look at the ranch, calculated the distance to the nearest Target, more than 100 miles away, and bailed after the first day. Since then, he'd kept a few "friends with benefits" on speed dial when in town for auctions or such. There were no misunderstandings in those situations. They were clear he wouldn't change, and he understood they had no interest in a life with him in the wilds of Wyoming. None of them were impressed that Yellowstone lie directly to the West, that his land shared peaks with the national park.

"See ya tomorrow." Tuck cuffed him on the back before turning to leave.

When the horn on Tuck's beat-up pickup blasted three short honks, Jace didn't look back but gave an over-the-head wave. After the slapping of the tires on the wet earth faded, Jace reached into the front pocket of his weathered jeans and pulled free the folded slip of paper.

It was a silly note from his sister that had planted the idea of borrowing a wife and made him call Sabrina. Jace scanned the sheet, reading his slanted scroll quickly, his gaze only stopping on his sister's bubbly script.

1. Fix west fence near stream
2. Weed out unhealthy herd
3. Parse out stock for the exchange
4. Prep for summer births from Heifers
5. Ranch vehicles need service
6. *Find a wife and be happy*

It was the word *find*, like he could do an Internet search and be provided a solution. Which in his case, all he had to do was dial up his college friend. It bothered him that Willow had written *be happy*. He was under the impression that he *was* happy. Yeah, it could get lonely out here, especially in the winter, but it all came back to compromises. Once spring hit full-on, he'd be going non-stop without a second thought about if he had someone to sit next to him on the fence or a helpmate who'd heat up his dinner on those cold rainy days that he'd be forced to stay out in the deluge. He wasn't so lonely he took for granted he had a place to come home to and a hot meal, even if it was canned soup. He'd seen people with less, and he wasn't about to sit here feeling sorry for himself because he required a wife and his sister thought he was unhappy. These were obstacles he needed to find a way around.

Jace was a simple man. He never asked for much and was grateful for what he had. He needed to remember that. Swiping his hand over his face, he followed it with a heavy sigh. Lately, he'd asked for a whole heck of a lot. He'd asked for a cure for his father. He'd asked for more time. It was plain greedy to ask for a wife, too, even if he did it under the guise of making a dying man happy.

The phone in the breast pocket of his thick Carhartt jacket vibrated. Jace smiled wryly. For all the remoteness of the location, he had cell service out in the field but spotty service in his house. How was that for technology?

A glance at the screen told him Sabrina was calling.

"Rina," he said, using the old nickname he'd given her in college. "I was just thinking about you. How's tricks?"

"You know I hate when you say that."

Her irritation was a pretense. Experience and a lengthy, true friendship taught him that. "Your call brings a smile to my face." They never spent time bickering about the insignificant.

"That's how you should start a conversation, Jace. That makes a woman all warm and soft."

Jace laughed and wished, not the for first time, he could have made something spark between himself and Sabrina. But nothing comes from nothing, and even sparks require an accelerant of some making.

"How's Pops?" She never failed to inquire.

"Holding his own. Hates not being out here doing the day-to-day stuff, but he knows that getting through this therapy will help maintain a quality to his life he wants."

"I'm sorry the trial drug didn't work. Did Willow go back to school?"

Jace wiped one eye with the corner of his palm. They all were sorry. Real sorry and heartbroken.

Willow, was finishing up her master's degree at the University of Washington. "Yeah, she keeps talking about transferring back here, but they don't have her program, and Mom won't hear of it. She only has six months left."

Which felt like nothing when you didn't have a ticking clock to face every day. If he should get 180 more days with his father, he'd drop to his knees and give thanks. He no longer had faith in what the doctors said. The disease seemed to have a mind of its own, accelerating faster than they'd expected.

"I hope I get some time in with your Mom and Pops while I'm there."

"You're coming? To what do I owe this honor?" Last time she came to the ranch was to hide out and nurse her broken heart. Jace couldn't think of that clown, Lawton, without wanting to punch him in the face. Dammit if the man hadn't caught them off guard. Spending four years being Lawton's roommate hadn't prepared Jace for witnessing Lawton's lilied-liver, chicken-butt cowardice first hand. That was Lawton Jones. Coward of the first order. Standing in his tux, throwing his belongings into his car, and begging Jace to tell Sabrina he was sorry. He just couldn't go through with it.

"This time it's for business. I found you a wife." There was no misunderstanding her matter-of-fact tone. The call had gone from friendship to business owner and client.

Jace's thoughts became a jumbled mess. A wife? Would she bail after the first week? How would Pops react?

"Did you hear me?" Sabrina's probe was gentle.

He grunted.

"But here's the caveat. I know when you called me it was more out of desperation to make Pops happy, but it's time you made yourself happy, too, Jace. You haven't been the same since What's-Her-Dummy left you."

"She has a name." Truth was he didn't like to say it either.

"Yes, and drives a minivan with those family stickers on the back. She has two kids and a dog. She's very happy reigning over the Junior League and Daughters of the American Revolution."

"So you've seen her?" It wasn't that he ached to know more about his old girlfriend. He no more missed her than he would that grizzly should it leave. But he missed the idea of her. Of the dreams he had when they were together.

"Unfortunately, I have. Do you think you're open to a little happiness?"

He'd have to be a nut to say no. "Sure."

"But it won't be instant. I can't just drop Meredith off, see you two get hitched, wave my magic love wand, and the two of you will live happily ever after. You're going to have to work for it."

He shrugged. "Sure," he repeated. He wasn't by nature a mean or poorly tempered man, and adding another female to the fold should be easy enough. If she knew what she was getting into, then what could go wrong?

That was a dumb question. Tons could go wrong.

"Sure," Sabrina mimicked. "You're going to have to do all those things you're afraid of. Things like share a bit of yourself, go on dates, ask her questions about herself, all those things you profess to have no time for. All the things you've avoided doing since Dumb-Dumb left."

"I'm not a Neanderthal." His mother would box his ears if he so much as thought of being rude. Yet, go on dates? What would they talk about? His life was nothing but cows and bulls.

Shit, nothing like realizing you were a boring-ass person. He didn't even have a hobby.

"No, you aren't a Neanderthal. You're a wonderful, caring man with a good sense of humor. You deserve to be happy, my friend, and I found the person who can give that to you if you're willing."

Jace grunted. This here was the real deal. He'd called her in a moment of weakness, moments after the doctor told them the clinical trial of new meds wasn't working and had exacerbated the symptoms. What they feared the most, losing time with Pops, had happened.

"Are you sure this is the right thing to do? Can't she just come out and pretend for a while? Who is this woman? Did you say her name was Meredith? What if she hates it here? What if we don't connect?" Because if he couldn't be honest with his friend who was now his matchmaker and who had, ironically, begged him not to date his ex when he'd first floated the idea back in their sophomore year, who could he be honest with?

"Meredith will need a gentle touch and some time. I'm not trying to liken her to an animal, but she needs the same tenderness you've shown those skittish horses of yours."

"Rina, this doesn't sound like the best—"

"Listen to me, Jace Shepard. You know I'm good at what I do."

This was, without question, true. He could list the friends she'd set up that were in happy, fulfilling marriages. It was ironic that the person love had betrayed was so good in the matchmaking and marriage department.

"If there were two people in the world who needed each other more than you need Meredith and she needs you, I have yet to meet them. Ever. The minute I talked to her, I knew she was for you. She's a beautiful person, and her mother and I served on several committees. I considered her mother a friend, a mentor. I'm trusting you with her. I have faith you can give her everything that she needs, and therefore will get everything you need in return."

Jace didn't want to think about what that meant. These days, hope seemed to be an expensive commodity. "You used to be a friend of her mother's?"

"She passed."

Jace understood. He'd supported Sabrina when she grieved with the passing of her father. He was going through his own process now as he watched his father slowly fade away. The sadness that was bound to live in Meredith's heart would be something he might not be directly familiar with yet, but he'd soon come to understand.

"How old is she?" Because some girl expecting instant gratification in everything would not do.

"She's eight years younger than us."

He did the math in his head and whistled through his teeth. "That's young." A twenty-four year old would really have a hard time living this remotely. His sister was only a year younger and constantly complained about that lack of "everything" when she was home.

"She's not like you're imagining. This is it, Jace. I know with all that I am she's the one for you. Are you ready for what I'm offering?"

Maybe they could find a common bond to unite them, more than losing a parent, and find a companionship. He thought of his situation in terms of his father's health and not the "forever" marriage was defined by.

He'd sure like to sit on this fence with someone and share life with them. He'd settle for an easy friendship. Would it be hard to make friends with this woman? Shoot, he had lots of female friends. This would be no different. Ok, maybe a little different, but not much.

"When?" he asked, his gaze reading the line his sister wrote on the paper.

Find a wife and be happy

"Friday, ten o'clock. That cute little church in town. Wear something appropriate. I can't believe I have to tell you that."

"What does she look like? Maybe she's not my type. Maybe she could just stay here at the ranch to see if she likes it before—"

"No. That's not how this works. I've sent you a picture. Check your email. Regardless, you need a wife. Meredith needs a husband. Let's get down to business and meet each other's needs. We aren't playing here. This is for keeps."

For keeps.

Those two words forced him to sit up straight. He really should confess that *for keeps* wasn't something he thought was attainable. Not that he wouldn't take it, but he wouldn't expect it.

Think of Pops.

What harm was one little white lie? "OK," he said, his voice drifting away with the wind.

"I beg your pardon? What was that?"

He could hear the smile in her voice. "I said I'm in."

Sabrina laughed. "I'm actually very excited. Not only will this be the first wedding I've ever attended for one of my matches, but I'm past ready to see you happy."

"Do I meet you there? Want me to come to the airport or anything?"

"No, meet us there. Make sure you go down to the county

clerk and get the marriage license. I've emailed you all the docs you'll need."

"All right. Anything else?" He cataloged it like he did all his business transactions.

"Didn't you say you had family or something that worked at the clerk's office?"

"Yeah, a second cousin. Why?"

"Any chance they'd be willing to code the information into the system inaccurately?"

Jace straightened. This was starting to sound a little sketchy. He didn't need anymore trouble, thank you very much. He had enough with the day-to-day of the ranch.

"What are you getting me into Sabrina?" He'd walk away if he had to.

"I'm only trying to give her some time away from her father. Make it a little harder for him to find her."

"Am I going to have a problem with this father?"

"No, you'll be able to handle him. It's Meredith that needs to learn to do that, and distance and time will help her. I promise, when the time comes, her father won't be an issue."

She always made good on her promises, and no one could read people better than Sabrina Holloway. He'd seen that first-hand, with the exception of Lawton of course. But everyone fails sometime.

"You're sure about this, Rina?"

"Unequivocally."

"OK, see you in two days." He shook his head in disbelief, surprised at how willing he was being led into this nonsense. A matchmaker and a mail order bride. Who said times were changing?

"You'll thank me soon enough, my friend," Sabrina said before disconnecting.

Jace opened his email and found the one from Sabrina.

Attached was a grainy picture of a young woman's profile. Though he couldn't make out her face, the lighting was poor, there were several things he was able to see. The fancy evening gown, the casual elegance with how she held a champagne flute, and opulence surrounding her. She looked...too fancy for a Wyoming ranch.

Tucking the phone back into his coat pocket, he shook his head, debating on whether to cancel on Sabrina. He stared at the empty space next to him. Would she sit on the fence with him? Like his mom had done with Pops? Or would this place bore her like it had done with others? Only time would tell.

But for now, it was time for the farmer to take a wife. Or, in his case—the cattleman.

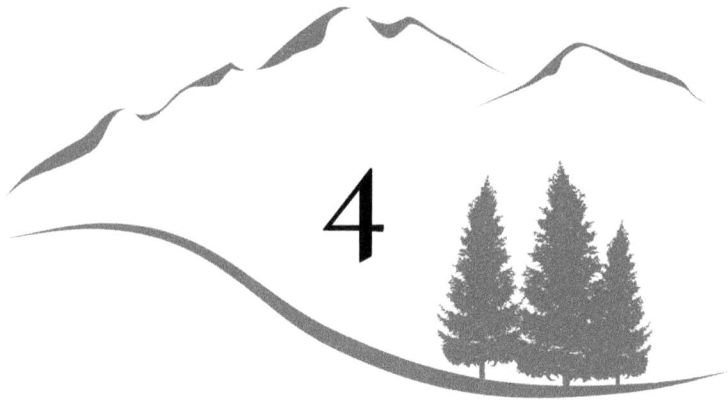

4

Pulling the cord on her window blinds, Meredith used slow, deliberate movements to block out the midday sun. She was desperate not to make a sound or stir the bubbling nausea in her belly. One sudden move or any loud noise, and it would release. Sighing with relief, albeit minuscule, she closed her heavy lids as she gently rested her head against the wall. She'd take her successes, however small, whenever and however she could get them. If she didn't get ahead of this headache, it would be a full-blown migraine before she knew it.

Who was she kidding? She was nearly at migraine status now. Sliding her cheek along the wall, she slowly turned toward her bed. Looking through one eye, she was able to make out the clock on her nightstand.

She had an hour. Maybe an hour and half before she was expected downstairs. A third evening event in less than five days was likely the culprit for her current state. But as this was an election year, the buzz regarding who would be running was high and, undoubtedly, her father wanted to ensure he was backing the right candidate.

It was Meredith's duty to listen, probe, and report back what the women were repeating. To glean out pillow talk. Doing so left Meredith with a desire to shower often and an ever-ready apology on her lips.

Oh no, it would certainly not do for Markus Hanover to be on the wrong side of this outcome, for he had too much at stake, depended too much on strong-arming others as a business tactic. To back the wrong person would result in a large dip in profit. Or so he liked to rant about these days.

She shuffled to her bed, as picking up her feet would require too much energy and jostle her stomach more than she'd like. She set the pillows up so she'd be upright when she got into bed. Lying down would be far too uncomfortable. Easing onto the bed, she managed to get herself into a comfortable position without losing her stomach contents.

Success!

She'd rest for a bit before forcing herself up to get ready. If her father hadn't said a million times how essential tonight was, she'd beg off. Plead if she must. But because tonight's event was hosting the cream of the crop of movers and shakers, Meredith knew her pleas would fall on deaf ears.

Letting her eyes drift closed, she tried to clear her mind of all the things that polluted it. Who did she want to be?

Ever since Sabrina had asked the question, Meredith had been trying to find the answer. When she took a close look at her life and her relationship with her father, she was unable to find any happiness, any brightness in the emptiness inside her.

Would she be able to live under a new identity, telling a story that wasn't her own? For the rest of her life? What if she met someone and wanted to marry him? Would tell him the truth? If not, could she sustain the lie? Truth was, she wasn't very good at subterfuge.

Just thinking about it made her already aching head pound harder.

Today, in the throes of the flashing, painful lights that intensified when her eyes were closed, waiting until autumn seemed like an eternity.

Taking deep breaths, Meredith tried to force a calmness over herself. She lightly massaged her temples, letting her mouth go slack, her breathing go shallow. She swallowed passed the nausea and let the ebbing darkness blissfully claim her.

A sudden banging, the loud sound reverberating through Meredith's head, pulled her from her sleep and forced her to jerk upright. Bile rose up her throat, its bitter taste only making her queasiness worse. When the bright overhead light went on, she ducked her head, covering her eyes with her hands.

"What are you doing?" her father bellowed.

Meredith was torn between continuing to cover her eyes or move to her ears as both his voice and the light were like an assault on her senses.

"I have a headache, Father." Her voice sounded rough, dry, but not without a pleading tone. "Could you please turn off the light?"

"Get up. We're late as it is, and you aren't even ready. Have you been sleeping all afternoon?"

She knew he was moving toward her by the sound of his heavy footsteps and could feel them reverberate around the room as they pounded against the wood floor.

When he stopped at her bed, she felt him loom over her. "I can't go. I'm not feeling well."

"Did you take any medicine? What about those pills Dr. Goodman gave you?" His tone was not of a concerned parent but was laced with irritation and frustration.

She'd seen him like this before. Soon he would spiral into anger and there would be no point in reasoning with him. Yet she tried anyway, hoping he was still merely irritated. "Those pills don't help, and they make me spacey."

"Meredith," he boomed. "I don't have time for this. Get up and get dressed. This is an important dinner. Lyle Brady is going, and he asked about you."

In for a penny, in for a pound her Mother had always said.

"Lyle Brady is an old man, Father. Didn't he graduate a year or two behind you in school?"

"He would still be a powerful ally to have on my side. The political climate is changing and—"

"No." She opened her eyes, knowing she needed to see his reaction, but the pain and energy required to do so was exhausting.

"No?" His voiced echoed through the room, forcing Meredith to wrap her arms around her head to block out the sound.

"I'm not going, and I will not be sold off to some old man to suit your business needs. What year is this anyway?" Hoping to steady her world, she let out a long exhale. Only, the churning in her stomach increased, the bile rising higher.

"Why can't you ever do as I ask?" he roared. "Just do as I say."

"Father, puh-p-please." She hated the begging, but she'd do it if it meant he would go away and let her be. It wasn't worth the effort to point out she'd done everything he'd asked, or commanded, since momma died. Being the daughter he wanted had never been and wouldn't ever be enough.

He grabbed her by the wrist, her hair getting caught up in the grasp as well, and jerked her from the bed. "Enough of this Meredith."

But the sudden movement was too much for her, and she recoiled, twisted away, and retched on the floor. Tears stinging her eyes, she fell to her knees and tried to catch her breath, control the heaving. Her wrist stung from his abrasive grasp, and her head ached from where her hair had been pulled from the scalp.

Never had he touched her like this. Yes, her father was a calloused, single-minded, distant person who'd come to her birthday parties when she was younger, but stood in the background. Even so, he'd taught her how to drive a car the year before her mother died, and for all his flaws, he'd never been aggressive. But the longer her mother was dead, the more bitter, angry, and resentful he grew. Even intolerable.

But he was her family. He was all she had left. Both her parents had been only children of only children, and there was no aunt or cousin with which to seek refuge.

Meredith reached forward and found the edge of her bed. She pulled herself closer and collapsed against it. Through narrow slits, she looked up at her father's red face.

"Get a handle on this, Meredith. This is unacceptable." He turned on his heel and marched out.

Left to clean up the mess, her throat burning from the acid of her vomit, she rested her head against the soft cotton of her quilt, using the cloth to absorb her tears. She couldn't do this anymore. Ever since her mother's death, nothing had been the same, and it looked like it would never improve.

In this dark moment, Meredith accepted she'd lost both parents. Hoping her father would become the man she wanted him to be, needed him to be, was gone. He was a person she didn't like, a person she didn't respect. Yet she was forced to live as he chose.

Not any longer.

Making a decision in this state could very well be a mistake of epic proportions, but what options did she have? As she saw it, there were two. The first, she could take what money she had and try to strike out on her own. But spending each day looking over her shoulder wasn't freedom she envisioned. The other, she could take Sabrina up on her offer. The idea frightened her, the unknowns were great, but it was an opportunity that couldn't be ignored. A stop-gap that gave her breathing room to figure out her next move. No reasonable person would force her to stay in a marriage she didn't want. Not all matchmakers had a hundred percent success.

Easing forward, she reached for her bedside table. She skimmed her fingers across the wood surface until she found the knob for the drawer, then slid it open. Inside was her old-fashioned address book. Though most people kept this info on their phone, Meredith liked having hers in a book. The strikethroughs and address changes of her college friends were vicarious little adventures she dreamt about, having let go of social media since it was too painful to watch people's lives move forward while hers didn't.

She wanted to be a strikethrough in someone's book.

Her fingers sought the cool, smooth sensation that was the telltale leather binding. After opening the cover, she felt for and found a small, thick card. She didn't have to see it to know what the embossed letters said.

Hope.

Meredith closed her eyes and tried to picture a new life. Would it be like her friend who married the Marine? Living all around the world. She didn't want to romanticize the idea, but the thought of living in a small, quaint European town had become a fantasy she struggled not to cling to. How could any reality compare to that?

She felt and found her phone on the top of the table and slid it toward her. It took three tries, but she finally dialed the number correctly.

When Sabrina answered on the second ring, Meredith said, "Please help me, Sabrina."

"Of course, honey. Tell me what you need." Sabrina's voice

had an immediate calming effect on Meredith. Perhaps it was because it reminded her of her mother's or because there was a quiet confidence, a streak of strength that Sabrina embodied that told Meredith she was doing the right thing.

"I need a new life. I want a new life. Help me." Meredith was pleased to hear the quiver in her voice fade as she spoke.

"Are you certain? I can help you get a new life, but I can't help you go back to this one if you chicken out. You have to commit to what I'm offering."

No one would fault her for fibbing. "I'm beyond certain. I even know how I'm going to get away from the house." Meredith shut her eyes, rested her forehead on the edge of the bed, and filled Sabrina in on the ruse she'd have to undergo to get away. "Can you make this happen in two days?"

5

Standing outside her father's home office, Meredith reviewed the plan for what had to be the millionth time. With each run through, a deeper calmness would wash over her. She had no doubt she was taking the correct course. For the first time in years, she was alive with excitement, and dare she think...hope?

Meredith slipped the oversize sunglasses onto her nose and pushed them into place. Her hair, pulled back into a tight ponytail, was intended to show off the paleness of her completion, which she purposefully left devoid of makeup.

She stepped into the doorway and cleared her throat. Experience had taught her that unless she demanded his attention, he would not grant it.

"Yes?" He didn't bother to look up from his newspaper, the front page of the business section exposed.

"I'll be gone for a few days, Father." She didn't lift the large, leather overnight bag that had been her mother's to emphasize her point. Instead, she stood quietly and waited.

He looked at her over the edge of his paper. "What is this?"

"I have an appointment for a sleep study. I called Dr. Goodman, and he referred me. It's time to get to the bottom of these headaches, and this is where we start." Her biggest gamble would be if her father called Dr. Goodman to confirm, but she was banking on his trust for the old family friend to supersede his trust for her. "I called him after the other night and expressed how, errr, disruptive these headaches are. This is what he suggested."

He slapped the paper closed on the desk. "And I'm just hearing about it now?"

Meredith's stomach churned with anxiety. "I didn't want to mention it yesterday because I was uncertain if I would get into the sleep study. He called late yesterday, while you were out, and confirmed. You came in so late I was unable to tell you until now." She knew she had to play this carefully, keep a blank poker face. "You can call him if you'd like." She straightened, locking her knees to keep them from shaking.

Please, please, please don't call she prayed.

His gaze searched her up and down, his eyes lingering on her face. "You don't look well." Following a sigh, he said, "If Dr. Goodman says this is needed, then by all means. You'll be home when?"

"In a few days. Maybe sooner if the study goes well."

"There's an auction coming up. Another charity for horses or refugee animals or some other nonsense, but some of the potential candidates for the governor's position will be there. I need you to be in top form that night. Keep your ears open. There's talk that one favored by the media really has an agenda not conducive to my business. You'll need to ferret that out. I hear his wife is a chatty box if she has enough drinks."

"I'll need a new gown," she said to keep with her typical response to his request.

"Of course." He picked the paper up from the desk, his attention back on the news. She was forgotten.

She took one last look around. This memory would be the only keepsake she would have of him. In her bag, tucked between her undergarments, was her favorite picture with her mother. Meredith wanted to take the entire photo album, but she feared it would be noticed since it was kept in the study on the shelf next to the TV. Meredith had also taken the pearl necklace and earring set her mother and grandmother had worn on their wedding days. Not because she wanted to carry on with the tradition. Marrying an utter stranger was surely not what her mother had envisioned when she showed Meredith the pearls all the years ago, but because her mother had said they were good luck and had made of point of wearing them on significant days, such as Meredith's birth. If she were going to gamble away the only life she knew, she was going to need all the luck she could get her hands on. It was anyone's guess as to what she would be walking into?

That thought alone gave her pause, and she stared a moment longer at her father, thinking perhaps she should say something kind for him to remember her by. But before she could think of anything to say, he gave her something to remember him by.

"Try to keep the budget on this dress down, Meredith. No shoes. For crying out loud, who knew I would have such a frivolous twit of a daughter?"

Meredith was glad for the large sunglasses that masked her expression and the unexpected sting of moisture to her eyes. With his parting words, she turned on her heel and walked away. There was nothing left to be said.

6

Escaping to Sabrina's was far easier than Meredith expected. She simply gave her father's driver the address for a medical office building known for sleep studies, to which he promptly delivered her, watching until she entered the building before pulling back into the heavy Dallas traffic. She then walked in the front door, across the lobby, and out a side door Sabrina had told her to look for. Not using cell phones gave the entire endeavor a clandestine air. She found it absolutely thrilling. Though Meredith trembled the entire drive to the building and as she walked out the side door to a waiting Sabrina, there was a taste of something so glorious, a freedom, that made breathing easier and her vision clear and crisp. The world around her exploded with energy. Colors were brighter; the faces of those walking by came alive and were more interesting. This vibrant world is what independence looked like when the person doing the looking had previously been told what to see. It was heady and intoxicating, and she giggled aloud as she dashed across to Sabrina. Her large high-end SUV spoke about the woman's personality. Meredith knew the discreet dark windows were also an indication of her privacy.

She slid into the passenger seat, holding her bag on her lap, and laughed again. It took a tremendous amount of self-control to not clasp her hands together with childlike delight so she tucked them under her bag instead.

"Are you sure you want to do this?" Sabrina asked.

Panic replaced elation instantly. Meredith turned to face Sabrina, fear squeezing her chest. "Are you having second thoughts?" The woman was going to have to kick Meredith out of the car if she'd changed her mind. Meredith had a plan, and it all hinged on Sabrina.

"No, sugar. I only want to be certain you understand what you're getting into. Going back will be very difficult. You can't—"

"I have no intention of coming back. There's nothing for me here."

"Not even your father?" Sabrina sat sideways in her seat looking relaxed. Her SUV idled quietly.

Meredith wanted to scream at her to drive. This lack of motion was frustrating. Could they not get on with it already? It was like having the billion-dollar winning lottery ticket just a breath away, and her fingers could not stretch any farther to reach it.

"He stopped being my father years ago. He reminded me of that the other night when my health was not as important to him as networking and making deals. I'm not a daughter to him. I'm a tool. Something to use to further his business, and I'm tired of it." Meredith wanted to slide her leg across the center console and stomp on the gas.

"Did you do as I said?" Sabrina asked.

"I left my cell phone there. Did a factory reset. I called you from the house line anyway. I deleted the redials. But it's like I told you. He won't call the police. It would be too embarrassing. He'll hire a private detective first."

"Which is why there can't be any way to track you. My one holdup is the marriage license. When that gets filed... Well, we'll cross that bridge then."

At the word marriage, Meredith's energy deflated much like a balloon. Quick and with lots of noise.

"Meredith, there is no need for such a distraught sigh. You are not leaving one situation for a worse one. I would not do that to you."

"How can you be sure?" This was her one fear. Her large—no, more like ginormous— fear. By nature, she was not a gambler, and yet here she was taking a huge risk. "How do you know this man won't be abusive or a closet something or other or—"

"It's like I told you on the phone, and I will tell you as many times as you need—I do an extensive background search on anyone who applies. This includes hiring a private investigator to go through your personal life and talk to everyone they can. This helps tease out issues. As you'll see in a little bit, you'll also have to undergo an extensive questionnaire, speak at length to a spiritual advisor, a sex therapist, a psychologist. The match underwent the same rigorous evaluation. Of course, we are rushing things because of your circumstances but—and I've never done this before—my instincts tell me this is going to work out fabulously, and they have rarely led me wrong." She pulled into traffic and drove in the direction opposite of Meredith's childhood home, away from the city and Victors Club. As the miles passed, the suburbs slipping away in the rearview mirror, the open landscape extended before her as if waiting with open arms, and the weight on Meredith's chest decreased until only the anxiety from the unknown remained.

It was only after they pulled into a long driveway that wove through several trees and opened up to a large, sprawling ranch that Meredith thought of something other than her own situation. She relaxed her grip on her overnight bag.

"This is where you live?" It was the loveliest home Meredith had ever seen and she, an addict to home and garden shows, had seen several. A large porch with several rockers ran the length of the white house. Black shutters gave it a classic vibe. It screamed "home," and Meredith's heart ached to have such a place. Once, when her mother was alive, they'd lived in a house like this, one that spoke of family and laughter and warmth. Back then, even her father's rough edges had been softened by her mother and the life she created for them.

"This is where I live. And this is where you will live for the next day or so until we can get you sorted out. Come on, I'll take you inside. We don't have much time, so the sooner we get started the better off we are."

Meredith followed Sabrina from the car to the porch. Although the ranch looked to be one of the working types, the place was quiet. Meredith scanned the lands around her.

"The barn and stables are about a quarter mile north. That gives me the privacy I need." Sabrina swung open the door and gestured for Meredith to proceed her. Inside was just as beautiful as outside. It was French country with touches of Texas—saddles on pedestals, a large Lone Star over a fireplace, and a moose and deer head hanging from the wall. Not too many to be macabre, but enough to let the visitor know the people who lived here were hunters.

Sabrina pointed to a large twelve-point buck. "Daddy shot that a week before he died. He'd been so excited. Waited all his life to get a buck with so many points." A wistful expression swept cross Sabrina's face, only to be quickly replaced by a curious one. "Things like that don't bother you, do they? Not everyone likes hunting."

Meredith shook her head. "Did your dad eat the meat or do it more for sport? Maybe I'm skewed, but my granddaddy was a hunter, my momma's father. He used to let me go out and scout with him. He taught me the importance of making good use of all the meat." It felt like a lifetime ago, as if the memory didn't belong to her, but was something she'd seen in a dream or on TV. Meredith swung her gaze from the animal to Sabrina. "I don't know if you recall or not, but they, my grandparents, died in the same accident with my mother."

Sabrina said nothing, but reached out, took Meredith's hand, and gave it a light squeeze. "Well, hun, I don't mean to rush you, but like I said, we've lots to do today. I have my book club coming in an hour, and I need to get you out of sight. Come with me."

Sabrina led her down a long hallway and up a short flight of stairs. At the top, they went through another door. When Meredith crossed the threshold, she knew she'd come into the office portion of the house. Though the room was set up like a cozy living space, the personality of the other portion of the house was missing. This was more...lackluster, or perhaps corporate. As corporate as it could get being on the same property. The only items of intimacy were the large 11x18 pictures on the wall, each framed with oversize, colorful mats that drew the eye toward the picture. Meredith quickly scanned each of them. Many were of different families, laughing or smiling for the camera. Some were on horses, lounging on a beach, or building a snowman.

"You can stow your bag in here, unless you want me to show you to your room. You won't be able to access it while my book club is here as your room is in the main part of the house. Most people feel better keeping their stuff with them in the beginning. Through here is the restroom." She opened a door on the east wall to show a lavish lavatory. The butter yellow color on the walls was homey and inviting. A large soaker tub and a vanity made from barn wood made Meredith coo. Like her mother, Meredith had once enjoyed bubble baths and a good book. The room was a stark contrast to the sterile and cold house her father had moved them into with nary a tub to be had.

"Over here is a small kitchenette. Please help yourself." Sabrina walked across the space and opened an identical door to show another well-appointed space. "Let's get you started. You want something to drink?" Sabrina walked to a large wall cabinet and swung open the wood door. She withdrew a thin laptop, and while closing the cabinet door with her shoulder, flipped the laptop open.

"I'd love a tea." Meredith looked around and tried to relax. For a brief moment, she could pretend she was staying with a friend. Had her life gone differently, it might be exactly what she'd be doing. But Sabrina's all-business attitude, though not unfriendly or abrasive, clearly showcased that sooner rather than later Meredith would be legally bound to a stranger, and all because her father turned into a crazy person after her mother's death.

"You want sweet or unsweet? Have a seat, hon. Get comfy. Kick off your shoes. You have a lot to do. Help yourself to whatever." Sabrina handed her the laptop. The screen was a pretty sky blue and white banner with the words HOPE across it.

"Sweet, please." Meredith sunk into an overstuffed butter-yellow chenille chaise lounge and pulled the laptop close.

"Click on the word HOPE. It will start the questionnaire that has two hundred questions. Answer the best you can. Go with your gut. You can mark any of the questions you are uncertain about with a star, and then you can go back later and answer. There is no right or wrong. It's about you and what you want and how you see your life. It usually takes an hour or so. Dr. Williams will be here shortly, and when you're done, you will meet with him. He'll pass you along to Dr. Fleming, she's our sex therapist, and by the time you are done with them, I should be done with my book club." Sabrina delivered the information as she moved around the room, opening blinds and making Meredith a drink. She placed a large glass of iced tea along with a plate of assorted mini sandwiches and petit fours on the table. "There's more in the kitchen and other stuff if this doesn't suit. OK?"

Meredith nodded.

"I'll leave you to it. Should you have a question, you can call me on that phone." She pointed to the old-school rotary phone sitting on the desk. "Dial one, and it will ring to where I am."

Again, Meredith nodded.

"If you want to back out, now is the time."

"I don't want to back out." But even to Meredith, her voice sounded small. "Honest," she said with more conviction. "But what if I don't like him or find him attractive?"

Sabrina shook her head. "If I showed you a picture, you would make a lot of conclusions based on that one image. You begin this with preconceived ideas. I like to keep those to a minimum. That's why I don't show pictures." Sabrina tapped the computer. "Once we go through with this, we will fly to your new home, and you'll be married right away."

Meredith swallowed. "I know. I have to stay at least a year or pay the fees." Which were more than Meredith had saved when planning her great escape. The amount was staggering.

"I take this very seriously. You are looking for a new life, and so are these men. They are just as lonely. Of course, they would never admit that." Sabrina chuckled. "Their circumstances make matching and finding a wife the 'typical way' more difficult, or they would've been successful in that endeavor. They trust me to be diligent and careful in my selection, just as you are trusting me to keep you safe."

"I take it seriously as well. I always thought I'd marry once. Maybe that was a young girl's fantasy born from too many movies about princesses and dreams coming true, but when I look at how my life is now, the only thing I see changing is me getting older. Or my father trying to pawn me off on someone that would make a good business match for him. Like Lyle Brady."

Sabrina cringed.

As Meredith shook her head, a lone tear escaped. "I'm more willing to take a chance on finding happiness with a stranger than I am with my father. How sad is that?"

Sabrina handed her a tissue and then squeezed her shoulder. "I know this is a giant leap of faith for you, Meredith, but let me show you something." She gestured to the walls. "Look at these pictures. These were all clients of mine. They found the love and happiness they were seeking. I know the folks posed for photos, but before I matched them, they were alone. Some were scared the life they were living was all they were going to get. Now they have this." She did a broad sweep of the wall. "You can have this."

Could she really? Meredith wasn't sure. It was hard imagining how this could be hers. Yes, she'd once wanted what these people had—a loving family. Meredith stared at one picture in particular. It was a family of four. The husband had a child on his shoulders, and the wife stood behind a second, older child and next to her husband. The camera caught them during an exchange, and the look passing between them, forever captured, was full of love and...familiarity. She could never have this. Not with her situation the way it was. She didn't see how it could happen. Sadness squeezed her heart and left her breathless.

"I'll let you get to it then," Sabrina said. The clicking of her heels faded away into the background as Meredith continued to stare and wonder about the couple, their story, and what brought them together.

She knew she couldn't ask for everything—freedom, a life, and a family, but what she could ask for was being happy with what she got. To not ache for more. She made a silent prayer, and if her mother was listening asked, "Please, I only want my own life. I promise to be happy with that."

7

Sabrina's statement about getting a lot done in a short time was no joke. It had been Meredith's fault the process had stretched into the late hours of the night. Once she got to talking to the spiritual advisor, it had opened a floodgate of pent-up emotions and fears. Following a well needed cathartic cry, Meredith had ended the night with a glass of wine and some laughs with Sabrina.

She knew the sex therapist was part of the process but, mercy, some of the questions were embarrassing. Confessing she was a virgin had been the worst, and talking with a complete stranger, albeit a nice motherly sort of stranger, about the stages of romance and how to claim a satisfying experience for both parties had nearly done Meredith in.

Hence the wine.

And the laughter.

She'd fallen into bed with the sudden awareness that, for all the stress the day brought, not a single headache or hint of one was had. No doubt, she was in a better headspace. Talking out her fears helped release some of the pent-up angst she was carrying. It made that out-of-control feeling dissipate, and in its place came a more focused grasp of her purpose. Talking about sex, however, made her freak the hell out. How naive she'd been to not even think about having sex with this man. Surely he wouldn't expect sex right away

The following morning, the evaluation process behind her, she held the freshly toasted slice of wheat bread with melted butter and promptly lost her appetite.

"We leave this evening." Sabrina said in her singsong, sugared voice as she cut a grapefruit in half. "Tomorrow is the big day. Did you want to pick up a dress before we go?"

"So soon?" Meredith slid the bread back on the plate. Intellectually, she had expected the quick turnaround, emotionally she wasn't ready.

Sabrina smiled softly and slid into the chair across from her. "I know this is scary, but I want to get you out of town as soon as we can. I worry we overlooked something, and your father will find you."

Meredith shook her head. "He won't start looking until tomorrow. Earliest."

"If everything goes as planned. But why postpone the inevitable? This is what you said you wanted to do. So let's do it. It's time to embrace your new life. Open up your hands, and let this life go, Meredith, and while your hands are open, keep them that way so you can receive a new one. You're getting married."

Marriage. There had been no dating that led to falling in love. No heated kisses or going further than that. Is this what it was like all those years ago when marriages were arranged, each person getting something from the deal? Funny how little the premise of an arrangement had changed, if it had at all. Meredith was curious to what her *groom* was getting out of the situation.

Dr. Fleming, the spiritual advisor had asked her what she thought of marriage. Truth was she had stopped thinking about it altogether a few years back. Her primary examples had been her parents and her grandparents, but they were the memories and perspective of a child.

Dr. Fleming said she was in the perfect place for a marriage. Her expectations weren't based on how she'd seen someone get treated as much as they were based on how she herself wanted to be treated. Her only caution? To make sure she stood up for what she wanted if she had to.

She didn't feel like she was in a perfect place to be wed. Her knees were shaking for Pete's sake.

Sabrina turned the laptop so they both could see the screen and access it. As Sabrina minimized the page, Meredith caught a glance of the images of two men. Her curiosity peaked. Were they her prospects? Though Sabrina said they would meet and be married tomorrow, perhaps Sabrina was still uncertain about the match.

Hopefully that wasn't the case because, if so, it didn't give Meredith much comfort. She was quite happy, thank you very much, to work under the belief this was an exact and flawless science and happily ever after could be found through the use of a computer test, discussion with professionals, and a leap of faith. The pictures of Sabrina's wall were proof of this.

"Here is a site with dresses. If you pick one soon, we can have a seamstress out to make sure it's perfect." Sabrina scrolled through the page quickly.

"This is a local boutique. I've seen some of their stuff." Meredith leaned closer to the screen. She'd passed the shop several times as she took her many evening gowns and shoes to the consignment shop, and more than once she'd been stopped short by the breathtaking loveliness of the gowns in the window.

But Meredith had never dared to dream when she'd gazed at the dresses. If she'd ever be given the chance at marriage, it would be long after she'd run away from her father and home.

Even then, marriage had never really seemed plausible since it was unfair to bring someone into the madness that was her life.

"Do you like any?" Sabrina dug a spoon into the pink flesh of the grapefruit pulp.

"They're all beautiful. Are people really getting married in colored gowns?" Splashes of color shaped like flowers were beaded on several dresses. Red, blue, green. Some were trimmed in pink. Others had trains in yellow. Stunning.

"Yes, people get married in what they want. You should, too."

Meredith wanted white. "I know I will have no one present from my side, but will he? And where will we do this? I'd feel silly in a ballgown-type dress. Is it warm or cold?"

When her gaze fell onto one, her heart skipped a few beats, but she continued to scroll through the rest, not willing to become attached to the first one that gave her pause.

"Cool. It will be in a small church in a very small town. His parents will be there." Sabrina stood and took her plate to the kitchen.

Meredith startled at the mention of his parents. His. Because he had no name yet. "Really, his parents?"

Sabrina smiled and nodded. "They're lovely people. I have to pop into my office to make sure all the last-minute details are working out. When you decide, simply click and fill out the size info. The rest will be handled." Without waiting for a reply, she left the room.

Meredith returned her attention to the simple all-white wedding gown. It was unconventional since it fell mid-shin instead of all the way to the floor. But then marrying a guy moments after meeting him without the excuse of Vegas or alcohol was unconventional in and of itself, so why should the gown be any different?

The dress would easily sell at consignment.

The idea struck her in the solar plexus. She didn't have to go through with the wedding. She could put some distance between her and her father and go on the run once she and Sabrina arrived in Small Town, USA. Yes, this thought had merit. She focused on the gown. Logically, she knew to select something that would be good for resale regardless of what she personally wanted —she wouldn't be wearing it for long if at all— but she really couldn't stop herself. One particular dress was calling her.

The skirt was made from organza and full with a flirty swing. The lace bodice was off the shoulder but tasteful and simple. The long sleeves would help to keep her warm—if she even wore it. Meredith was in love. She was tired of ball gowns and itchy taffeta. She wanted something fresh and, dare she say, a tad flirty. The fun vibe the dress gave off without being tacky was the feel Meredith hoped to capture. New, never used wouldn't last long at a consignment shop.

Without another moment's hesitation, Meredith clicked the button and filled in the measurements. When she was done, a message popped up on the screen that the shop would deliver the dress in less than two hours, and a seamstress would accompany it. No wonder Sabrina's fees were enormous. She was given the options of accessories, shoes were essential, and she selected a small clutch but wasn't sure why. Hosiery and underwear were the last to be selected, and more than once Meredith checked over her shoulder. Nothing spoke more of modern day than one selecting their trousseau online within a moment of clicks.

When she was done and closed the screen, a small tab caught her eye. Checking for Sabrina again and finding herself alone, Meredith clicked the tab.

On the screen were photos of two men. One done in head-shot style, likely for professional reasons and seen on corporate websites, and the other was a personal picture probably snapped by someone's phone. The quality wasn't poor, just not as pristine as the other.

Headshot guy was cute in that awkward nerd way. His glasses were thick-rimmed but managed not to overpower his face. A lock of inky black hair fell over his forehead, his expression much like a deer caught in the headlights. It was comical. Meredith was sure his expression matched her own, for all the getting-down-to-business she'd just done with purchasing the dress, there was a freaked-out person inside her screaming, "Wait, slow the horses!" while no one listened.

The other man was outside, a bluer than blue sky behind him. His skin was tanned but not weathered, as if he were a person who spent lots of time outdoors but knew to wear sunscreen. The photographer had caught him mid-smile. A dimple teased at one cheek, and laugh lines lightly etched his face. His hair was not as dark as the first guy but caramel brown and lightened by the sun. His demeanor was darker than the first. Mr. Glasses looked as if he'd fumbled looking for a pen, but this one, the cowboy, looked the sort who could defend his home by wielding said pen as a weapon. There was something formidable and no-nonsense about him that Meredith found appealing, yet terrifying at the same time. Would he be domineering like her father? Surely, Sabrina would not do that to her. Her gaze darted back to the dark-haired man. His disheveled appearance, even in a picture where one was expected to be their best, was comforting to Meredith. She refused to look at the other man and willed that this gentle, scatterbrained, appealing twin to Jeff Goldblum be the man Sabrina picked for her. Though it would be easier to run from the cowboy, less guilt.

She slammed the computer lid down when she heard Sabrina's heels clack on the tiles of the floor. Pushing the computer away, she stood with her plate in hand.

"All done? Let's get you packed and ready to go. The shop will be here with the dress soon, and we'll fly out a few hours after they leave."

"Do you think rushing this is wise?" Meredith's plate trembled in her hand.

Sabrina took the china from her and rubbed her back. "I know it's unnerving. But soon you will be starting a new life. One that can bring you a lifetime of happiness if you allow it. It'll require some work and patience."

Meredith nodded, hoping her newly crafted plan wasn't obvious to Sabrina. She wasn't sure how that would be possible, but Sabrina had a sixth sense about her.

Starting a new life is what Sabrina had said. Yes, Meredith would be finally getting the life she wanted, one that would give her freedom without the baggage of a husband. She hated that she would be in the hole with what she owed Sabrina, but had every intention of paying her back. One day. Meredith chose to ignore the niggling thought about how her actions would be shafting two people.

8

I f today's events were any indication how this marriage was going to turn out, Jace wasn't very hopeful. A flat tire on the truck, a coyote in the hen house, and Tuck had reported more missing cattle. The last place he needed to be was anywhere but the ranch.

Yet here he stood, hiding behind the corner, having come up on Sabrina and the woman, Meredith, unexpectedly. Not wanting to interrupt, he took the moment to take her in, this person who he would soon be legally bound to.

She was pretty in a way that most considered classic, though far too thin. A month on a cattle ranch would thicken her right up. Her glossy chestnut hair was tied up in some kind of formal arrangement he was certain his sister Willow would be able to label. Her features were not petite or overlarge but suited her perfectly, her nose straight and even. There was no button nose or heart-shaped mouth, no coquettish fluttering of lashes or feigning shyness. Instead she stood slack-mouthed and stared at the mountains. Normally he'd find her reaction encouraging, but he knew with one look she wasn't hearty enough for this lifestyle. It would get to her, like it had to the others before her. Maybe not the first broken fingernail, but certainly the second, because for all her loveliness, he couldn't erase the image of her in a fancy gown from his memory. She was out of her element here, and he should save them all a bunch of trouble and back out.

"I don't know if I will ever get tired of seeing that view. It's incredible," she said, the awe obvious in her husky voice. His chest filled with pride, and he thought about stepping from behind the corner to explain that she was looking at and assure her that, indeed, the view never did get old, but then he remembered that most everyone liked the view, at first, but not enough to stay.

Pops had a year if the doctor's predictions were accurate. That's all he would ask. He tapped his Stetson against his thigh. He wasn't so foolish to bank on forever, but if he could get her to stay until Pops was gone...yeah, until then.

Pops would take one look at Meredith and pat Jace's back. Jace considered the merits of being up front with Meredith who, as far as he knew, was going into this intent on forever. Not that he'd consider that very likely. No, she was the type that could be broken by the ruggedness of living out here, and he'd be smart to be up front with her with hopes of striking a mutually satisfying bargain. He'd have to do it when Rina wasn't around.

He ached between the shoulders. Christ, like he needed any more stress. Jace took a chance and sneaked another peek. She looked like a skittish filly, ready to flee. Yet the coiled tension she was emitting didn't put him off like he'd expected. Had he come across her in any other setting, he'd have approached her. There was something he couldn't yet identify that drew him toward her, and that's why he decided to go through with the wedding.

OK, maybe that part about approaching her wasn't true. He'd have *thought* of doing it. Wondered if they might have made a

connection, but like Rina had said to him on more than one occasion, he'd gotten lazy, allowed previous failed attempts to skew
his perspective. Not that he was going to admit that to her
anytime soon. He likely would have recognized Meredith's skit-
tishness, attributing it to a need for flight, and would have
written her off. It was hard letting someone in only to watch
them leave.

"Let's go in, Meredith. It's chilly out here," Rina said and
tugged Meredith's elbow. She turned away slowly, possibly
longing for one last look and, dare he hope, falling for his hometown? It wasn't a lot for most people, but it was everything to
some.

"It's a cute town," he heard her say as she followed Sabrina
inside, the door closing behind her and cutting off any further
conversation he might eavesdrop on.

She thought Bison's Prairie was cute, but how would she feel
when she realized it consisted of the basics? Three churches, one
housed in a barn, a grocery store, hardware and feed store, one
bakery, one flower shop, a diner, and a small hospital that was
really a medical clinic.

He leaned against the building and tried to process it all.

He was getting married. He'd worn his best gray suit, the one
he only brought out for the high-profile meetings he had when
he went to the auctions or stock exchange. He'd even gone the
two hours up to Billings to get a new tie, something lighter than
his usual somber style and had settled on a pale blue one that
complimented the suit. While there, he'd picked up a simple
white gold wedding band with diamonds running the length.

Girls liked diamonds, right? It would be a nice impression. At
least that was the plan.

Jesus, who was he kidding? Deep inside, a part of him hoped
this chick would stay. That he would be one of Rina's success

stories, but thoughts like that got him nothing but heartache, and he'd be smart to make a deal and stick to it.

"Hey, Peeping Tom. You coming in or what?" Sabrina appeared next to him, startling him from his reverie.

He jumped and swung his gaze to her. "What is wrong with you sneaking up on a man like that?"

"What is wrong with you peering around the corner like a ten year old? You lost your manners or something?"

"So you saw me, did you?"

Sabrina crossed her arms and raised one brow, her hip jutting out to the side.

"I thought it would be awkward coming up to you all like that. 'Hey, I'm Jace. Guess we're getting married today.'" He met her gaze for gaze.

"You just wanted to check her out without her knowing. You forget that I know you, Jace McAdams Shepard."

Jace had the good sense to duck his head.

"And where are your parents? Why aren't they here? I know Willow is in school, but shouldn't your parents see you get married? Your momma is going to be livid as it is." There was no change in her posture.

"What do I say Rina? Hey you all, I just met this here girl, and we're getting married. Care to come witness?" Jace stuffed his hands in his pant pockets where his right hand toyed with the ring box.

"Okay, you have a point there. But they should be here. Tell them what you want. I suggest the truth, but it's your life. Regardless, Pops will be brokenhearted to miss this."

Jace knew she was right. He nodded, met her gaze, and then shrugged. "What do I do?"

"For a man so good at business and cattle, you sure are lousy with people."

"Forgive me for not knowing how to handle my mail-order bride situation," he said.

"Touché. Come in and meet Meredith and then go get your folks. How's that for a plan?" She uncrossed her arms and held them wide for a hug.

He stepped into them and pulled her close. "Thanks for being such a good friend."

"Thank me when you're celebrating your anniversary and wondering how you ever lived without Meredith. Name a child after me."

"What if I have all boys?" He liked the idea of sons, something he hadn't really allowed himself to imagine.

"I'll accept Sebastian or Sabine or—"

"Never gonna happen." They stepped apart and headed for the church. He put the Stetson on and adjusted the sightline. When they reached the door that opened into the church classrooms, he grabbed for it before Sabrina could and paused as he grasped the knob, his palms suddenly moist, his mouth dry.

"Wait, let me go in alone." This would be the time he'd need to bargain with her. He couldn't do that with Sabrina around.

She tilted her head, studying him. "Are you sure about that?"

"One hundred percent." Twenty-five was more the truth.

"Okay, I'll just go...." She looked around.

"To the diner for some coffee. Maybe stop by the clinic and tell my folks you're here for a surprise. They'll know soon enough."

Sabrina nodded. "Okay." She patted his chest. "Good luck." Then brushed passed him on the stairs as she left.

Jace blew out a breath then swung the back door open. When he stepped inside, Meredith jerked to a stand, her hands behind her back. Her suitcase on the floor was open, clothes spilling out. They made brief eye contact, and in that second, he read her disappointment.

"You," she whispered. Though the look was quickly gone, he didn't need to see it again to know she was more enchanted with the view than him.

"You going somewhere?" From where he stood, this appeared to be the case. When he'd come in, she'd looked to be stuffing clothes into a small bag. Still wearing her long white coat and her purse on her shoulder, it was clear to him she was attempting to make a quick escape.

Her eyes were wide, and the bluest he'd ever seen. Her pretty mouth hung open, nothing coming out.

Jace whipped off his hat and slapped it against his knees. Shit. This would be the record. She hadn't even met him and was trying to bail. "What's the plan? Slip out the other door? Grab a cab?" Jace ran a hand through his hair and sighed.

She slammed her mouth closed and nodded.

"Well, you're out of luck. We don't have cabs here. Just a bus stop, and the one bus that comes through already left for the day."

Meredith dropped what she'd been holding behind her back, a small backpack, and stepped toward him. "I'm sorry. I know I'm awful, but the gravity of this...this... Don't you think this is insane?" Was that a tremble in her lip among the controlled tightness of her expression?

"Yeah, it's insane. But that's not a new revelation. The idea was insane from the onset." He sighed, putting one hand on his hip. "Was this your plan all along? To get this far and bail?" He needed to know. How had Sabrina called this one wrong?

"I'm sorry," she said before promptly bursting into tears, covering her face with her hands. She mumbled her apologies again.

Well, shit.

"Here Meredith, why don't you sit down?" When he touched her elbow, he expected her to pull away, or at the very least jump, but instead she let him guide her to a chair. She sank into it, her face still buried in her hands. Though her sobs were quiet, they seemed to be coming from a well deep within, for her body shook each time she let one free.

Jace sat on his haunches before her; he placed his hat next to him. Pulling an old handkerchief, one that used to belong to his granddaddy, from his breast pocket, he placed it on her knee. "Here you go," he said while patting her knee.

Removing her hands from her face, he watched her gaze dart from him to the hankie before she lifted it to her tear-ravaged face. "I'm so sorry."

"Because...."

She covered her face with the off-white linen and shook her head.

"If you don't want to be here, you don't have to be. This'll be hard enough, I imagine, if you'd rather be somewhere else. I won't keep you against your will." Disappointment was present, not that he hadn't expected it, and Jace was ready to move on. Get back to the ranch.

She shook her head. "That's not why I'm crying. I mean, yes, I'm scared to be here." When she pulled in a deep, ragged breath, her delicate little shoulders shook.

"Are you willing to share why you're crying?" He kept his voice low and easy, not urgent, but the truth was he wanted to snap at her, at Sabrina, or anyone.

"There's too much. I feel...." She covered her chest with her hands. "I can't even figure it out."

"Let's try it a different way. If you were to get married today, what would make you happy?"

She looked up at him, then brought the hankie to her nose, and for a moment, he wondered if she'd stopped breathing.

"I always pictured my mother being with me when I married. She would hand me my bouquet and give me last-minute advice, and maybe I wouldn't feel so alone," she whispered. One hand played with the hem of her skirt, folding it over her knee repeatedly.

Jace took that hand between his. "I'm very sorry. Rina told me she passed. I can't imagine what that must feel like." His gaze met hers, and Jace knew she needed their first common thread. "Pops, my father, is sick. ALS. You know what that is?" His voice cracked, emotion changing his normal baritone into a hoarse whisper.

She nodded. "I did a fundraiser for it once."

"Watching him deteriorate eats me alive." It was something he hadn't dared speak of since he knew there would be no way to keep his voice from showing the depths of his sorrow, and he'd been right.

She snaked her fingers between his and squeezed. "I'm sorry."

"He wants me settled before he dies." He let the words hang between them. "Threatened to cut me out of my inheritance over this."

"That's why I'm here?" It was part question and part realization. "I wondered what could be so wrong with a man that he'd need to marry a stranger."

Jace didn't know whether to be insulted or not.

"I have a proposal." Jace laughed. "No pun intended."

Meredith's wobbly smile encouraged him to continue.

"I need a wife and you need what? To get on your feet? To hide?"

"An opportunity to start over."

Jace wasn't precisely sure what that meant, but he could work with it. "How about we help each other out. You help me make a dying man happy, and I help you with that opportunity."

She bit her lip before saying, "Continue."

"Let's go through with this. At my place, you'll have the time and freedom to figure out whatever it is you need to figure out."

Something he'd said stirred a change in her. She sat up straighter, became more self-possessed.

"You would marry me to make your dad happy and then let me go when...?"

"Yeah, I would." He didn't like fooling Pops, or Mom for that matter, but he wanted these last days with Pops to count. Hell, he'd marry a bear if it was what Pops wanted.

"Listen, I've known Rina for years. We went to college together, and she's one of my closest friends. I don't want to disappoint her, and I know she talks about forever and all that, but I want you to know if you aren't happy here, you can leave. My only request is if you decide to stay, it's for as long as my father is alive."

"I have nowhere else I can go," she said and started up again with the hiccups and sobs.

"No family?"

Following a slight shake of the head, she said, "None to speak of."

Her response filled him with a thousand questions. Maybe it was because he was a man, and protection was an inherent trait, or maybe because he was a big brother. Not that he was thinking of Meredith as a little sister. He was ashamed to admit that even as she sat before him, he had to continue to avert his eyes from her legs. Her long slender calves begged to be stroked. Shoot, everything about her seemed to cry out for touch. But more than anything, he wanted to put his arm around her, tell her everything was going to be okay, and then make it so.

"You have here. I have a ranch with cattle, and that can be your home for as long as you need it."

Fresh tears streamed down her face, but the shoulder-wracking sobs were gone. "Would you really let me leave? After all this has been set up?"

She really was very pretty. Beautiful, actually. There was nothing flashy about her, not one attribute that was remarkable, but the combination of smooth, untanned skin and large blue eyes mixed with a gentleness in her demeanor stoked a long-banked fire that resided deep within him.

Who would hurt such a gentle creature that she'd enter into a lifetime union with a perfect stranger simply to get away? The thought of it was astounding. He tried to imagine Willow doing the same thing, and the thought made him want to call her to make sure she was happy.

"It can be isolating on the ranch. Lots of time to yourself. I'm willing to give you my home if you are willing to give me your word you'll stay for my father."

Her brows winged closer. "Isolating how?"

"You'll have to experience it. Maybe you won't find it to be true." Jace shrugged, but he knew he didn't believe that, nor was he able to make it sound like he did. "There's poor Internet. The days are long with chores, idle time is limited. Everyone plays a role that matters, though, and you would be no different."

Watching Meredith, he wondered if the people she had left behind cared she was gone. But that no longer mattered because he cared. She was here now, and soon, if she were willing, she would be a part of his family. He took that responsibility seriously, even if it was only for the duration of Pop's life.

"I want you to know that I'd like to go through with this, but only if you want to." Jace studied her. No truer words were spoken, and the worry that she might say no surprised Jace. His gut told him this mutual arrangement could work. He might actually pull off getting a dying man to believe he'd found happiness. It sounded awful, the trickery, but living with Pops being sad because Jace wasn't married would be far harder. Crazy old man and his wishes.

She needed a place to belong and, if he was honest with himself, and today would be a perfect day for that, there was plenty of room for her here. "Do you think you might be interested in this offer?" He held firm to her hands. "We're looking at a year, maybe more if we're lucky to have Pops that long."

"I think I could really like it here. It's beautiful and peaceful." She nodded. "I need peaceful." If she loved the scenery in its current state, he couldn't wait to see her reaction to the full colors in late spring and early summer. Or the orange of autumn.

Jace sat back on his haunches, easing the tension from his calves. "I'm an honest and loyal man, Meredith. I'm not looking for a fast paced, exciting life. I like the slow pace here. Cattle's about all the excitement I can handle. Maybe a bear or two." He smiled. "You think that's something that'll work for you?" All things she needed to know so when she started getting squirrely about leaving before Pops was gone, he could point out he had warned her.

She looked in the direction of the window, and then nodded before turning her attention back to him. "I'll give you my word I'll stay for the time your father is alive. I keep my word, and it looks easy enough to be here. I think I could like it."

It wasn't perfect by any stretch of the imagination, but it would do. "Okay then. Try it is." He bounced slightly on his heels, but stopped when she pulled her hands from his, tucking one under her leg.

"I'd give you this back." She gently waved the handkerchief before him. "But I'd like to wash it first."

"If you're all right now, I'll just step out and collect my folks." He waited for a sign. When she nodded, he stood before her.

"Should I just wait here?"

He patted his pockets in mock exaggeration. "You didn't lift my truck keys did you? Still hoping to make a getaway?" Perhaps not the best joke to make to a woman feeling apprehensive about starting a new life with a complete stranger, but to his surprise, she laughed. An easy, melodic sound that made him chuckle as well.

"Are most women really that desperate to get out of this town? Should I be forewarned?" The hint of a smile told him she was teasing.

"Well, it's not for all people. Some folk who grow up here leave, and some come back, and on the occasion someone stumbles upon us, they might stay, too. We have the basics. No mass shopping chain."

She pressed her lips together while looking up at him through her lashes. "So you're saying you're experiencing a population boom simply by me being here?"

Jace tossed back his head and laughed. "Yep, that about sums it up." Their gazes stayed on each other briefly, both enjoying the easy moment they'd just experienced, until Meredith looked away.

"I should freshen up," she said while looking around the room.

"It's the door over to the left." He indicated with his chin. "If it's all right with you, I'll go now."

She nodded then stood. Her proximity was closer than he'd anticipated and normally, instinct would have him step back and out of her personal space, but neither of them moved. If he stepped half a foot closer, he'd be able to tuck her nicely in his arms, put his chin on her head. Maybe Rina was right. They were a good fit, at least physically.

"I have one request."

Her eyes widened at the word "request."

"I'd like to avoid the specifics with my parents. Just say we met while I was in Texas at auction, emailed a few times, and decided to do this. I'm aware that I'm asking you to lie, but it's for a good reason."

She blinked slowly. He wanted to point out that fudging how this all came about was likely the most insignificant of their issues, but it was only right that he be upfront with her.

"I don't want my father, or mother either, worrying about why I did this."

"I understand. Thanks for being honest with me, Jace." She said his name with hesitation, as if she was trying it out. He liked the way it sounded coming from her.

"I'll be back in fifteen." He stepped back and nestled his hat on his head.

"Maybe you have a getaway car around the corner?"

Smiling, he shook his head. "I'll be right back." He stepped from the church and jogged to the flower store across the street.

Mrs. Williams, Tucker's mom, was sitting behind the counter, her hands clasped before her as if she'd been waiting on him.

"Hey, Mrs. Williams, I need some help." He leaned one hip against the counter. He had a suspicion she knew what was going down over at the church and might be miffed about not being invited.

She crossed her arms. "Go on."

"What's that saying women use when they're getting married? About old things? Because I need you to help me put all that together. I'll need a bouquet, and I'll need you to you at the church in thirty minutes to see me get married."

9

It was him! The one she'd hoped *not* to be matched with, and he had busted her shoving clothes in her pack.

Left alone in the church classroom, Meredith had known it was time to beat feet. Freedom was calling. She would have preferred to strike out on her own in a big city, get lost in the masses, but it wouldn't be the case here. Having driven through main street to get to the church, Meredith knew a stranger would stick out in the cute western town. She'd seen tie-ups for horses outside some of the stores. So charming. As soon as Sabrina had stepped from the room, Meredith had tossed what she could into her pack, setting out a change of clothes, knowing a woman in a wedding dress would be like a lighthouse beacon on a foggy night.

Being on her own had to be easier than living with a stranger, right? Even if the stranger had been the nerdy guy, she'd planned on leaving. When he, Jace, stepped into the room and caught her, she was struck with two things: panic and butterflies. Panic because her instincts told her she was right about him—he'd be a force to be reckoned with—and butterflies because his picture hadn't done him justice. He was breath-stealing gorgeous. There was no way she could stay. She didn't know how to be around someone who made her stomach quiver every time she looked at him.

When he told her there were no cabs or buses, Meredith briefly had considered hitchhiking. Until a second later, when it dawned on her that she was picking potential death over marriage. How many crime shows had she seen on TV where the hitchhiker lived? Mm, she couldn't recall one, and she was a crime show addict.

She was so ashamed. Of her actions, her desperation, and indecisiveness.

Her surprise had gotten the best of her when he'd stepped into the room. She hoped she hadn't shown her disappointment when realizing her life was not likely to be that of Charlotte Lucas from *Pride and Prejudice*, destined to spend her days as she pleased in a sitting parlor. No, this man would make demands on her, and that thought alone had caused her hands to tremble with anxiety. It was inevitable, for she would not be able to avoid confrontation. This would be no easy transition away from her controlling father to a passive, mild-mannered stranger.

Dr. Fleming had said she needed to stand up for herself right away. That's what she would do.

She would not run. That was plain stupid. She would take the deal. It was the best option.

After quickly repacking her suitcase and hiding the backpack —she didn't want Sabrina to see it—she escaped to the restroom where she stood before the sink and pushed from her mind thoughts of home and Texas. This would be home now, for however long. She'd landed, albeit temporarily. This was a good thing, right? So why did tears threaten to fall once again? She was one step closer to her goal. Now if she could learn to ask for what she wanted.

Dabbing at her eyes with the hankie, she found her attention drawn to it, her thoughts straying to the man with the light gray eyes who'd held her hand when she cried and offered her a handkerchief for her tears. There was gentleness in him that told her she would be all right if she stayed.

The handkerchief was a simple square of linen, but it spoke of so much more. The frayed edges and slight off-color stain in the corner told the story of use. Whether for tears or sweat, it showed a history of cleaning up messes.

And now it was cleaning up the mess that she was. Funny, though, she didn't have to be. Not at this moment. Not in the next. Fresh start. It was hers for the taking.

Even the headache that had threatened to come earlier while she was about to enter the church was nowhere to be found. A horse had neighed, and she'd turned to search for the animal, suddenly swept away in the memories of a better, more carefree time of her life when she had taken horseback riding lessons from her grandmother. There was something about this place. Something that spoke to Meredith.

It was the mountains standing tall and strong against the elements. Presenting with a range of color, some peaks light, others dark, they welcomed and cautioned. The foothills extended out as if arms stretching to embrace the land and her. They gave her strength, odd as that might sound. In order to form, they'd pushed through years of earth and resistance to rise above the fray and now presided over the landscape majestically.

Meredith was ready to form. To become the person she was meant to be, though she had no desire to preside over anything except her own home. And her life, of course. That was why she'd done this insanely impulsive act.

She recalled how her mother used to whisper words of encouragement, always cheering her on, boosting her up.

You can have anything you want Meredith. You only have to be willing to ask for it.

She sure hoped asking for this would not be a future regret.

For the past ten years, Meredith had been surrounded by people and had felt wholly alone. At this moment, in this place, she was acutely aware she had no one but herself. It was really a new, fresh start.

Who was she and who did she want to be?

Heavy footfalls, likely from boots, snapped her from her reverie. Where was Sabrina? Had she decided to leave without saying goodbye?

Meredith knew if she walked out there and let that rough-skinned but gentle-touch cowboy make all the decisions, she would eventually be living a life she hadn't wanted and would be no better off than she was with her father.

The contrast was to be bossy and demanding, mannerisms that went against the very fiber of her core, and her gut told her that wouldn't be successful. Jace, the people in his family, and even she would probably end up disliking herself if she embodied that behavior. No, Meredith needed to strike a balance.

A rap on the door made her jump. "Are you in there?"

If a person's voice could tell a story, Jace's would be a western. It was deep with a hint of huskiness that was likely due to yelling out of doors for extended time. But it sounded like something one heard when they watched old movies of cowboys and wagon trains. His drawl, though not Texas southern like she was used to, spoke of a slower pace of life. Or perhaps this was what she wanted to believe.

Or maybe his story was a whole lot of sexiness. He certainly sounded like it. Or what she thought sexy might sound like. Not that she knew. He was raw and rough around the edges, and she had no trouble picturing herself locked in his arms. Sexual energy rolled off him in heady waves that made her feel loopy. Until this very moment, she hadn't given her own sexual identity much thought. She knew she was missing out on it. Knew she wanted to try it. But it was all academic. Something she had thought about after watching movies or reading a book, even when discussing it with Dr. Fleming, it had still been abstract.

Jace Shepard brought it to life. To the real world and made her yearn in a foreign way.

He rapped on the door again.

"I'm here." She finished touching up her makeup with one last stroke of her blush brush across her cheek. The simplicity of the act at a time when nothing was simple brought a small chuckle forward. Not that she needed the color. Thinking about Jace and sex was all it had taken to add a hint of pink to her cheeks.

He stood before the door holding a simple bouquet of snow-white hellebores with dusty miller wrapping around it. A sky blue ribbon tied the bouquet together. The Stetson she'd seen him holding earlier was on his head, and though it worked well with his suit, it changed his appearance. The fierceness she'd first seen when he stepped into the room was no longer the image of a cutthroat businessman, but that of one who lived by the rules of a rugged land. He looked less cattle rancher and more cowboy.

Jace shifted, his gaze darting from her to the flowers. "Ah, I thought you might like these. Mrs. Williams, the lady who owns the flower store, said all brides should have something blue, and I wasn't sure if you had anything blue or borrowed. I, ah, there's a few more that you should have, too, but I forget what they are."

"Something borrowed, something blue, something old, and something new."

"Yeah, that's it. So I took a chance that you didn't have anything blue." He thrust the flowers at her.

"I don't." Her hand trembled as she took the small bundle. It was stunning in its simplicity and beauty. "It's beautiful. Thank you."

"How about the others?"

"Well, these are my mother's pearls." She touched the delicate strand around her neck. "This can be something old. If you let me hold on to this handkerchief that will be my something borrowed." She opened her hand to show the fabric she had clutched there.

He nodded.

"I'm all set then." This was as authentic as her wedding was going to get and as close to her dreams as possible.

"Ah, it seems that while we were in here...talking, Rina made herself useful and invited the entire town to the service." He pointed over his shoulder to where the chapel was. "It's nearly full. I don't want to cause you any undo stress, any more than you might already have that is, but if we hurry this along, we'll beat the rush. I'm betting in the next thirty minutes, it'll have a crowd bigger than Sunday service."

Suddenly, Meredith felt a bit lightheaded. "How many people usually come to Sunday service?"

"About two-fifty. But we're timing this well because it's before lunch so not everyone close by can get off. It's when people have to stand and watch that things tend to get rowdy."

Meredith stepped back and leaned against the wall. She fanned herself with the bouquet. "So we better get a move on it then."

Jace smiled. "I'd like you to meet my folks before we do this. You okay with that?"

She nodded. It only made sense. How awkward would that be to meet afterward?

"I'll also get Rina."

He stepped back. She held his gaze, and something akin to

familiarity passed between them. Or at least she thought he felt it, too, because his brow had furrowed slightly. Certainly, they shared this moment in common, but Meredith's gut told her it was more than that. Deeper. Whatever it was left her feeling a little less alone, if only a tad.

No sooner had Jace left than Sabrina arrived. Her smile was wide, and she clasped her hands together in excitement.

"Oh, Meredith. I have to confess that I'm looking forward to watching the two of you come together. You should know that Jace is one of my closest friends. It's why I have so much faith in the two of you. You look beautiful, honey. Did Jace give you these flowers?" She gestured to the bouquet.

"He did." She couldn't help but smile.

Another side door opened, and a tall woman dressed in a long suede skirt, plain shirt, and large belt walked in. Her dark hair, fringed in silver, was pulled up into a large, loose bun. Her skin was like Jace's and looked tanned but not weathered. Behind her was a man, undoubtedly his father as the resemblance was amazing. Same eyes, height, hair, and smile. His steps were slow, more labored and planned. He was dressed much like his wife with simple slacks, plain dress shirt, and a large belt with an even larger buckle with a bucking horse engraved on it. He wore a gray Stetson like Jace.

"Mercy, Sabrina. You blow into town and always bring with you some surprises." The woman went straight to Sabrina and folded her in a hug. "I hadn't even realized Jace saw you the last time he was in Dallas, much less met someone." She gestured to Meredith.

Briefly, Sabrina gave Meredith a questioning look.

Jace removed his hat and ran a hand through his hair. "Well, Ma. It was like this—"

Meredith sprung forward. "I'm not usually so impulsive by nature, but your son's charms and Sabrina's outstanding character reference and gloating stories of him give me comfort in knowing we're doing the right thing. I know we've only known each other a short time, since he was at the auction." She directed that last bit to Sabrina. "But who needs time when something feels right? I feel like I've known him a lifetime, and now I'll get a lifetime to get to know him. I'm Meredith Hanover." She stuck out her hand and made her smile larger, all the while hoping she wasn't going to burn in hell for lying to these people. Jace's father stepped forward and took her hand in his. "I'm Wes Shepard. You can call me Pops. It's a pleasure meeting you."

His hand trembled in hers, his clasp weak, his fingers squeezing intermittently. She made sure to act as if she didn't notice. "He looks just like you. I could have picked you out anywhere."

"He acts like him, too. Stubborn and bossy." This from Jace's mom.

Meredith waited for Wes to pull his hand away from hers before she turned to face Jace's mom.

"I'm Marjory." She didn't extend her hand, but instead opened her arms and folded Meredith into them like she had Sabrina. "I won't lie and say I'm not surprised, but I like the sight of you already. That last one looked more conniving than a coyote. 'Member her, Rina?" Marjory stepped back and scanned Meredith up and down.

Sabrina came to stand next to Marjory. "I do, and I also remember trying to talk him out of dating her."

"You're a pretty little thing. Almost delicate. We're gonna have to thicken you up. You're not a vegetarian or anything like that, are ya?"

"Leave her alone, Ma. You'll get plenty of time to grill her later." Jace came into the room carrying a collapsed wheelchair.

"I'd have done all this sooner had I met her *before* you all decided to get married."

Jace stiffened and shot Meredith a look she interpreted as a silent plea for help.

"I'm afraid that's my fault. My father is very protective," Meredith said in a rush of words and was pleased to see Jace's shoulders relax.

"Is he here?" Marjory asked.

"No ma'am. I'm afraid he doesn't support the idea." Meredith figured her time spent watching criminal investigation shows was paying off. Lying about a few facts was easier to keep track of than a whole mess of them. She was safer sticking to the truth, even if it made her sound like a flighty, impulsive girl.

"And you're here anyway?" Marjory still held Meredith's shoulders.

"Yes, ma'am. I can only hope he'll come around at some point." She wasn't sure if that was a lie or not.

"Here's your wheelchair, Pops." Jace pushed the arms to the side to lock the seat in place.

"That darned thing? I don't need that. Just chuck it in the trash outside." Pops didn't bother looking at it.

"You know I can't do that. Your therapist said—"

"My therapist is a twenty-something dingbat from California who can't wait to get out of this small town and 'hang ten.' Whatever that means. He's probably taken a beating to the head from all that surfing."

Marjory rolled her eyes. "We'll just leave it here in case you need it. You know I like a contingency plan, Wes. Now take my arm and escort me out to the chapel where we can watch our son get married. You make sure you film that Rina, or Willow will have a fit." Marjory didn't wait for Pops to come to her. She went to him, tucked her arm through his, and stepped in closer. Slowly, they made their way into the chapel.

"Come on, son. Isn't it bad luck to see the bride before the service?" Pops called over his shoulder.

When Jace caught her eye, he thanked her with a nod and a smile. Then he followed his parents out the door.

Meredith smiled, so much for running away.

10

The scariest words at the ceremony were not, "I now pronounce you husband and wife." They were, "You may kiss the bride."

Jace turned to her, took off his hat, clasping it with both hands in front of him, and raised his brows in question. Meredith stepped forward and nodded slightly.

The good folks in the church leaned forward.

As he lowered his head, she caught the slight upward tick of his mouth. Knowing he was okay with kissing her, even possibly looking forward to it if the smile was any indication, made the fluttery sensation in her stomach beat madly. Excitement undulated through her, fear following at its heels.

Everything she knew about being kissed was either from watching television or what she experienced in high school. By college, her father was restricting her time in the company of others, specifically men. She'd been sheltered far too long and now, before her, was a man who could do more with her than a chaste kiss in front of his hometown.

He was her husband.

Please let him be a good kisser.

Meredith swallowed. Her hands shook from both the anticipation of his touch and the realization of what she'd done, so she clutched the bouquet harder.

What did she know about how to have a healthy relationship with a man? One who she was growing increasingly attracted to. One who left her mouth dry and her palms wet. Yes, she'd been kissed before. She'd even contemplated second base with a boy in her trigonometry class, but that was high school, and this? This was the big league. In actuality, this could be for keeps. More importantly, she had every right to him.

Thinking that made her feel antiquated and prudish. Just because they were married, she could now touch him? Perhaps, though, this was important since their situation was unique. She was his wife. He was her man, and when his soft lips pressed to hers, the earth on which she stood trembled, and she lost the ability to breathe. Kissing him was better than any book she'd read or love scene she watched. Her heart accelerated as every nerve ending sizzled, and she was consumed with the urge to pull him closer, deeper.

"Meredith?" he murmured as he drew back. "What are you thinking so hard about?"

"I, uh..." She felt as if a fireball exploded before her, her skin hot and damp.

Jace chuckled. "Yeah, me, too." He popped his hat back on his head, took her hand, and then turned to the crowd.

"If you all will excuse us. Thank you for coming."

Meredith was certain he was about to expire from the intense burning coming from within her.

"Aren't we going to celebrate?" someone called from the pews.

"That's the plan. As soon as I can get her back to the ranch." Jace stepped down from the altar, pulling her with him.

The crowd laughed. Her knees wobbled.

"Now come on, son. You know we all want to share this day with you." Marjory turned away from them and faced the crowd. "Since we were given virtually no notice, I'd like to invite you all to the diner for some coffee and dessert."

The crowd cheered and began to shuffle toward the parish doors, leaving Jace and Meredith stuck at the back of the line.

Jace sighed. "Looks like we'll have to revisit those thoughts later. Mom will never let us escape."

If she was good at one thing, it was working a crowd, pretending she had nowhere else to be when she really wanted to be anywhere else.

With his hand now resting on the small of her back, he guided her down the aisle and back into the church classroom. "Let's grab your coat." He opened the closet and gestured to the long cream-colored coat hanging inside.

After taking it from the hanger, he held it open for her to slip on. Though layered enough to offer warmth, it was too pretty for the rugged country. It would go in the closet with his suit, only to be used if she went with him to Texas for auctions and not likely then, as it was too heavy for that climate.

"You do have other coats?" The lack of knowledge that he possessed about her was astounding. He'd already learned some important things, like she fit perfectly against his side, her lips were uncharacteristically soft, not yet chapped from the change of seasons, and she sighed deeply when he'd kissed her. A sound so becoming he'd wanted to keep at it and see what other noises she'd make.

She slid into the coat and smiled at him over her shoulder, her blue eyes bright and sparkly. "I was just thinking I might be unprepared for here."

He nodded to the two suitcases stacked against the far wall. "I'm assumin' both of those are yours."

"Yes." She held the lapels of the coat closed.

"I'll put them in the truck. Take a moment and enjoy the silence. It's gonna be chaos at the diner. I'll do my best to hold back the rush, but they're all gonna want to get close to you and pump you for information, hoping it'll be them that gets the juicy tidbit of gossip." He adjusted his hat on his head.

She raised a brow. "Should I drop little things here and there? Take this story to a new level or stick to the basics? We met at the stockyards in Ft. Worth, and it was love at first sight?"

Jace rolled his shoulders. What did love at first sight look like? He rubbed his hand down his face. In college, when he'd fallen for a girl, he'd been all in. Meaning, he'd had a hard time keeping his hands to himself. There was no question he'd like to do the same with Meredith, but the circumstances were different here. He'd have to tread lightly, make her feel comfortable, and try not to scare her away. The remoteness of the lifestyle had always handled that for him.

"Ah..."

"Other than the real reason why we're married, what else explains our actions other than instant love?" She bit her lip, looking adorable as hell. "I'm sorry. I shouldn't have said anything. It's up to you how this is handled." She looked down.

Jace was puzzled by her apology. "This is your story as well. You need to be comfortable with it."

She shook her head. "I'm good with whatever you decide."

Jace pressed his lips together. The last thing he needed in his life was a woman who would want him to make all her decisions. He made too many of them already, and there was little energy to make more.

"Meredith, if I told folks I was rescuing you in exchange for sex, you'd be good with that?"

Pink stained her cheeks, and she shook her head.

"Or that you're homeless and illegal, and I did it to keep you in the country?"

Shaking her head, she rolled her eyes but said nothing. He was pleased to see a different response from her. It hinted to a personality other than the capitulating one he was witnessing right now. He wanted the one he'd seen earlier when they first met, the one planning on skipping out. That girl had courage.

"See, it does matter. So speak up. Now, let's walk and talk. We linger any longer, there will be rumors of a baby coming in the winter." Grabbing her suitcases, he moved to the door and held it open.

"I can get them." She reached for the cases.

"I got them. You want to stay in for a moment or go on outside and get a look at that view?"

She opened the door, and he was right behind her as she stepped out of the church.

"It's a stunning view. Do you have this from your house?"

Jace looked at the mountain range. "Pretty much, but from a slightly different angle."

She stared at the peaks, colored in shades of lavender and orange from the wildflowers. The mountains as a backdrop to this beautiful woman was a sight he feared he could get used to quickly, an image he wouldn't be able to forget. It suited her. The colors and the landscape. Like the land, Meredith appeared one way, easy and manageable, but underneath, and he hoped his sense of her wasn't wrong, there was a resistance. A fight. She would need that in order to survive out here, and he hoped he'd get to see it before she left.

With more force than necessary, he tossed her bags in the truck. Not married an hour, and he was already thinking of her in terms of before and after she left.

"Let's say that we met, we *connected*, we had a common interest in being married and connecting as we did." He wagged his brows. "Decided to give it a go." He shrugged. "Why not? People get married for lesser reasons."

She nodded.

Jace faced her. "Listen. I know I said I'm a nice guy, and I am. But I'll bulldoze you in a New York minute. Not because I want to, but because life moves at a rapid pace for me here. There's always something pressin' to get done. You need to speak up and hold your own. That's how we do it out here." He met her gaze, then nodded. "You good with that?"

Meredith's eyes widened. "I can do my best," she said softly.

"That's all I can hope for." He took her hand in his, glanced at her to see if she was good with it, and then led her to the diner. When they entered, a loud cheer went up through the crowd, and he couldn't contain his smile. Glancing at his parents, the pleasure on their faces made this whole new adventure worth it.

The woman his mom played Bunko with pulled Meredith away. They stripped her of her coat before enveloping her into their fold. He was the recipient of several slaps on the back as he made his way to Pops.

He pulled out a chair and straddled it, the back against his front. "You okay with me getting hitched Pops?" He really wanted to know if the spontaneity of it was going over all right.

"She's the nicest girl you've ever brought home. If first impressions are anything, hers is a damn good one. Little gun shy, but that eases with time."

Jace nodded, watching as Meredith fielded questions. After a handful of minutes, something about her shifted. He saw it happen. The smile on her face transitioned from an uncertain but natural one to a demure, insincere one. It never wavered. Her posture was more rigid, and she looked disconnected. She was checking out. Her reaction to the landscape and his parents had sparked a tiny ember of hope that maybe she'd like it in the small town of Bison's Prairie, but her expression was saying otherwise.

"Give her time," Rina said. She looped her arm through his and tugged him from his chair.

"Of course."

Rina steered him toward the makeshift drink table. He had to give credit to the folks that threw this "reception" together at the last minute. A large punch bowl with scoops of bobbing sherbet, the trademark of any proper Bison Prairie event, was the centerpiece.

Rina sighed. "No, Jace. *Actually* give her time. I know you're watching her and already making contingency plans, but how about you go into this without holding the past actions of others against her?"

Jace pulled back. "What's her story?"

"Ask her. When you're alone tonight, maybe you should spend it getting to know each other."

"I already know her mother's passed." Though he wondered about her father. He preferred to think she was looking for a home instead of running from one. That thought gave him comfort, awful as it was. He could compete with "nowhere to go." His place was pretty sweet if he did say so himself. It embodied home in ways that drew others in. When the woman of his past had left, they'd said they'd miss the house the most.

Sabrina elbowed him. "It must be killing you to be all social and make nice with people."

"Making nice with you takes all my energy." He faced her. "Tucks gonna kill me. I said I'd be back shortly and left him in charge. I shoulda had him come in for the wedding."

Sabrina broke into a large smile.

"What?"

"What?" she echoed.

"What's with the smile?"

"I'm just real proud of myself, and if you go about this right, I'll be real proud of you."

"Any advice?" He'd be a fool not to be nervous about all this. Heck, if their initial attraction didn't continue and their interactions became awkward and stilted, how would he explain that to Pops? He reached passed the punch bowl and poured two cups of coffee, then handed one to Sabrina.

"I just gave you advice."

"That was advice? To go about it right? C'mon. You can do better than that." Jace glanced around the room and found Meredith chatting with his mother. Though she looked much like before, there was a slight squint to her eyes and once, while his mother was looking away, she rubbed her temple. He poured another cup for her, wondering if she even liked coffee.

"Think of her as a scared filly and work your magic." Sabrina clapped him on the back, causing a splash of coffee to slosh over the top and hit the table.

"Right now I think she's getting a headache, and I should try to get her out of here before she starts to run or buck." He took a step.

When Rina touched his elbow, he paused. "She doesn't know how to buck, but if she did it, it would be a beautiful thing." She raised a brow then let go of his arm.

He made his way to Meredith, pondering Sabrina's words. They hadn't been here long, but coffee had been doled out, and behind the counter, plates of pie and cake slices were quickly lining up. They would be able to leave soon.

When he reached her side, he bent close and said, "Can I get you an aspirin? A piece of pie?" He held the paper cup out.

Meredith glanced at him, her light blue eyes cloudy with discomfort, then at the cup. She shook her head, wincing slightly as she did. He needed to get her away sooner than later. He set the cups aside.

"Ma." He pulled his mother into a hug. "I'm sorry I sprang

this on you, but thanks for being understanding. I'm gonna take Meredith to the ranch now. You'll handle the crowd?"

She held him tight before releasing him. "You all need to have some cake, and then you can go. You will have the rest of your lives to do what you have in mind."

This was a new spot for him, torn between his mother's request and this new and unfamiliar need to take care of Meredith, his wife, basically a stranger. He wasn't sure what to do or say. Yeah, he wanted to get Meredith home and maybe recapture some more of that sexual interest that poked out when he'd kissed her at the altar. He'd like to explore that further, but she didn't look to be in the best of shape and was fading fast.

"Ma, I think Meredith is overwhelmed."

She looked over his shoulder then nodded. "I'll grab some cake, and you can make quick work of it. Trust me on this. Give the town a little something, so they'll leave you alone. You know how old-fashioned these people can be." She squeezed his shoulder before spinning away. Presumable to get cake.

Mrs. Carson was yammering on about knitting, not really caring if she had Meredith's attention. Jace leaned close to Meredith and whispered in her ear. "My mom is getting us cake. We'll do a thing where people share a bite, smile, and get out of here. You good with that?"

She nodded. "I can stay as long as you like."

Jace frowned. Her words did not reflect the vibe he was getting. Not that her actions did either. It was something else. Something he didn't know how to label.

Hell, this married business was hard. All this guessing and second-guessing. He rolled his shoulders. Chances were high he was going to jack this up royally.

His mom approached carrying a large slice of red velvet cake. She thrust the plate at him and a large brown bag, too.

"Here's dinner and some extra dessert for later tonight. I love you." She kissed his cheek. "I don't know why this has all come about, but I mean to find out. If you married this sweet girl to make your father happy, to have someone cook at the house, or for any other reason than you are madly in love with her, I will skin you alive." She met his gaze, gave him her famous stink eye that used to leave him cowering, all before turning to the crowd.

"Can I have your attention please? Jace and Meredith are anxious to be on their way. I'm sure you all understand." There was a low rumble of laughter through the crowd.

Jace placed the bag on the table next to him and handed Meredith the fork. He raised a brow in question, but he knew she'd lie and say she was fine. She'd gone a few shades paler since they arrived, and the weight of a clicking clock pressed upon him. There was no logic as to why he felt like he needed to get her outta here. He just did.

"Ready?" He stepped closer.

"Always," she said, not looking at him.

"Ladies and gentlemen, allow me to introduce Mr. And Mrs. Jace Shepard."

A cheer went through the room.

"They're going to share some cake, throw a bouquet, and then split. Please stay and have some cake or pie on us." Mom pointed to him, shifting the focus of the room from her to them.

Jace held his fork and the plate between them. He scooped off the corner then faced Meredith. The corners of her eyes were crinkled, hinting at a squint, a look he'd seen before in Pop's expression when he fought off pain.

Jace shoved the cake in her mouth, catching some of it at the corner and forcing it to smear slightly on her cheek.

Meredith startled, her eyes widening, and stepped back. She blinked several times before her attention was fully on him. He winked and smiled, hoping she'd recognize he hadn't meant to do that.

The crowd was quiet. She adjusted the fork he'd given her earlier so she could scoop up some cake then stepped closer. When a wicked gleam came into her eyes, excitement flared through him. Getting to know her naughty and nice sides was going to be his pleasure. As her hand with the fork moved toward his mouth, he knew he was about to take the lump sum to the kisser, but then something in her shifted.

It was astonishing to watch the visibly obvious as the uncertainty crossed her face and shuttered her expression. She fed him as gently and sweetly as possible, making sure not a morsel went anywhere but in his mouth.

Jace was disappointed. Not because he thought his actions made him look like an ass, his new bride with cake on her face, but because he knew this wasn't what she wanted to do and had suppressed her initial desires and reaction.

Was this wounded filly an abused one? Anger coursed through Jace at the mere thought. He wanted, no he needed, to let Meredith know she was safe with him, with his family.

He slid the plate on the table and took the fork from her hand. Addressing the crowd but looking at her, he said. "Thanks for coming you all. Its time I take my bride outta here." He lunged at her, catching her off guard, and flipped her over his shoulder, fireman style. Meredith squealed.

"Throw the bouquet," someone yelled. He felt Meredith rise up and assumed she tossed the flowers because many of the women in the room cried out in excitement.

He headed straight for the door, snatching up Meredith's coat as he walked out. He marched down the street toward his truck, the anger fueling his steps.

"All right. We're out of sight. You can put me down," she said between breaths as she bounced along his shoulder.

Jace said nothing but walked the three blocks in silence.

"Jace?"

He reached his truck and flipped her over, setting her against it, tossing her coat into the truck bed. "Listen to me, Meredith. I don't know what's happened to you in the past, but you're safe here. Nothing is going to happen to you here. I promise."

Meredith shoved him in the chest, pushing him away. "Really? Because it feels real safe to me when you're all up in my face."

11

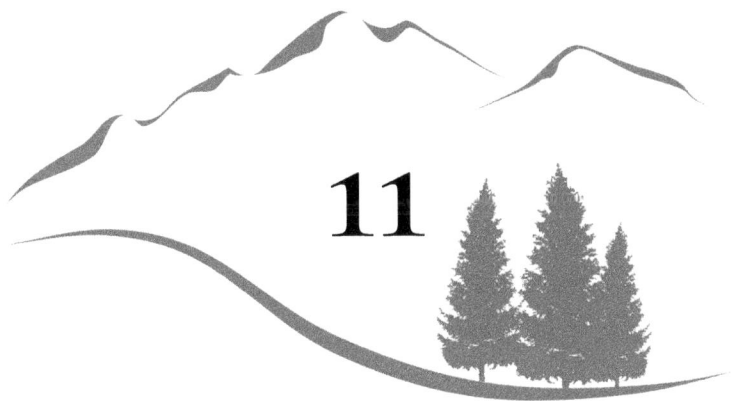

She tried. She really did try. She wanted to get to know the town folks, but the mingling and light chatter did her in. Like a person with post-traumatic stress, she had felt the headache come on and had emotionally retreated in an effort to ward it off.

Clearly, Jace was angry with her. He might say she was safe, but with his hands on his hips and the way he leaned toward her, the message didn't jive with the words.

Being bossed around was getting tiresome.

So she'd told him so. Before she had thought about what she was doing, the words had tumbled out with the same force she had used to shove him back.

Jace stepped away, his arms going slack from his hips. He ducked his head, giving it a slight shake. "You're right."

She barely heard the words, too afraid of what was to come next. Her father had raged at her the times she stood up to him, so much she'd stopped until that last night when he'd shoved her.

"I beg your pardon?"

Jace looked up and met her gaze. "I said you're right. I won't deny that I'm angry, but I can see why you might think I was angry with you. I'm not, and I'm sorry for getting in your face." He gave a gruff, bitter-sounding laugh. "This married thing is hard."

"I beg your pardon?" She was stuck on the apology, having not expected it.

Confusion crossed Jace's face. "What?"

Meredith shook her head to clear her thoughts. "What?"

Jace smiled. "Did I say something that I need to clarify? I'm not sure I can remember all that I did say." He rubbed his chin.

"You apologized." She returned his smile.

"And I meant it." He took off his hat, rubbed his hand over his short hair. A dark brown lock fell across his forehead, giving him a charming look that could only be classified as rogue.

"No one has ever apologized to me. I mean, in a situation like this." She smiled, big enough to show some teeth. Apologies were nice.

Jace held his hat with both hands and ran one along the rim. "Can I ask a personal question?"

Meredith shrugged. "We're married. I think you're entitled to a few."

They shared a laugh. Hard to believe this morning she'd judged Jace to be more than she was ready for, but so far he'd been nothing but nice. Granted, people who wanted something from another person were always nice.

Jace shifted, glanced at her, then looked away. "Ah..."

"Wow, this must be one humdinger of a question." The anxiety she'd fought back earlier began to spread upward from the pit of her belly. She pressed a hand to her side. Soon it would reach her head and bring on the migraine.

"I'm just gonna put it out there, okay?"

She nodded and clenched her teeth.

"Has someone hit you, Meredith?"

Instantly, the anxiety dissipated. "What? No." She thought about the last fight she had with her father. "Not in the way you must be thinking."

"But someone laid their hands on you in anger?" Jace straightened, his knuckles going white.

Meredith sighed and leaned back against the truck. Out of the corner of her eye, she saw her coat and pulled it from the bed, slipped it on. For a moment, during their brief heated words, she hadn't felt the chill of the spring day, but now the crisp, cool air was sinking into her bones.

"It was one time, and it was my father. He grabbed me by my arms and shoved me."

"Jesus." The muscle in his jaw popped. "Is that why you're here?"

"That's what helped me decide to be here."

Jace nodded.

"It wasn't just that. There's more to it, of course. It was a bad situation all around, and my health was starting to deteriorate. Headaches." She pointed to her temple. She didn't want him to think she was flighty, had one scuffle with her father, and did something as extreme as marry a stranger. His good opinion was important to her. The people of Bison Prairie had greeted her with kindness because of Jace and his family. That had not escaped her attention.

Jace rested one arm on the side of the truck. "Tell me about these headaches. You were getting one in the diner, right?"

"Best I can figure is that they come on with stress. They're migraines. Debilitating ones. I was getting them all the time. Almost daily. The life I left wasn't good or happy."

"I figured it wasn't or Sabrina wouldn't have introduced us had it been otherwise," he said.

Sabrina. It was her word that gave Meredith credit. Not

Meredith's. She shivered and wondered what it would be like to have the trust and faith of this man.

"Hey, you're cold. Let's get into the truck, and I'll take you home." He gestured for her to walk around the car, then followed behind her. He opened the passenger door and helped her inside, making sure her coat was not hanging out before closing the door with a soft but solid click.

Meredith tucked her trembling hands into her coat pockets. What was next?

Her mind went to the one topic everyone thought of after their wedding.

Honeymoon.

Sex.

Did he expect to have sex with her tonight? She tried to picture it, and though she had no difficulty picturing Jace without a shirt, she couldn't begin to see herself as the other participant in the event.

They drove down a long stretch of road, a highway, before turning down another long two-lane road. She didn't know if they were close to his house but with each mile, she felt as if time was running out. She'd soon have the answer to her sex question. She needed to decide if she was going to do *it* or not. She didn't want to freak out on him. Wanted even less to make a fool of herself. She knew she needed to bring up the topic. Waiting to see how it played out might be an option, but that gave her heartburn.

Meredith wasn't sure she had the courage to have the much needed conversation with him. She'd used up whatever courage she had earlier with her one retort about his anger. Like a new runner with aspirations of a marathon, Meredith was going to have to build up her nerve bit by bit. She nibbled at her lip and tried to work out what to say, then moved to chewing her thumbnail.

"We should get to know each other better. Why don't you tell me something about yourself," Jace said.

She paused her nail chewing. "I'm really boring."

The open road was before them. To each side of the car were trees that fell away to clearings with the occasional house set way back from the road. Some were surrounded by fences, and cattle spotted the landscape in the distance.

"I doubt you're boring. Give me something." He dropped one hand to his lap, resting it on his upper thigh.

Was that a sign? A clue as to what he wanted?

She accidentally bit the pad of her thumb, not knowing what he meant about giving him something. She'd seen enough movies to know guys liked to get frisky in cars, let the girl do the work, but she wasn't the person to do that. Or at least she didn't think she was. She'd never even had a finger near her nether regions; a blowjob was way far out of her repertoire.

"Let me see your hand?" He held out his, waiting.

Meredith wiped her damp palm on her coat before slowly putting her hand in his.

He wrapped his fingers with hers, brought them to his lap to rest on his thigh. "Relax, take a deep breath."

A deep breath? She couldn't even take in a shallow one as all her air was stuck in her upper chest, panic about to take over. They turned onto a driveway that looked to run miles before them. The entrance was grand. Large beams supported by beautifully crafted, dusty red bricks pointed the way. An automated wood gate swung open to allow them entry. Fencing ran the length of the road for miles beyond what she could see. There was no house in the distance, but she knew they were at his ranch by the large twisted-iron sign that hung from the top beam touting they'd arrived at Three Peaks Ranch.

He squeezed her hand, and a tremor ran through her. He adjusted in his seat, their hands moving closer to his crotch and

Meredith knew—she just knew—he wanted something. A hand job at the very least. She'd read plenty of books that talked about the insatiable libido that consumed men.

"I can't sleep with you," she blurted out and then jerked her hand from his and buried her face in them. She was a hot mess of a woman with her social anxiety and all-consuming uncertainty. He should have the marriage annulled and find someone else who was less a dumpster fire.

"You can't today or ever?" His voice was even, as though he'd asked a simple question. "Is this sandwich turkey or ham?"

Meredith looked at him through her fingers. "I'm sorry. I have no tact. I meant to say that we just met and..." She impersonated a fish as she searched for words, lips moving but nothing coming out.

Jace smiled and slowed the truck to a crawl. "I'm not going to force you to do something you don't want to do. I'm not that kind of man." He bent forward so their eyes could meet. "All right?"

She closed her eyes and nodded.

"Look," he said.

She opened her eyes and peered at him through her fingers. He ticked his head toward the window. Dropping her hands, she looked through the windshield at the most breathtaking view she'd ever seen. Variegated shades of green covered the land with spots of happy yellow wildflowers. The mountains, three distinct peaks that lay just beyond, were giant slate gray forces looming over them. She leaned toward the window to get a closer look.

"I hope you like the view. Maybe it's better than the one in town?" he said softly.

Without looking away, she reached out her hand and touched his upper arm. "It's stunning. Please tell me it never gets old." She glanced at him and found him staring at her and not the view.

He shook his head. "I've been here my entire life, with the exception of being away for college, and I'm not sick of seeing them yet."

She smiled, looking between the mountains and him. "I can't wait to see the changes the seasons bring," she said more to herself. The land was untamed, but solid. Its story new, she guessed, with each season. She wanted to be like the landscape. She wanted her story to be fresh but solid. She wanted to have a story beyond what was written so far.

She sucked in a strong, relaxing breath and smiled. Here was a version of freedom. Not the one she pictured, but definitely the chance to be the person she thought she could be, the person her father had no interest in but her mother had helped create before she died. Starting today, she wasn't going to be the sum of her past but the whole of her future. Each day would be a new version of Meredith, created from her own desires and dreams. No more Meredith Hanover, doormat. This is her time to really figure out a new true Meredith.

"Meredith?"

When she looked at Jace, something shifted. He was smiling at her, and a dimple peeked out from his cheek. The energy pulsing through her increased, sending shock waves of something foreign but exciting right to her core. It pulled her to him with such a force, there was no denying it. She caressed his cheek, her thumb stroking the dimple. Their eyes held as he turned his mouth to her palm and delivered a gentle kiss.

Heat shot into her palm, up her arm, and surged through her body. He laid his hand to hers, pressing it into his face, and kissed her palm again.

"Jace," she whispered.

These feelings, this headiness of want were so overwhelming, Meredith wasn't sure how to handle them. She'd never been in this situation before. She knew what she wanted to do, more, wanted him to do to her, only she wasn't sure how to make that happen.

Meredith let her eyelids drift down until they were closed and hoped he would read the sign correctly.

A low rumble of laughter penetrated her haze of need, and she snapped her eyes open. Jace was staring at her, a full grin across his face. He bit the inside of her palm with a small nip then entwined his fingers with hers and pulled her hand from his face to his chest.

"Let's lay some ground rules, Meredith. Anytime you want me to kiss you, you just come up and take a kiss. I'll never turn that away." He jerked her forward, and she came to a stop against his chest. He cupped the back of her neck.

"Now you can close your eyes," he whispered before putting his lips to hers.

He didn't kiss her roughly, but not gentle either. His kiss was weighted with need, or perhaps that was what she felt.

Need.

An insatiable desire to explore and learn. Though nervous, she had nothing to lose.

She removed her hand from his and wrapped her arms around his neck, situating herself closer. He snaked an arm around her back and pressed her against him.

Meredith was sure the heat would consume her, and she'd expire in a ball of flames.

When his tongue swept through her mouth, she was a goner. Moaning, she adjusted to face him head-on and felt his hands on her rear as he lifted her up to straddle him, the steering wheel at her back, her wedding dress and coat pooling to the sides.

"If we had met out or through mutual friends, I have no doubt we'd be doing this exact same thing right now," he mumbled against her lips.

What a great fantasy. She was like any normal twenty-four year old, making out in a truck with a hot guy.

It felt so right and so wrong. It was glorious.

He trailed a path of kisses across her jaw and down her neck. Wanting him to touch more of her, she arched to give him greater access. His hands came from around her waist to run up her sides, coming to rest level with her breasts. His lips hovered over the pucker of skin at her throat, then he brushed them softly against it. "One day I want to know why you have this." He kissed the scar again.

She never wanted to talk about the scar. With it came too many bad memories. "If we'd met out, there would be no chance we'd be doing this. My father wouldn't let me out of his sight." She sighed when he did a suck-kiss on her collarbone. "Thank God, my father isn't here." She dragged her hands through his hair as he moved lower and kissed the swell of her breast. His thumbs stroked over the top of her dress, teasing the nipples underneath.

"Sounds like you didn't get a lot of opportunity to make out in a car," Jace said as he moved a sleeve off her shoulder, lowering the neckline. His lips followed the path down.

"I've never made out in a car before," she said, trying to not pant.

A loud blasting horn made her jump away to the other side of the truck.

12

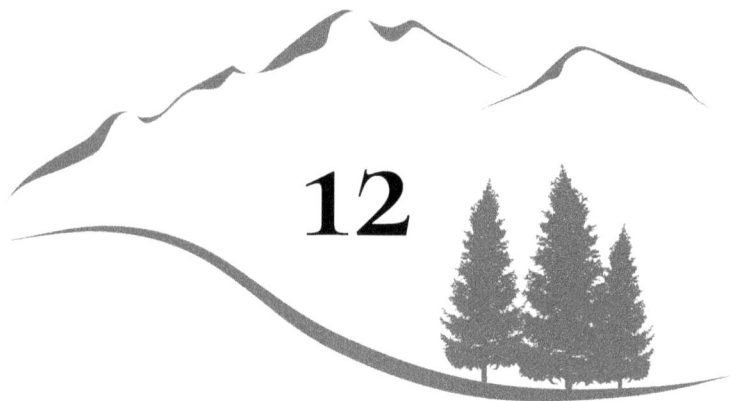

Movement from across the prairie caught Jace's eye. Tuck's truck was coming his way.

"Shit," he mumbled, reached over, and pulled her dress back up her shoulder.

"What?" She'd gone from looking satiated to panicked in one breath.

"It's okay, but my ranch manager is headed this way. I'd rather he not know what we were up to." Meredith sat up straighter; her once perfectly styled hair was cascading wildly around her face, curls resting on her shoulder. She was flushed, her lips swollen from his roughness, her eyes light. She looked like a woman who'd been sexed. He couldn't wait to see how she looked once he got about doing it properly.

She jerked the seatbelt across her in a rush.

He took her shaking hand in his after she clicked the belt into place. "Meredith, it's okay. Tuck and I have been friends our entire lives. He's a nice guy who's likely wondering where I've been and why I haven't done my share of the work today."

"You didn't tell him you were getting married?" When he shook his head, anger flashed across her face.

Her indignation pleased him. Hidden within her, ready to be set free, were a backbone and an expectation of how she wanted to be treated. He would enjoy watching her come into it. So long as it wasn't directed at him like it was right now.

"I stupidly hadn't thought the act all the way through. Had I foreseen it would have gone like it had, I would've had Tuck and his wife at the ceremony."

"Oh." Her lips made such a cute *o,* he wanted to kiss her again. "Sorry."

"I'm sorry for the interruption." He shifted in his seat and straightened the front of his pants. Meredith blushed and looked out the window.

"Maybe it was a good thing?" she mumbled.

"How so?"

"Don't you think it would be a mistake to...to...you know." She clasped her hands together. "Mix business with pleasure."

Jace wiped a hand down his face and blew out a breath. "No, I don't. I think it would make things more believable."

"Do you really believe that?" Her blue eyes sparkled against her flushed cheeks.

Getting frisky looked good on her and, yeah, he really wanted to be right about it making things more believable between them if that meant they could pick up where they left off. But he wasn't right. He knew that.

He punched the steering wheel with his palm then said, "Yeah, you're right. It could cause serious complication."

"I'm so embarrassed," she mumbled, then looked away.

"Why?" He tried not to focus on any part of her body. As far as he was concerned, every part of her was begging for him to kiss it. But she'd brought up a good point. There would be no avoiding each other if this ended awkwardly and there was a high probability of that happening. They barely knew one another. Sex in the cab of his truck might not be the best way to start out this arrangement, whether his body wanted to or not.

He had to think of Pops.

She let her head fall back, resting it on the seat, and looked at the ceiling. "What you must think of me. First you catch me trying to skip out, breaking my word to Sabrina, then we strike a deal to help each other out, and now I'm all over you. Not a very clear message."

He understood what she was saying; it was important to her not to be thought of negatively.

"It's clear we've got some chemistry between us. Maybe it'll help convince my folks that our marriage is genuine."

She rolled her eyes to him. "Do you think we can pull this off?"

"Having sex? Hell yeah."

When pink color stained her cheeks, he chuckled and said, "I think we take it day by day. How does that sound?"

"No, ah…" She gulped and leaned toward him. "Sex," she said in a lowered voice. "I'm not the type… I haven't ever… I wouldn't be able to compartmentalize." She shook her head.

Jace tried to decipher what she was saying and wondered if it was possible she was a virgin. He slowly nodded. They needed more time to get to know each other, and she needed to get her feet under her–so to speak. "Day by day sounds good."

Tuck honked several times and pulled up to the truck heading the opposite direction so their driver's sides lined up. Jace lowered his window.

"Dude, where you been? Shits getting real here. Fence is down in the east pasture, and we're missing some heads." Tuck looked past him to Meredith. "Whoa. Hey." He scanned what he could of her and gave Jace a wide-eyed, questioning look.

"Tuck, this is Meredith. She and I got married this morning."

Tuck's mouth dropped open before breaking into a wide grin. "You're shitting me, right?" Tuck slapped the steering wheel.

Jace shook his head. "Sorry man, I would have had you there if I realized it wasn't going to be the private ceremony I wanted." He glanced at Meredith. "The private ceremony we wanted." He smiled at her.

"Hell, man. Congratulations. Mandy is going to kill me. You know that right?" Tuck leaned back in his seat and looked across Jace. "Congratulations, Meredith. It's nice to meet you."

"Thank you. It's nice to meet you as well." Her eyes darted between Jace and Tuck's. Sooner or later he'd like to hear her story and learn why she was so nervous around others. Preferably sooner.

"So about the fence and the cattle..." Tuck said.

"Let me get Meredith to the house and situated, and I'll head out there with you and get it fixed up."

Tuck nodded and, following a wag of his brows, drove away.

"I hate to leave ya like this, but we can't afford to lose any more cattle." He cruised slowly down the drive.

"Anything I can do to help?"

"Can you teach cows to move away when a bear comes close? 'Cause that's the problem I'm having." He grinned, happy that she offered to pitch in.

"I would think they'd be scared. I know I'd be scared." She shuddered.

"Sometimes." He shrugged with indifference. "Sometimes they fight back, but mostly they're used to a variety of wildlife and can be slow to clue in."

They turned a bend, and behind some trees sat the house. It was a two-story with a wrap porch that his great-granddaddy had built, and he shared a bit of his family history with Meredith.

"That's it. That's home." Jace smiled.

"I love it. It reminds me of Sabrina's house. I've always wanted to sit on a porch like that and drink coffee—"

"Watch the sun rise or set."

Meredith nodded eagerly. "Exactly. Have you always lived here?"

"Yeah, I couldn't live anywhere else but here."

She faced him, her eyes wide. "Four generations?"

He nodded. "It means a lot to me."

"I can see why. It would to me as well." She looked from the house to across the yard at the large barn and the three corrals next to it.

He pulled up to the detached garage. A covered walkway led the way to the backside of the house, but this family had traditions and, pretend marriage or not, he was going to adhere to them.

He jumped from the truck with every intention to go around and get her door, but Meredith was already sliding out of the truck from his side, and the sight filled him with longing. What if Meredith were really his girl? Yes, she technically was. But that was in name and not in years. Jace forced the thoughts back. He would not get attached to the idea of Meredith always being around. She liked the house; she didn't seem put off by the remoteness. Chances of her sticking around until Pops passed were getting better. He wouldn't ask for more.

Tuck pulled in behind him and got out. He took off his hat and extended his hand to Meredith. "Welcome to Three Peaks Ranch, Mrs. Shepard. It's a pleasure to have you here."

"Thank you—"

"Tuck. You can call me Tuck."

Jace took Meredith by the elbow and steered her toward the front door. "I hate to leave you here to fend for yourself. I'm not sure how long we'll be." He led her around to the front and up the stairs, then stopped to faced her. "Listen, I know this might seem weird, but it's a Shepard tradition to carry the bride over the threshold." He lowered his voice. "I know our circumstances are different, but would you mind?"

Meredith shook her head. "I believe it's a tradition for many people in our nation."

"Yeah, but not like this." He bent and tossed her over his shoulder fireman-style. Her fabulous fanny in the air, his hands holding her sexy legs at the calf.

"Jace," she called out laughing.

"Get the bags, will ya, Tuck?" he called over his shoulder as he kicked the door open and stepped across the threshold.

13

J ace gave her a quick tour of the house, and following an awkward where-do-I-put-these moment with her bags, deposited them in what looked like a guest room. He then disappeared into the room next to hers, she assumed his, because he stepped out minutes later dressed in well-worn jeans that fit snugly over his back assets, a flannel shirt, a wool jacket in navy blue, and his grey Stetson. She'd nearly drooled openly. Instead, she leaned against the wall to steady her knees lest she jump him like the licentious woman she really was. Their time in the truck proved that.

He guided her to the kitchen. "Make yourself at home. Unpack, get settled, and eat anything. I'll be back as soon as I can. The house is heated, but if it gets too cold, build a fire." He hesitated. "Sound good?"

She turned away, embarrassed she didn't know the first thing about making a fire, much less how to cook. "What about you eating? We left the food they gave us at the diner."

Taking from the pantry a container of what looked to be beef jerky and some energy drinks, Jace held them up. "Don't hold dinner for me. I'm real sorry about this."

She moved behind the island and forced a smile. "Don't worry about me. I'll be fine."

He arched a brow. "You sure?"

"Absolutely. I'm going to change out of this dress and snoop through your drawers."

"All right then. Sounds like a plan. I'll be back soon." He nodded as if to reassure her, took one step backward, smiled again, then spun on his heel and bolted from the room.

Sticking to her words, she did as she told Jace and changed into jeans and a sweatshirt, It took less than ten minutes to unpack her bags. Downstairs she went through the pantry and fridge but decided on a peanut butter and jelly sandwich. Meredith hadn't so much as boiled water in her life, and standing in front of the six-burner range made her feel woefully out of her element. Would she be expected to cook? She supposed it couldn't be all that hard. Maybe she'd ask Jace for Internet access and could look up some recipes.

The house was quiet with the exception of bugs outside calling on the night. She was a stranger in a strange home and land with nothing to do. She didn't even have a book to read. She'd tried watching TV but was too restless, too distracted by her thoughts to focus.

Instead, she laid on the couch and thought of Jace.

She ran her hand over the areas that Jace had kissed, touching her lips and the top of her breast, remembering the heat, then scolding herself for being foolish about some kisses, lovely as they were. She and Jace had made a deal to play house, and it would do no good for her to get reality confused with fantasy. Even if the fantasy portion warmed her to her very center and gave her those intoxicating butterflies that made her giddy. Yes, heady stuff indeed were his kisses.

Her father had wanted her to connect with someone like Lyle Brady, a man so cold, ice shivered when he was nearby.

How could a father love his daughter so little to want that for her?

Meredith shook her head. At least she was here. She was getting a chance to figure everything out.

She explored the family home, walls covered with generations of Shepard's working the land and going to rodeos, at weddings, and family get-togethers. All smiling, happy, with arms flung around each other's. Sabrina was in a few.

It was stupid to be envious of her, but Meredith was. Not only because Jace had his arm flung across her shoulders and they were laughing, but because Sabrina had a life Meredith had only dreamed about. She was loved enough to be on someone's wall along with baby pictures and awkward school photos.

All that had ended for Meredith when her mother died.

She touched the wood frames, wiped the beginnings of dust off a baby picture. She'd be stupid to deny she wanted this, a wall that showcased her life and showed love and laughter. But she would have to wait awhile before she opened herself up to the possibility of love and family. She reminded herself there was still time. She was just getting started and, sure, she might find all she wanted here at Three Peaks Ranch. Or she might not. What if she tried to make this place the solution and then his father passed and Jace asked her to leave? Meredith turned away from the wall. No. She shook her head. No. She would not sell this newly found freedom by forcing herself into a family position—all for security.

She would let things happen the way they were meant to.

The doubts ate at her, making sound reasoning hard. She was skewed and more vulnerable after what she and Jace had shared. At least she knew that much.

She moved to the picture window in the living room and pushed back the soft floral curtains. The house had a woman's touch that Meredith found comforting, like the framed cross-stitched art on the wall, the runner over the buffet in the dining room, and similar cross-stitched pillows on the leather couch. It worked for her just like the view outside of the sun sinking behind the mountains did.

Her exploration of the house ended in a back room that looked to have been the family room but was now a bedroom. Going by the equipment, a bench, adjustable bed much like a hospital one, and the rack of clothes pushed to the corner, this was where his father slept. As comfortable as they'd tried to make it, there was no privacy. Feeling like a trespasser, she backed from the room.

Time passed at an agonizingly slow pace. She found a computer and took a chance that Jace wouldn't mind if she used it. The speed was worse than dial up. Deciding she should try something, Meredith searched on how to start a fire, but found the instructions too intimidating. She didn't know if the flue was open, and the off chance it was closed, it was April after all, was a risk she decided against. She imagined Jace coming home to a house of smoke of her doing. No way.

Instead she found a Jane Austen book in the study at the back of the house where the computer was. Clearly Jace's study. His jacket over the chair, a coffee cup on the desk corner, and books and papers across the surface. Her gut told her this was where he spent his time when he was in the house. Unlike the immaculate house, this room looked lived in and the space felt private. Much like when she entered his father's bedroom, she was left with a sense of not belonging. Not wanting to be caught there, she quickly grabbed the novel and scuttled out. Settling on the couch in the front room, she covered herself with a wool blanket and tried to relax. Tried to get lost in Mr. Darcy, but found her mind wandering to what transpired in the truck, and her attention was constantly drawn to the front window. At some point, around when the moon was at its highest, she fell asleep wondering what was keeping Jace.

14

It was not unlike fence mending to be time consuming, especially if they were old and deteriorating. The fences that were down were not the oldest on the ranch. That detail belonged to the west side. These looked to have broken under a weight.

Likely from the same grizzly that was determined to cause Jace grief. He considered whether it was time to call in Fish and Game to try to trap him. Every cattle lost was dollars from his pocket, and whereas Jace respected the circle of life and the power of the giant bear, he also liked to eat and had his sister's college to pay for. This bear was quickly becoming his key problem. Soon the ranch would have the calves running. Letting them range on a wide belt of land was what they'd always done. This year he'd have to rethink that plan.

Jace entered the house from the back, coming into the kitchen. He was sorta hoping there would be a plate of food waiting for him, but the kitchen looked untouched, save for the jar of peanut butter still on the counter.

Well, hell.

Here it was his honeymoon, and he'd spent the evening and better part of the night rebuilding a fence and herding cows back onto his land, not wanting them to roam on the government's prairies. He had very little recourse there; no one liked a bear killer, even if the beast was stalking Jace's stock. For Jace, that was asking for more trouble than it was worth. Many activists didn't like the centuries-old deal ranchers had with the government regarding use of public land. Their intention was to preserve the natural resource, and Jace killing a bear would give them fodder. Jace understood that. He believed in preservation and wildlife responsibility, too, but right now he needed to preserve his income.

He found Meredith sleeping on the couch and debated whether to carry her upstairs or leave her. He decided to let her be. She looked peaceful and comfortable, and if he carried her upstairs, that would just open a shit can of awkwardness he didn't have the energy to deal with. Not feeling right about leaving her, he decided to stay as well. He dimmed the light and stretched out on the overstuffed chair beside her. Kicking off his boots, he slid them quietly to the floor before letting his head fall back with exhaustion. He'd slept many nights here, his father in the next room, Jace on hand to assist should Pops need to use the restroom or something. His mother was exhausted, and he'd tried to offer relief whenever he could. He wondered how this would all work with Meredith here once his parents moved back from town now that Pop's rehab was almost complete. There were no immediate answers as sleep crept up quickly and took him down.

He woke when someone nudged his shoulder. When he jerked upright, Meredith jumped back.

"I'm sorry. I didn't mean to startle you." She wrapped her arms around herself.

"Sorry. Normally when someone wakes me, it's because

something is going wrong." He rubbed the sleep from his eyes, his face cloaked in morning stubble. "What time is it?"

There was a hint of sunlight peaking over the mountains outside.

"I have five on my watch. I heard a truck come up the drive, and I thought I'd better wake you." She sat on the edge of the couch.

Jace stifled a yawn. He could swear he'd just shut his eyes five minutes ago. "That's Tuck. We usually get started around now." He stretched and caught a whiff of something. Sniffing his pits, he grimaced. "Sorry. Not the picture of a magical honeymoon, I imagine."

"That's okay, you seem really busy. Are the fences okay?" She shook her head. "That's a stupid question. I meant did you get the fences worked out?"

Jace laughed. "Yeah, but I knew what you meant." He sighed, stood, and stretched again. "Looks like I got a wildlife problem. Bear."

Meredith's eyes grew large.

"Speaking of which, do you know how to shoot a gun?"

She shook her head.

"Let's make sure we fix that right away. I don't want you here alone without being able to protect yourself."

Meredith looked out the window and scooted down the couch closer to him.

"I'm not trying to scare you, Meredith. I think in my entire life a bear has only come up close to the house twice, and both times we were able to scare it away. But better to be safe and prepared than not."

She nodded slightly. "Sure. That makes sense."

"Listen, I'm desperate for a shower. Think you can scare me up some food while I do that? I'll meet you in the kitchen in ten minutes." He didn't have time to wait for an answer and made quick work getting ready. True to his word, he was back downstairs and in the kitchen in the time he said.

Meredith stood at the island with a plate. On it were two slices of bread with peanut butter.

"What's this?" He wiped water from his neck. Having hurried, he hadn't fully toweled off.

"It's protein and the only thing I know how to "scare up.""

Jace nodded several times and then burst out laughing. "I'm sorry," he said and took the plate. He tried to stifle the laughter when Meredith looked devastated, her face crumbling with every laugh.

"I'm not laughing at you. I'm laughing because I just assumed, and well...you know what they say about assuming. Here I had these fantasies of coming down to a giant breakfast, and you hand me peanut butter bread. It's not even toasted." It was priceless really and a good lesson. Oh, how Willow and his mother would love to see him get handed a plate of bread. His mom had nagged him to death about learning to cook, and he'd chauvinistically assumed he'd find a woman to do that. Here he was married to one who didn't know how.

"I couldn't find the toaster," she squeaked, a tear leaking out.

Jace was instantly somber. He put the plate down.

"So, you don't know how to cook?" He scratched his beginning beard. In his haste, he'd forgotten to shave.

Meredith shook her head and swiped away the lone tear. "No, I don't." Her chin lifted in defiance.

"Me either," he said. "Mom's been up my craw about learning, and I told her there was no need. With her around or if I ever married, that was taken care. That's why I was laughing. I'm sorry Ma missed this because it would've made her day. Not that we're going to tell her or anything."

Meredith sagged against the counter, her wrecked face now

reassembled into a beautiful picture of loveliness. "I thought you were laughing at me."

"I'm sorry. I hope you'll find I'll never do that. Not spitefully."

He slid the bread from the plate and took a bite. "It's good."

When she laughed, it was a light, flirty sound that gave him instant wood. He moved to stand on the other side of the island. He needed to think of something else other than the sweet sounds she made when he touched her because that chain of thought was starting to get him overheated. He looked at the bread.

"I'm guessing then you had someone cook for you. Is it because you have no interest in knowing how to cook or...?" Food. They'd talk about food. How sexy could that be?

She looked to the floor before meeting his eyes and nodded. "We had a cook."

He glanced at her hands. They were pristine. Smooth. Unlike his mother or Willow whose hands showed their use.

Ranch hands, his mother called them.

Meredith had socialite hands. It was going to be a long, tough year for her polished nails.

"I see a lot of canned goods in the pantry, but not a lot of fresh food in the fridge." She bit her lip, and he swallowed hard.

Her action instantly brought him back to his attraction to her. Who cared if she didn't have ranch hands? So long as she put those hands on him, he'd be perfectly fine. She nibbled her lip, and he wanted to do the same. He wanted to be close enough to her that he could suck on her lip and other things his mouth might find.

Jesus H. Christ, he was a horny asshole. Here she was trying to have a conversation with him, one that had made her cry earlier, and he was thinking about breaking their pact and getting her naked. But keeping his mind in the gutter helped him ignore the tiny, nagging doubt she was too pampered and would find this a difficult place to live. That she'd want to leave any day now. He imagined trying to explain that to his parents.

His mood instantly soured. She was here one full day and already it was complicated. Sex, no sex, married but not really married. He needed to focus on something asexual like...cows. He needed to remember why he was doing this—Pops. He needed to not be distracted by her lips...or anything. He shuffled on his feet, ate the last bite of the bread while he tried to remember what they were talking about before he ventured down this tangent.

"I can't cook either, but I can open up a mean can of beans or soup. And over a campfire, I can grill an insanely good steak. I can flip burgers on a grill without burning them. You know, those sorts of things, and salads probably aren't that hard, my sister makes them all the time. That's just chopping, right? That's not mixing ingredients, but even then, how hard could ingredient mixing be?"

Meredith traced the pattern on the counter. "I don't know. I'd like to try it, though."

"You should try it. Experiment away. I'm going to be outside for most the day. I can show you real quick where to get the eggs. Did I mention we have hens and chickens?"

She shook her head. "You don't mind if I mess up your kitchen?"

"It's your kitchen, too," he said and took the other piece of bread off the plate.

"We could maybe try some cooking things together." Her words trailed off as she ducked her head.

There were plenty of things he wanted to try with her. "If I get any time free from corralling cattle and riding the perimeter, then that sounds like a plan." He didn't foresee any of that happening, but he couldn't tell her no.

Meredith smiled. "Duh, you have super busy days, which is why you're up at the crack of dawn."

Thinking about the day ahead of him made Jace yawn. "Yeah, they do stretch into the evenings often as well."

"Um, so if there's any time to take me out and ride the grounds with you, I'd love that. I may not know how to cook, but I do know how to ride."

"Really?"

"Yes, I've been riding since I was a kid."

Jace folded the bread, ready to cram it in his mouth. He could see Tuck out by the barn getting the horses ready. They needed to look at all the fence line and see if they could get a lead on the bear. "Well, that's a start. I think we're onto something here." He winked. "Riding is going to come in real handy around here. Let's make a list. I need to teach you to shoot."

"And I'll experiment with mixing ingredients. Likely baking before cooking."

"There's a difference?"

She rolled her eyes. "Yeah, even I know that."

He looked around the kitchen. "I'm guessing you've not started a fire before either?"

"No, sorry."

"Let's start there. Take the chill out of the morning. Then you can try one this evening if you want. Come on, I'll show you real quick."

He shoved the bread in his mouth, adjusted the crotch of his pants, and then led her into the living room and showed her how to make a fire. She was too cute for words, making her notes, echoing the sequence, naming the chimney parts after he did.

He watched her while she poked at the logs in the fireplace, and the urge to call in sick was overwhelming. Who could blame him? This was his honeymoon.

"Listen, I won't be in for lunch, but I'll be back for dinner. If its peanut butter and crackers and a can of beans, that works for me."

With a sheepish grin Meredith said, "I couldn't find the can opener so it'll be likely peanut butter."

Jace laughed and tucked a strand of hair behind her ear. "I do know where that is. Second drawer by the stove."

He got lost into the deep pools of her azure eyes, and she blinked back at him, her expression a reflection of his curiosity. Just one kiss. Where would it lead? When she leaned toward him, he stepped closer, his thumb stroking down her neck as he let go of the long lock of her hair.

Her eyelids fluttered.

Just one quick taste. He knew he shouldn't do it. They agreed it would cause nothing but problems, but the decision was out of his control. Something bigger than him, some force he wasn't able to name, pushed him in her direction. He brushed his lips against hers. One, twice, and a tad longer on the third time.

Outside a horn gave one long blow followed by three short ones.

Meredith jumped back, covering her mouth with her hand. "We shouldn't...."

He nodded, stepping toward the door. "Yep, we shouldn't." But man he really wanted to.

15

Desire was a new thing for Meredith. Well, sexual desire. She'd long thought that emotion wasn't in her since she'd never been remotely attracted to any of the people in her father's circle, but Jace, he'd woken those urges that had been dormant for so long.

And all he had to do was take a shower.

She was worse than a sixteen year old after her first kiss. She was crushing on Jace Shepard something fierce. Maybe it was because she liked the way he made her feel when he drew out those desires, or maybe it was simply the way the water from his shower clung in beads to his hair and how the scruff of his chin made him look softer, yet rougher, and she liked the idea of both.

His dimple deepened when he'd laughed earlier, something she found knee-wobbling sexy, and between that and the bit of peanut butter that had clung to his upper lip, she'd had to fight the urge to lick him.

She'd never had a sexual fantasy, but standing in the kitchen with him, she'd pictured sex on the countertop. If it was anything like what they'd started in the car, they could repeat it any and every location, and she'd be satisfied.

Wait. Hold up. Thoughts of that nature weren't smart, and Meredith wanted to play this smart.

Needing a distraction, she decided to do as he'd suggested and made herself at home. She took a shower, exploring her body in ways she'd never done before. Seeing herself as a woman for the first time. A woman with needs and urges.

A woman who could ask to be satisfied.

That one simple fact terrified her. She knew it could bring her so much pleasure, but so much pain as well. Undoubtedly, everything that encompassed sex was out of her wheelhouse and though she was beyond curious to learn more about Jace, his man parts, and how she felt pressed against them, she wasn't so naive to believe sex wouldn't muddy the water.

After the shower, Meredith, feeling refreshed and rejuvenated, set out to make something for them to eat. In the small pantry off the kitchen, she found a freezer full of beef, no surprise there, and a cookbook in an old sideboard on the far wall. Flipping through the pages until she saw a recipe she liked she settled on a savory dish that had few ingredients and, therefore, less opportunity of error. She explored the kitchen, trying to get familiar with where things were located. She was laying out the required cooking and baking accouterments when she noticed a pickup driving toward the house. It wasn't Jace or Tuck's truck since they'd left on horses hours earlier.

Was this one of those times where she might need to know how to use a gun? She did feel a bit vulnerable. She followed the truck's path, having moved across the house to watch it park by the garage, and when Jace's mom got out from the cab, Meredith sank back against the wall with relief.

The tall woman reached for the door, then paused, her hand raised to knock. Not wanting his mother to think they were inside doing naughty things, Meredith flung open the door and smiled widely. "Boy, am I glad to see you." And it was true. Having someone else around was nice.

"You are?" Marjory stepped into the house and smiled.

"Absolutely. Jace has been gone all morning, and it's just me with my thoughts." Meredith tucked her hands in her back pockets, something she'd always done when she was nervous, and it drove her father nuts. Said it wasn't ladylike.

"Do you mean to tell me my son is out working, and you all haven't even been married twenty-four hours?" The older woman shook her head. "Where did I go wrong with that boy? He was never dropped on his head that I can recall, but he sure acts like it. Do you know he was seven before he learned to tie his shoes, and I still can't get him to cook. I have failed as a mother, and you are paying the price."

"That can't be true. He's very nice and considerate. That's more important to me than cooking." She wanted to share this morning's incident but remembered Jace's request not to tell his mom.

"Any coffee still in the pot?" Marjory asked while hanging her coat on the hook by the door.

Meredith shook her head. She'd spent some time staring at the coffee pot, wishing it would magically produce the dark nectar of life but hadn't worked up the courage to give it a try. With the Internet not coming up, she decided to err on the side of less risk. Ergo, no coffee.

"We'll have to fix that right away." Marjory bustled to the kitchen. "What's all this?" She pointed to the items Meredith had put out on the counter in prep for dinner then stopped at the cookbook. "You want to make Hamburger Pie?"

Meredith nodded and slid into a seat at the island.

Marjory's attention was on Meredith who tried not to squirm in her seat as the older woman appeared to be studying her.

Marjory smiled kindly and said, "Well, honey. I know it's called a pie but it's actually more like a casserole and this—she held up the small pie tin— is too small. You'll need a deep dish pie plate if you want to make it round and cut it in triangles."

"Oh, okay." Meredith went to the cabinet that held the pie plate and pulled out a bigger one. When she set it on the table Marjory held up an egg.

"You washed this, right?"

Meredith swallowed and nodded.

"Once you wash off the bloom—that's the protective coating— you need to store them in the fridge. They're okay to sit out with the bloom on."

"Oh, I'm sorry. I didn't know." Talk about feeling inept. Not that Meredith thought she should know these things, but she really wanted to make a good impression.

"Of course you didn't. Life on a ranch is different than life in the city. Ranch cooking with fresh product can differ as well. Go into the freezer and pull out the beef to let it defrost. It'll make cooking this meal easier." She tapped the cookbook.

Meredith hurried off to the deep freezer wondering if there might be a blog or something about learning how to function on a ranch. All the shows she watched on the cooking channels never mentioned fresh eggs versus store bought. Or even defrosting for that matter. She grabbed a package wrapped in white paper with beef scrawled across the top, then took it to the kitchen and handed it to Marjory.

She was given another kind smile from Jace's mom. "This is stew beef. That's what this word is." She pointed to the illegible scrawl. "Not that you can make it out. You'll need ground beef. See if you can find me what looks like it might have a G in the word." She handed back the package, and Meredith felt heat creep up her neck. She searched the freezer and settled on one she thought started with a G.

"I have a confession to make," Meredith said as she handed Marjory the other pack of meat. She was breaking Jace's trust but felt she needed to. She wasn't going to master the kitchen on her wits alone and loved the idea of help so she shared the story about her lack of kitchen skills and the conversation she and Jace had earlier in the morning. He was right. His mother did find great pleasure in their situation.

"Not that I want you to go hungry, dear, but it serves him right. That explains the empty coffee pot. Come on, I'll show you how to get that going, and then we can go over some basics if you'd like."

"I would love that, and coffee sounds amazing. Let me find some paper first so I can take notes." She hurried to Jace's office and took a notepad from the drawer, a pencil from the desk. A crinkled slip of paper under a geode caught her eye.

It was a list.

1. Fix west fence near stream
2. Weed out unhealthy herd
3. Parse out stock for the exchange
4. Prep for spring breeding
5. Ranch vehicles need service
6. *Find a wife and be happy*

Obviously the last one wasn't in Jace's handwriting as it was too girly and loopy, probably his mother or maybe Sabrina. Meredith wasn't going to read into it. Life on the ranch as Jace's wife was a fantasy she could get lost in. The safety of the ranch, a loving and doting husband, and a family that embraced her. Most everyone would want that. The picture of it was crystal clear in her mind, as if it were a memory. But it was nothing more than an overactive imagination.

He was not loving and doting to her. This number 6 on his

list was not his wish, but someone else's and she was no sooner keen on building a second life of pretense than she was to return to her father.

Nodding in determination, Meredith tucked the list under a pile of loose papers and picked up the notepad. She hurried to the kitchen, but stopped short when she saw a new picture hanging on the wall of family pictures she'd admired yesterday. It was of her and Jace after they'd been pronounced man and wife. They'd turned to face the crowd, and if Meredith hadn't known the circumstances of their union, she'd say the couple in the image looked happy.

"All right, Meredith," Marjory said when Meredith joined her in the kitchen, feeling warm and fuzzy from the picture in the hall. "You ready to get down to business?"

"Thanks for hanging the photo up. I didn't know anyone was taking pictures." She stared at the older woman, wondering what she thought of her son's unexpected marriage.

"Thank God Sabrina had the wherewithal to ask the newspaper's photographer to attend. I didn't even have the presence of mind to use my phone's camera. I'm so glad we have a few pictures."

"There's more?" Meredith was anxious to see them.

"Yes, I'll email them to you. Give me your address before I leave."

Meredith didn't have an address. How ridiculous was that? She was so poorly prepared for the world.

"Did you mention coffee?" The last thing she wanted was for his mom to know that.

"I did. You want to start there?"

Meredith nodded.

"Coffee is easy enough. Finding the preferred taste will take some finagling. Since our men work long hours, they need strong coffee." She pushed the maker toward Meredith. "The water and grind should be proportionate."

"So equal amounts."

Marjory laughed. "Hell no, child. Though I'd like to see that pot of coffee go down some rancher's gullets. Some of these folks around here are lazy, and they might actually do some work." She pointed to the north. "Old man Beasley is a prime example. Does the bare minimum. Lets his cattle come onto our land and pushes ours out. Neighbors here call each other when they see bears or coyotes on the land, but not Beasley."

"Maybe he's too old?" Meredith took a guess.

"Nope. Graduated the year behind me. Was as lazy in school as he is now. Grouchy back then, too. That's how he got the nickname 'old man.' 'Cause he acts like one."

"Jace said there was a bear that broke down some of the east fence. Fixed it last night."

Marjory was silent, nodding that she heard. She dumped two scoops of grounds in the filter. "That bear has been around a long time, coming onto the property. I think he's old or sick or both, and that worries me. Bears like that don't behave like they're supposed to." She handed Meredith the scooper. "No weak-ass coffee for us, honey. Two tablespoons for six cups of water, but if the guys are working close, then double that and make a large pot. They'll be in and out all day drinking it."

Meredith liked the sound of that. Seeing Jace as he worked. Watching those large shoulders doing whatever he did around the house. She felt her face get hot so she ducked her head and made notes about the coffee.

"Hey, would you mind showing me how to get eggs? Jace said he would, but he's swamped."

Marjory patted her on the back. "You're gonna do well here, girl. I can feel it in my bones. Come on, I'll show you some of the chores while I ask my own favor of you."

Marjory showed her the chicken coop. Not only how to get the eggs but when and what to feed them. She talked about the coyotes and the foxes and making sure the gate to the coop was always closed. They fed the horses and the barn cats as well, all chores Marjory had handled before going into town with Pops.

"Jace has been doing all this in addition to the other stuff?" Meredith asked, because she wanted to pull her weight. Not tool around the house aimlessly.

"Yes, and that brings me to my favor. I know the timing stinks, but Wes is being discharged in two weeks, and he wants to come home. I want to come home. Would you mind if we did?" Marjory threw out seed for the hens.

"Why would I mind? This is your home." Meredith couldn't imagine saying anything else.

"No, hon. It's now yours. That's what Wes's mother said to me when we were married, and now I pass it down to you."

What a crazy tradition, one that left Meredith feeling itchy in her skin. What would Marjory say when Meredith left? And if she, Meredith, took the house, where would Pops and Marjory live? The room at the back of the house with the hospital bed?

Meredith shook her head. "No. This is all our homes. Wes's bed is here. Your bed is here. I have no claim. Just tell me what I can do to make the transition easier." It was hard going from such a stingy, demanding father to a giving and caring mother-in-law. Meredith didn't know how to resign the emotions of it all.

"It's going to be awkward with our room now downstairs. I need to warn you. It will make Jace feel like he has to do more. I'm expecting you to help him see that he doesn't have to carry the entire burden."

Meredith nodded. "I can do my best."

Marjory laughed. "Yes, with my stubborn son, that's all I can ask for."

Finished with the outside chores and carrying a basket full of eggs, they made their way back to the big house.

"What's that?" Meredith asked, pointing to a standalone cabin on the other side of the barn. It was in direct view of the larger main house, but set off enough for privacy. It, too, had fabulous views of the mountain range.

"That used to be the ranch manager's place, back when employees lived on the ranch. We used to have a bunkhouse, but it burned down in a summer storm."

"Does anyone live there?" Meredith gave it a second look.

"Nope. Been empty for years. Jace talked about moving out to it at one time, but then Wes got sick, and well...here we are." A sadness pulled at Marjory's face, deepening the downward lines around her mouth. She looked tired. Though she might come across as put together, the telltale circles under her eyes and the occasional sighing of fatigue gave her away.

Meredith placed a hand over Marjory's arm. "Please let me help."

Marjory patted her cheek. "You're a dear. Your parents must be so proud of you."

It was so nice to be spoken to kindly and touched with gentle hands. Though it made her yearn for her mother all that much more.

"My mother died when I was sixteen. I'd like to think she'd be proud of me now."

"Now?" Marjory looked at her quizzically.

"I see now that I spent a lot of time in denial. In grief maybe. Now, here, I'm starting to leave that behind, and I think that's what she would have wanted."

"And your father?"

Meredith shrugged. "Maybe he's still stuck there. I don't know. But we don't speak anymore."

Marjory flung an arm around Meredith's shoulder and side-hugged her. "You have us now. You're a Shepard, and we Shepard's love fiercely and loyally, laugh as much as we can, and fight just as often, too."

"Sounds marvelous." And it did.

At the back door Marjory stopped and stared at a dry patch of land, some unruly bushes, and frowned. Sprigs of grass were shooting up in patches, it's haphazard care out of place on the well-maintained ranch.

"What did that used to be?" It was too close to the house to be the burned-out bunkhouse.

"My garden. Every year I planted fruits and vegetables. It was something for me. Something I enjoyed." She shook her head sadly. "This year there has been no time."

Meredith inspected the area, imagining it in rows of glorious produce, picturing herself helping. She needed a way to fill the day. Cooking and egg gathering weren't going to be enough. Unsure if she was about to do the right thing but willing to try Meredith made an offer. "Can I give it a go? I know absolutely nothing, but if you tell me what to do, I think I might be able to manage it."

Marjory beamed. "Do you really think so? If you can get them in the ground this week, we have a good shot of getting some goodies. I'll be able to help when we move back."

"I can't make any promises. I know not the color of my thumbs." For good measure, she wagged them.

Marjory laughed. "It's better than nothing."

They spent the afternoon in the kitchen, Meredith taking copious notes on both cooking and the garden. When Marjory left before the sun set, Meredith was overwhelmed in an exciting and invigorating way. She had something to do, and it was all of her own making. No one was forcing her and, yeah, she was helping others, like she did with the charities, only this time she would see the impact. This time it was strictly because she wanted to help.

First order of business? The manager's cabin. She made her way to the small log cabin to check it out. A quick inspection showed that a little hard work and elbow grease was all it needed to be comfortable and habitable. It was in remarkably good shape. She had an idea and couldn't wait to tell Jace when he got home.

16

More heads lost. A certain percentage was expected every year, but he'd be damned if he hadn't tried to get that number lower, and here it was higher. He and Tuck managed to move the herd from far out closer to Mr. Beasley's land back toward the homestead. It wasn't ideal, but action had to happen, and short of putting a man on them twenty-four seven, he had no other solution.

He'd laughed when Tuck suggested a GO-PRO to possibly capture what was happening, but in truth it wasn't the worst idea.

On that note, he'd cut Tuck lose and had headed home himself, a new and wonderful mix of excitement and pleasure adding haste to his steps. Jace was used to working long days, because why not? What was there to do when the day ended? He'd come home, open a can of something, shower, and then fall into bed in preparation to start it all over again the following morning. Before his parents had moved into town for his dad's therapy, he'd come home to them and an active house. He was now realizing how lonely it had been with them gone.

The porch light was on, as was the one in the front room. When he steered his horse to the barn and around the house, he could see the kitchen light was burning as well. Jace smiled. He was tempted to throw off the saddle and toss some hay to Pal, his horse, but the beast had worked hard and deserved better. Pal didn't care that Jace was having trouble delaying his own wants and needs.

Following a quick brush down and feeding, Jace made his way to the house. His Stetson off his head, bumping against his thigh, he tried to make his appearance less disheveled by raking his hair back with his hands. He and Tuck had rode hard today and, following a quick whiff of his shirt, smelled like it, too.

Once inside, he called out Meredith's name.

"In the kitchen," she called back.

"I need a shower. I'll be right back." He thundered up the stairs and took the quickest shower of his life. Apparently he was setting records with bathing these days. Soon he'd be wiping himself down with a rag and calling it good.

Downstairs, when he entered the kitchen, he found her bent over the oven taking something out and was immensely pleased he'd hurried so he hadn't missed this moment. He liked his woman a little thicker, but he found the curve of her ass very appealing.

"It smells good in here." The island was set with two plates, a bowl of salad, and....

"Do I smell coffee?" He was pulled to the machine like a horseshoe to a magnet.

"Yes, it's still good." She stood, moved to the island, and slid the hot plate onto the surface. Her long hair was pulled back into a ponytail, her face pink from the oven heat. She was a knockout, looking like she belonged with her worn jeans and his flannel shirt took his breath away.

She caught him staring at her, and she looked down. "Oh, I

borrowed your shirt because I was working in your mom's garden and got mine dirty. I hope—"

"It suits you." He grinned.

She grinned back.

Instant hard-on. That's how pathetic he was. It must be male DNA because he was raised by a woman who didn't tolerate gender profiling and stereotyping, but damn if he wasn't all proud with a puffed-out chest to find a sexy woman in his kitchen, making dinner for him, wearing his shirt.

"I'm glad you're home. I have lots to share." She gestured for him to sit.

And this woman was waiting for him. Hell, if he wasn't so hungry, he'd clear the island of its plates and take her on top of it. Her presence wielded that sort of power over him. Cripes, he needed another shower, a frigid one, or a distraction. He searched the room for something else to focus on and set his attention on the food.

"You had a nice day?" He slid into a seat.

She nodded. "I know this is nothing fancy, but I'm hoping it will get better." She took the stool next to him.

"What is it? It looks good." He cut a wedge from the savory-smelling dish, his stomach growling as the whiff of seasoned beef hit his nose. He wasn't sure what it was but, hell, he was hungry enough to eat just about anything. He didn't really care what it was.

She beamed with pride. "Hamburger pie and salad."

Without trepidation, he took a bite. The bottom was a bit overcooked and dark but he'd eaten squirrel and rattlesnake before so this was going to be easy to choke down if it was no good. To his surprise, it was tasty.

"This isn't that bad. I actually like it." He took another wedge.

"Your mom came around. She tried to get me to do something more adventurous but I figured a handful of ingredients is a good place to start."

"Mom was here? Why didn't she call me? Did you mention that you...you know...about the cooking?" He loaded his plate with salad. It'd been months since he had food that wasn't from a jar or can.

"I suppose she came to see me and yes, I told her. It came up."

He stopped eating. "And what did she say?"

"A lot about coffee and little about the garden in the back. I'm going to work on it with her when they move back. Which should happen in a couple of weeks, right?" Her shoulders rose, and she grimaced as though the info might make him upset. Damn, she must have lived a life that was constant walking on eggshells.

"She said two weeks?" Jace slapped his knee with pleasure. "Damn, it will be good to have Pops around."

Her shoulders dropped, and she picked up her fork to eat. "It will be nice to have someone around while you're out all day."

Jace put down his fork. "Are you okay with starting the garden? It might be harder than you think. Frustrating for sure." He didn't want Meredith to bite off more than she could chew. He wanted her to find life easier here than wherever it was she'd come from.

She dismissed his concerns with a wave.

"She asked my permission to move back. To which I said 'don't be silly' because this is their house. They can move back anytime." She smiled and quirked a brow. "Right?"

"Yeah." He liked the idea of Pops being back on the ranch, sharing in discussion about all the issues. But the added stress of having his folks here, his father needing twenty-four hour care, would add strain on all of them. Jace shifted in his seat, resting one hand on his thigh. "It'll be hard having him here. Hard watching Mom work her tail off caring for him. Hard watching him struggle to get around the house. You up for that?"

"Part of the reason I'm here is to give your father something. A...?" She gestured for him to fill in the words.

"A sense of peace about me and my well-being."

"Right, and I understand where you're coming from with that. So let me do my part. This is the first time in years I've felt useful, and I really like it." Her brows knitted with worry. "Your mom and I had a wonderful afternoon, and I think she needs to be here just as much as your dad."

Jace searched her face, looking for any sign she was less than sincere, but came up with nothing. If there was anything more appealing than someone being invested in another person, he wasn't sure what it was. Without hesitation, he pulled the stool she was sitting on closer to him, resting his legs on either side of hers, trapping her between them. She bit her lip.

"What?" he asked.

"If this is too presumptuous, please say so, but I had a look at the old ranch manager's cottage, and I think we could live there and let your folks have this place. This is their home."

Jace was awed by her thoughtfulness. The girls of his past, the ones he thought could be his future, would never have considered living in a small log cabin with rustic plumbing. Here Meredith was ready to give up the big house for something a fraction of the size. One minute he's thinking she's too pampered and spoiled without a basic knowledge of cooking, and the next she's digging in and making meals and putting his family first.

Determined. That's how he'd describe her.

"I'm not sure how this is all going to play out between us, but what you've just said does something to me, Meredith." He slid a hand up her thigh and watched a lovely shade of pink color her beautiful face.

She looked up at him through her lashes. "Something good?" Her low voice matched her flirty look.

The space around them crackled with an electric charge. Jace knew if he gave into his desires, it would consume him soon. He was ready to get lost in it and her.

"Yeah. Real good. There's something here, don't you think?" He stroked her cheek with one hand and used the one on her thigh to make lazy circles with his thumb, hoping to remind her of what they'd already shared.

She nodded.

He eased his hand to cup the back of her head and draw her forward. He brushed his lips over hers softly, then firmer a second time. Her hand came to rest on his arm as she shifted closer, teetering on the edge of her stool. Much like they were teetering on consummating their marriage. The air around them grew thin, leaving them to suck in slow, deep breaths at first, but as each kiss passed, their want hitched higher, beating a heavy pulse inside them, chanting for more, more, more.

In the truck the other day, Jace had blown Meredith's mind with simple touches and caresses. Well, some stroking as well. She'd naively thought it couldn't get any better than that heightened state of dizziness he made her feel. But this moment? It was not unlike the pounding need for his touch that she'd come to understand was her attraction for him, but more an internal, crazed sense of frenzy to get her hands all over him.

He'd come down from the shower, just like this morning, with his shoulder-hugging T-shirt, his butt-cupping jeans, and she'd wanted to jump on the island and ask him to make her his dinner, dessert, and breakfast. The awakening within her was wondrous and frightening at the same time.

So many questions she wanted to ask, so many words she wanted to use to beg him to do more to her. Give her more. Take her further. Show her everything.

He plunged his tongue in her mouth, meeting hers, and she melted into him. His fingers were on the buttons of her shirt, and when he got to the last one, he slipped the shirt off her shoulders, his long fingers caressing her skin as he ran them down the length of her arms before sliding them to her back where he deftly released her bra.

Combined with the shocking pleasure and intimacy of his thumbs stroking her breasts and the cold sweep of air across her skin brought common sense screaming caution in her mind like a loud obnoxious warning bell. Meredith jerked back, gasped, and covered her hands over her chest.

"What are we doing?" She hoped he could explain their actions in such a way that demanded they see it through. She desperately wanted the entire experience. However, that didn't mean she should have it.

Jace dropped his head, then sighed deeply, before looking up at her. "I'd like to say we're two adults, married to each other, and there's no harm with what we're doing."

"But?" She hunched down and quickly drew her shirt back up, clutching the sides together and covering her chest.

Jace winced slightly. "Um, have you ever done this before?"

She tried for a blank expression, hoping her naivete wasn't so obvious. "This—like get married and fool around? No."

Jace continued to watch her, waiting for the answer to the question she knew he was really asking. She shook her head and sucked in a deep breath, as if it would make the heat spreading over her cheeks cool.

"Not with anyone?" he asked.

She shook her head again and swallowed, her eyes focused on her knees.

He reached for her face, cupped her chin, and then raised her head. "There's the 'but.' You've never done this before, and you can't begin to know what you're getting into. But your first time should be all you need it to be. But the circumstances are unusual and that could be affecting our judgment."

"And whatever this is...chemistry maybe—"

"Is fleeting most likely." Jace held his gaze with hers. "And the last thing I'd want is to make being here harder than it need be. It's important to me that you stay for Pops and that you find life here easy enough."

Meredith pulled away, shifting back in her stool, her hands still clutched to the folds of the shirt. "Sex would likely complicate that."

"It definitely would." He looked away toward the food. "We should eat before this gets cold."

Meredith smiled, his subject change was likely an attempt to not make this moment any more awkward than it already was, but what was she supposed to do? Button up her shirt and dig in? She hadn't developed that sort of casual worldliness...yet.

"Actually, I snacked all day so I think I'll go up and try to get some rest. It's been a full day and there's lots I want to tackle tomorrow."

"Are you sure?" He stood when she did.

"Positive." She used one of large, lots-of-teeth false smiles in hopes to ease any of his doubt. "I'll see you in the morning." Without waiting for a response, she hurried from the kitchen and nearly broke into a run when she hit the stairs. Once behind the privacy of her bedroom door, Meredith let the embarrassment overtake her.

Ugh. It was all so confusing. What she wanted, what she should want, and what she should do about it all. She'd need to think it through and make a firm resolution about how to proceed. Pressing her ear to the door, she waited until she was sure he didn't follow her and crept back out, making her way to the bathroom where she got ready for bed. Back in her room, she laid in bed with the lights out, staring at the window and the beams of moonlight flooding in and asked herself what it was she wanted from this experience. It was much longer before she heard Jace clomp up the stairs, then pause outside her door. Meredith's breath stuck in her throat until he moved on to his room.

Even knowing he was close made her palms sweaty and her heartbeat erratic, and she knew fighting a heart's—or maybe in this case their bodies'—desires was going to complicate their situation just as much. It was more an issue of which complication would be easiest to live with. Keeping sex out of the deal was probably for the best. Her common sense told her that.

Therefore, with solid determination, she made a promise to herself to behave before falling into a fitful sleep full of dreams of Jace's rough hands all over her body.

17

J ace stood next to Meredith's bed, hesitating to wake her. Cripes, she was beautiful. Her hair spread around her, her lips slightly parted, and her bare shoulder peeking out from the covers were enough to make him revisit the conversation he'd had with himself most of last night. Hell with sleeping, he'd spent the time tossing and turning, trying to convince himself to keep his hands off her. Deep inside him lived a fear that if they consummated the marriage, it would inevitably force her off the ranch.

Yet, here he was considering slipping between the sheets with her and making promises he was certain he couldn't keep just to spend close time with her. The memories of every touch—from the first at the church to last night in the kitchen—stayed with him. They clamored to be relived and new ones discovered. He pushed all that aside and reminded himself why he sought her out this morning.

He wanted to show her the ranch and continue to forge the friendship that was forming between them. This is what they needed if they were going to make it through these last few months with Pops. He was counting on her, and developing that trust and friendship would go a long way to easing his worry she might hate the ranch and bolt at any minute.

He nudged her shoulder and whispered, "Hey." Instant heat to his body just from the one touch.

She rolled away from him.

Jace laughed "Want to see the sun come up over the plains? It's stunning."

She stretched and buried her face in her pillow.

"Come on. Wake up." He used his palm to give two quick prods.

"Are you serious?" She looked at him with one eye open. "What time is it?"

Jace chuckled. "Well, using my skills of deduction and seeing as how I asked if you wanted to watch the sun rise, I'd say it's about thirty minutes until sunrise."

She swiped at him. "It feels earlier."

"Come on, get your lazy ass outta bed, and get dressed. Not much else prettier than a spring sunrise other than a sunset."

She made like she wasn't happy about it, but sprung from bed and shooed him out of the room so she could dress, but not before he got an eyeful of her long legs in the fancy silky shorts she slept in. He hadn't made it to the bottom of the stair before he heard her come out. Wow, she'd been quick about dressing, and he was impressed. His sister, Willow, took what seemed like hours to do any part of grooming. He'd assumed a city girl like Meredith would be no different, if not worse. In the kitchen, they worked as a team to get the coffee going and pack a few snacks. Jace took a coat from the hall closet and handed it to her.

"Here, use this when you're working on the ranch. That pretty cream thing won't last a day." The coat, a heavy Carhartt, was one of his favorites, but he liked seeing it on her more than he wanted to wear it.

They drove in silence to the side pasture and parked so the bed faced the direction of the sunrise. They sat in the back with wool blankets across them as they sipped coffee and waited.

When the fading night moved away to allow for the multiple shades of blue and yellow to crest over the earth, Meredith sat up and set her coffee aside.

Dark blue became bright, light blue became white, and yellows burst around the edges.

"What do you think?" Jace asked from behind her.

"I've seen pictures in magazines," she whispered but hated to disrupt the moment. As the minutes passed, the world came alive. Birds began to sing. In the distance, a cow lowed. "But they don't capture this. This is..." She shook her head, unable to find the words.

"Worth getting out of bed?" He chuckled.

As the sun broke over the horizon, Meredith closed her eyes, leaned forward into the beams of sunlight, and soaked up their warmth as it fell over her. She pulled energy from this new dawn. She could do this every day. Here she could breathe. After feeling the sunrise deep into her bones, she sat back and opened her eyes. Color exploded around her.

"You are so lucky to have grown up with this."

"Yeah, I think so, too. That's why I won't leave."

She turned her attention to him. "Why would anyone?"

Jace's laugh was more a cynical bark than amusement. "You'd be surprised."

"No wonder your parents want to come back."

"I think it would be good for Pops." Jace poured her more coffee.

"Have you thought about what I suggested? The manager's cabin." Meredith sipped at the delicious brew that *she made*. Only her second pot, and it was perfect, if she did say so herself. Maybe slightly weak, but completely palatable. How lucky

Marjory told her how many scoops to add per cup of water or she'd likely be drinking brown water or black sludge. Probably brown water since she had the tendency to under-do everything, thanks to her father.

"Let's go take a look at it," Jace said. "Ready to leave?"

She glanced back at the sunrise, which was seconds from ending. "I'd like to do this again."

"We should make a point of doing sunrises in each season. They're all incredible."

"Deal, now let's go to the cabin." She slid from the truck bed, taking the blanket with her.

The drive back was quick, and she waited with eager anticipation as Jace walked through the cabin, pulling open closet doors and staring for far longer than she thought necessary at the bathroom. He came to stand before her, his hands on his hips, and shook his head.

She was instantly deflated. "You don't think it'll work for us?" Maybe he didn't want to be this close to her; the setting would be more intimate than the house.

"I think it would be great for us, actually. But my folks will never go for it. There's this tradition about passing down the house, and they'll want to pass it down to us, especially while Pops is alive to see it." Jace ducked his head and stuffed his hands in his pockets. "But all this place needs would be a rehab of the bathroom, and my folks could live here. It's perfect, really. No stairs, lots of space. I could build on a sun room to the back and give them more space." He looked around and nodded. "Yeah, I think it'll work, and it was a great idea."

Meredith beamed and clapped her hands in excitement. "I'll start cleaning it out today."

Jace shook his head. "Don't go nuts. When I have someone redo the bathroom, it'll make another mess."

She pointed at him. "Good point. But I'll at least wash what I can. When can you get someone out here to do the restroom?"

Laughing, he wrapped an arm around her. "How about we go into town for dinner, and I can talk to a few fellas at the diner?"

Meredith pushed him away, surprised by how natural it felt to have his arm around her. There was something very pleasing about the familiarity of the entire exchange. "You better get to work then so I can get my stuff done. The sooner we do, the sooner we can start on this and give your mom and dad the privacy they deserve." She spun on her heel and left the building.

"Where you going?" he called after her.

"To get the eggs." It was freeing to have a task. She liked participating, and knowing she'd come up with the solution for his parents made her stand tall with self-pride. She was not as her dad wanted her to believe—useless. She wasn't some pawn to be used in his machinations. She was a person with purpose, and now a life. Meredith fairly skipped to the coop. Letting herself into the gate, she made sure to latch it behind her. The space was large, nearly half the length of a football field, and gave the flock range to roam. The coops ran down the center of the space.

After snagging the basket from the fence, Meredith lifted the roof from the first coop and took out the eggs like Marjory had shown her. She hoped Jace was watching.

At the second house, she flipped open the roof, stuck in her hand, and let out a blood-curling scream.

Meredith hopped around the yard, chickens scattering at her feet, flapping her hands in the air wildly, and pausing only seconds to wipe them down her jeans. A basket of broken eggs lay on the ground.

Jace raced to her, jumping the fence. He caught her by the shoulders and gave a small shake. "What's happened? Are you hurt?"

"I touched it! I had it in my hand." She gave a violent shiver and wiped her hands again.

"Touched what?" Jace grabbed her hands and inspected them.

"The snake. Bleck. It's a big fat snake." She jerked her hands from his and spit on them, rubbing them together immediately following. "I will never get that feel out of my brain. So gross."

Jace laughed and pointed to the hen houses. "Which one?"

"The second." She moved back.

Jace lifted the roof then smiled at her from under his arm. "Milksnake. Old wives' tale is that they drink milk from the cow's teat. Not poisonous."

"Oh, my God. I don't even want to think about that." Meredith fanned herself, not wanting to show weakness, but had the urge to plop to the ground.

"You know why he's still in here?" Jace reached in, and with lightening quick reflexes, pulled the snake out. It dangled and coiled from his hand.

Meredith dropped to the ground. "Uh, because he was hungry?" She thought she might puke.

"That's what brought him here, but not what kept him. He's too fat to get out the small hole he came in through." Jace pointed to the bulge in the body of the snake.

"What is that?" Meredith asked before covering her mouth.

"Looks like two eggs. Greedy bastard. If he wants eggs he'll have to do his share of the work around here."

"What are you going to do with him?" She rose from the ground, brushing off her jeans, but making sure not to get too close.

"I'm gonna kill him. He's likely got a den nearby and will be back often. I can't have him eating the chicks."

Meredith gulped. She scanned the yard and started counting

the little chicks. Unfortunately, she had no baseline to know if one was missing.

"You okay? You look a little pale." When Jace stepped toward her, she scurried back.

"I'm a little freaked out."

"By what? The snake or the killing?" He made a large circle around her, heading toward the gate.

"All of it I guess." She folded her arms around herself.

Jace held the gate open for her, the snake still wiggling in his hand.

"You go on ahead," she said.

He sighed then looked at the snake. "I can't let him go. He'll be back."

"I'm not asking you to let him go." She waited for him to walk away before going to the gate. Jace went to his truck and took out a shotgun before heading toward the copse of trees down on the east side of the prairie.

"Where are you going?" she called, walking behind him but keeping a fair distance.

Jace turned and stopped. "Listen. I'm sorry you find all this disturbing, but this is life on the ranch. You don't like it, you should go now because this here is nothing compared to what can happen. I'm sure there's an angry tirade about our anti-quated ways and cruelty to animals but—"

"Are you telling me to go home?" She stopped in her tracks.

"I'm saying that you should leave sooner than later if this kinda thing is gonna bother you." He nudged the snake with the tip of his gun.

Meredith searched for words, but most of the ones that came to mind were some she'd never said before. Clearly, she was feeling strongly about something, and it wasn't the killing of a snake.

"You're an ass." She swiveled on her heel and marched home,

mumbling those stronger words she wanted to say earlier. She'd hit the first step of the porch when the shotgun firing caused her to jump. She looked out across the prairie and found him looking in her direction, the gun pointing toward the ground. She stomped up the stairs and slammed the door, hoping the sound would echo across the range as much as the gun had.

She paced the house, looking for something, anything, to channel her anger through. She should leave? Is that how it worked here? They had a deal, and he was backing out of it? Her reaction was more disturbing than making his father happy? It made no sense.

She thought they were becoming friends, but now she should leave over being grossed out by a snake?

Men were weird.

She stomped into the kitchen and stared at the stove. As if she was going to make him any breakfast. She ate a banana and two pieces of toast while she gathered cleaning supplies, finding long latex dish gloves under the kitchen sink.

She stomped back outside and refused to look for the dumb-dumb. Passing the chicken coop, her footsteps faltered. Any eggs that had been gathered were on the ground, but there were five houses left to be cleared of eggs. She really wanted to get them. She didn't like leaving the chore hanging. Setting the bucket of supplies on the ground, she put the dishwashing gloves on and went back to collect the eggs, pausing to check out each coop before sticking her hand inside.

Once the eggs were collected and stored back at the house, she went into the cabin. While taking down the curtains, she let the bucket in the sink fill with hot water. With the light shining in, she could see the areas that needed the most work and was making a mental list of where to start and how to progress when the front door flung open.

Jace stomped in with the shotgun in hand.

He didn't frighten her, though. Now, had her father done the same thing, that might have scared her.

"Come with me," he demanded.

"Please."

He paused and looked around like he thought she didn't hear him correctly. "Ah, um, I said come with me," he repeated.

"No, I mean you should say please." She'd been bossed around enough to last her a lifetime. She mixed cleaner into her water then dragged the bucket to the corner. After dipping her rag and wringing it out, she began to wash the windows and sills.

"What are you doing?" She heard him shift behind her but refused to look at him.

"I'm cleaning the cabin." She pointed to the bucket. "This is cleaner." She pointed to the window. "This is a window. I'm trying to get the two of them to work together since they both sort of need each other." She finally looked at him when she said. "So far so good. Let's hope the window doesn't think the cleaning towel is judgmental and made from thin, useless fibers." She swung back to the window and scrubbed until it squeaked.

"Ah, am I the window or the towel? Because earlier outside I was an ass."

Meredith hesitated, wondering if she should back down. In reality, they barely knew each other. Though she knew he'd never get aggressive like her father, and after the finger-in-face incident on their wedding day, he seemed to mindfully choose his actions. He set the gun to lean against the side counter and tucked his hands in his pockets, his Stetson not so low on his face she couldn't see his expression.

She bit her lip, the anger so ready to spill from her. He'd negatively judged her, and it had hurt.

Jace sighed. "Why don't we get in the habit now of saying

what we think and feel and worry about the collateral damage later."

It was the collateral damage that scared her. Granted, an argument wasn't as severe as losing a wife and mother in a plane accident, but the aftermath of that had changed her world drastically. She knew that an outcome's severity could never be predicted.

Jace crossed his arms. "Listen, I'm not trying to be short, but I got some things to do and I wanted to make sure—"

"You just assumed I was judging you about your lifestyle and decisions with that stupid snake instead of asking me anything," she said in a rush of words, shouting over him.

"It was clear you didn't approve of what I was doing."

"Exactly what did I do to make it clear?" She tossed the rag into the bucket and then crossed her arms.

"You nearly passed out. You went all pale and shaky." He looked...smug? She leaned in to get a closer look. Maybe it was the shadows from the hat because, by God, if he was going to be smug, she was going to come undone.

"Did you think for a moment that maybe I was pale and shaky because I'd just picked up a snake unintentionally? Something, mind you, that I have never done before, and I had no idea what kind of snake it was or what it would do to me. You just assumed...and well, you know what they say about assume. Except this time I think assuming only made an ass out of you."

She took a step closer, and he pushed up his hat. "You can't tell me you were happy with me killing the snake. Lots of city folks believe animals have rights, and in some cases that is true, but this reptile—"

"Again assuming. I didn't and still don't care what you did to the snake. I only asked because I wanted to know what typically happens. My main focus was to get my hands washed as quickly as possible because I was pretty skeeved out."

"So you don't care that I killed the snake?"

Meredith snorted. "I wasn't friends with the snake. He wasn't my pet. It was the first time we'd met, actually."

Jace narrowed his eyes, looking confused.

"Do I sound ridiculous? That's because you do as well. Why not ask me what I think about something and if, by chance, I have an issue, maybe discuss it with me. Educate me. Yes, I grew up in the city, but I'm not so shortsighted that I can't understand someone else's perspective."

Jace's mouth went into a thin line. He took off his hat and brushed back his hair before setting his hat back on. "This is where I should apologize to you."

"Yes, it is." The weight of worry lifted from her.

"Well, then. I'm sorry. You were right. I was an ass." He gave her a small smile.

She gave him a bigger one back. "Should I record this moment? For prosperity and record keeping?"

Jace chuckled. "You might." He took another few steps closer until he was in front of her. "I suppose this was our first fight." He took another step and backed her against the wall.

"I suppose it was. Should we be concerned that it's not been forty-eight hours, and we're fighting?"

He shook his head. "I hear good things happen after couples fight."

"Like what." She stared up at him, her breath caught in her throat, anticipation eating her up. Her decisions from last night evaporated from the heat of her need.

"Things like this." He ducked his head and wasted not another second pressing his mouth to hers, caressing her with his tongue.

Meredith wrapped her arms around his neck and melted into him.

"Maybe we should try this just once," he murmured against her lips.

"It's worth considering," she said while stretching closer to him.

The sound of a horn repeatedly blowing outside as it came closer broke them from their intentions. Jace leaned and looked out the window she'd been cleaning.

"It's Willow," he said, following it with a heavy sigh. "Get your game face on. If my sister were a dog, she'd be a pit bull. She's tenacious."

Meredith pressed a finger to her swollen lips before straightening her shirt and then patting her hair. "Do I look disheveled?"

Jace scanned her before grabbing her hand and tugging her to the door. "Yes, but that's a good thing. It'll help with getting her to believe our story." Once out the door, he slowed his stride and slung an arm around her shoulder. Willow, a tall dark-haired girl in a skirt, flowy shirt, and cowboy boots was half way up the stairs to the house when Jace let out an ear-piercing whistle. She stopped short and swung around, then bounded back down the stairs toward them.

Meredith nudged him with her elbow and whispered, "All my stuff is in the guestroom."

Jace grunted. "You get her coffee and keep her distracted. I'll move it all." He dropped his arm from her shoulder and lifted them out so his sister could fling herself in them.

18

Willow brought more energy to the house than Meredith thought humanly possible, though she'd been duly warned. After introductions, the two women made their way to the kitchen while Jace made some lame excuse to go upstairs. Once inside, Meredith pretended to not hear his frantic shuffling above them.

Willow was tall, like her brother, and had that air about her, a college student who knew everything and had the world at her fingertips. She talked incessantly about her professors and classes and how excited she was to be graduating soon.

After Jace joined them in the kitchen, looking flushed from rushed exertion, he filled Willow in on the plans for the cabin. She instantly volunteered to help get everything ready and offered to plan a housewarming party for their parents. Thankfully, Jace nixed it.

"Does Mom and Pops know you're here?" Jace probed.

"Yep, I stopped there first. Dad's ready to be done with therapy. I told them we would all try to meet them for dinner in town."

Knowing Willow would be on the ranch for a few weeks before returning to school for her summer session made Meredith tense, her stomach knot with worry. Would she and Jace be able to pull off their ruse while she was here? Meredith tried to see it as good practice for when the entire family was home, but that did nothing to assuage the churning mess in her stomach.

Though she knew it was silly, Meredith found it impossible to not resent Willow slightly. She was living the dream Meredith had always had. A loving, supportive family, her chance away at college to figure herself out, and the world in front of her. Logically, Meredith understood her resentment should be directed at her own father and the hand life had dealt her, but the tiny tinges of envy were there. Only two years younger, Willow, who did everything with one hand as she held her phone in the other, had the full, rich life Meredith had craved. Meredith knew her time for that had passed. Even if she returned to school tomorrow, it would not be an experience like Willow's. Being married was now part of her history, of who she was.

After a long day of making chit chat—Jace, the lucky dog, got to be out of the house all day working with the livestock and keeping an eye out for a bear—Meredith was steps from collapsing into bed. She shuffled down the hallway and came to a screeching halt outside Jace's bedroom door. He'd remained downstairs to harass his sister about school. She'd forgotten they'd moved her stuff over, hoping not to tip their hand. Meredith wondered if Willow couldn't be trusted, but as much as that girl rattled on about anything and everything, possessing the tidbit about Jace and Meredith's bargain would surely find its way out of her mouth.

Sighing wearily, Meredith pushed open Jace's door and groaned. From the look of things, Jace must have flung her stuff into his room, not caring where it would come to rest. Clothes were on the floor, over a lamp, but mainly on the bed. He had managed to put the picture of her mother on the nightstand, and her heart softened when she saw it.

Too tired to care about cleaning up and too nervous to be found awake when Jace decided to come to bed, Meredith tossed everything in the large rocking chair in the corner of the room. Once the mess was contained, Meredith saw Jace's room for the first time. It was simply decorated, heavy wood furniture surrounding the queen bed that was covered by a blue, gray, and red plaid quilt. It was all him. Smelled look him, stood quietly like he did, and made her want to take her clothes off. Of course, that might have more to do with the bed and her fatigue than anything. She found her toothbrush in his en suite bathroom and quickly completed her nightly ritual. After slipping into her paja-ma's, she slid between the sheets on the side of the bed closest to the bedside table with her mother's picture. Unfortunately, she found relaxing impossible as she lay stiffly on her stomach, an elbow stretch away from plank position. Her mind imagined what would happen when he came to bed. She stared at his empty side and wondered what it would be like to share a bed with Jace.

For her, this definitely put a hitch in the frequently discussed hands-off policy. Her mind was already filled with a variety of fantasies.

Meredith flopped on her back and sighed loudly. This was ridiculous. She was all jittery and jumpy, straining to hear if he was coming or not. As she saw it, she had two options. She could jump him when he came to bed, but even that wouldn't remove the awkwardness, just change it. Or she could do like she'd seen several times in the romantic comedy movies she watched. She would put a barrier between them. After she slipped from the bed, she searched for extra pillows and blankets to make the wall. Yeah, she knew the couples in the movies never stayed on their designated sides, but this wasn't any silly scripted movie. In his closet, she found another comforter that was long enough to work. Staying focused on her task at hand, she didn't even pause to smell his clothes. He'd probably walk in and catch her doing just that if she did. She rolled the comforter and placed it center of the bed, over the sheets but under the quilt. Then she climbed back into bed, resting on top of the sheet as an extra protection, and unsuccessfully attempted to force her shoulders to relax. She was tossing and turning, mumbling her frustrations, when Jace stepped into the room. She hadn't even heard him coming.

"Is this how we're doing it?" he said in a lowered voice, his attention on the center of the bed.

She gulped and looked up at him over the edge of the quilt. "Yes, we need something. Don't you think?"

He scratched behind his ear as if he was considering her words. "Need something because my animal magnetism is so strong you'll be unable to resist?" He gave a lopsided smile.

Meredith rolled her eyes and sat up. "You tell yourself whatever it is you want. I still stand by us not complicating things further with...um...you know." Her legs were crossed under the covers, and she wondered if that made her little white lie exempt?

"Sex," he said.

"Shush," she followed immediately with urgency. Though he hadn't said it loudly at all.

Working quickly on the buttons of his shirt, he had it off in record time. Meredith tugged the quilt up to her chin. Sitting in the rocker, he slid off his boots, letting them fall with a thunk to the floor, then he stood again and reached behind his head to pull off his T-shirt.

Jumping Aunt Hannah, he was a sight to behold. Meredith's knees began to tremble, and try as she might, she couldn't avert her eyes from the ripple of muscles running across his stomach.

When Jace undid his pants, Meredith slammed her eyes closed. His low chuckle was all she needed to force them open. He stood before her in dark boxers.

Well, that answered that question, and knowing it made her feel closer to him, like they were a couple who had layers of intimacy.

"Don't get all worried. Willow is in the next room, and the walls separating ours from hers is thinner than I'd like. If we're going to have some fun, I want to do it when we can let our hair down." He went to the bathroom door and stopped before entering. "You are a noisy woman, and I'm willing the bed can get pretty loud. Why would I not want that?" He wagged his brows before entering into the bathroom then closing the door.

Meredith's body went hot. Frustrated, she tossed onto her side, her back to where he'd sleep. When he came out, she didn't try to engage him further, not wanting any more imagery to add to her already rampant imagination.

She could tell by his movements he was standing on his side of the bed, and following a soft swoosh of clothing, he climbed in next to her. He'd taken off his boxers and was in bed. Next to her. Naked.

To make matters worse, he was asleep and snoring within ten minutes while she lay there watching the time click away on the clock on the bedside table.

19

If Willow was suspicious of Jace and Meredith, she never showed it. Meredith liked that about her and appreciated being treated like everyone else. Meredith found Willow's joie de vivre admirable—in the mornings—but by late afternoons, the abundance of energy would wear on Meredith and a headache threatened to push through. Not getting a full-night's rest didn't help either.

Yet, Meredith couldn't complain. Something lovely was happening in those dark hours where she and Jace would lie next to each other with a rolled blanket between them. They were talking. Every night the conversation would start out about the progress of the construction in the cabin but always lead to the livestock, the expectations of the ranch for the season, and often times they laughed about the bear messing with the herd, joking how the animal seemed to know the ranch's schedule and always seemed a day ahead of them when striking the herd. It was through these quiet shared moments that Meredith knew—regardless of the outcome—she'd done the right thing leaving home. Her life had purpose, and living each day with that knowledge filled her cup.

Until about midafternoon when Willow's yammering depleted her energy. By that point, Meredith would escape to the garden or the barn to find a chore and quiet haven.

At the top of the second week, the construction crew was a day from finishing the cabin, the kitchen was clean from breakfast, Jace and Tuck were out in the field, and looking forward to alone time, Meredith took her freshly topped-off coffee out into the garden to water and weed and get lost in the activity.

She stopped short when she saw Willow had infiltrated the garden, elbows deep in pruning and weeding.

"Oh," Meredith said, searching for something more articulate to say. She'd yet to be alone with Jace's sister and feared a round of twenty questions was inevitable. Willow would see right through their story. Shoot, maybe everyone else already did, too, and were just being nice, but Meredith knew Willow wouldn't be the type to politely ignore the obvious. She was frank, outspoken, comfortable in her skin, a well-loved young woman who liked to call peoples' bluffs.

"Sorry, I like to keep busy," Willow said with a smile before returning her attention to the plants.

"Yes, me, too. I thought you were studying or something."

Willow snorted. "That's my whole life. Books and more books. Notes and lectures. Don't get me wrong, I like school, and I try to keep it positive for my family, but I'll be glad when it's over. It's nice to do things like this." She swept her hand over the dirt around her.

"Well, I'll leave you to it then." Meredith turned on her heel.

"Or you could stay and help. We could get to know one another better."

Which was precisely what Meredith was afraid of—the probing and high probability that Willow would see through her, find her lacking, and tell her family Meredith didn't belong. It was silly, Meredith knew that on some basic level, but that didn't mean it couldn't happen. It was easy to feel like an imposter in a group of people when you felt like one inside your own body.

"You can take that side." Willow pointed to the end rows. "I haven't done that yet."

Meredith set her cup on the table, took in a deep nerve-steadying breath, and joined Willow in the garden.

They worked in silence for a bit, Meredith wondering what the best course of action would be—keep her distracted with idle chatter, something she wasn't very good at, or let it play out. She went with the latter.

"You and my brother are cute together," Willow said.

And so it begins.

"Thanks."

"It's nice to see him happy."

The statement reminded Meredith of the list she'd seen on her first night at the ranch. *Be happy.* Meredith looked at Willow and found she had her full attention.

"I hope he's happy. I know I am." Meredith hadn't really given it much thought but realized her words were true. She loved living on the ranch, using her hands, and being part of something bigger that was good. The air suited her, the work was rewarding, and the family...well, a person couldn't be more thankful for a bunch of people who'd been strangers a few weeks back.

Willow smiled wide and sat back on her heels. "I'm not going to grill you about how you met or anything. Mom said Sabrina and you are friends, and I can do the math. Not that I've ever been told what Sabrina does for a living, but I figured it out. Anyway." She waved her hand dismissively and shook her head, her smile even bigger. "Outside this family, Sabrina knows Jace better than anyone. If she paired the two of you together then, for me, that's as good as God sending a cupid down and shooting you both in the butts with a connected arrow."

Meredith blinked. What did one say to that? She had no idea, so she smiled instead. "You have an amazing family."

Willow's smile wavered; she blinked rapidly and nodded her head. "They are great."

"I didn't mean to upset you." The headaches that she'd thought she lost until recently poked at her edges, trying to break through.

"It's not that." She shook her head again. "It's seeing Pops. It's hard. Don't tell mom, but I didn't sign up for summer A session." She shrugged and looked away, wiping the corner of her eye. "I wanted to be home. I'm afraid I'm going to miss something. Everyone wants to keep on going like everything is all right, but it's not all right. I can't sit in class knowing my dad...."

Large tears rolled down her face, falling into the dirt.

Meredith swallowed the lump in her throat. "Did Jace tell you my mother passed away when I was sixteen?"

Willow shook her head. "He just said you didn't have family."

A small, bitter laugh escaped Meredith. "It's kinda true. My father is still alive, but he's...well, anyway. One day my mom was there, and the next she wasn't. I'd give anything for more time. I'd give anything to sit with her and just enjoy the space she's in." Meredith let go of the tears she'd been holding back and, magically, the headache evaporated.

Willow nodded. "Yes, that's all I want."

"I get it. You let me know how I can help." She reached across the space with her palm up. Willow placed her hand in Meredith's, and they squeezed.

"Look at us, crying in the garden," Willow said, gripping tightly.

Meredith laughed. "No one has to know." Mercy, she felt like a heel for being so petty and resenting of Willow before.

A low rumble echoed through the garden and vibrated the earth. Puzzled, Meredith looked up at the clear blue sky.

"It's the herd. They're coming in. Doesn't sound like all of them, though. Come on, let's go watch." Willow jumped up, wiped her eyes, and then dusted the dirt from her pants. Meredith followed suit. Out by the barn was a large corral-like, pie-shaped contraption.

Meredith pointed. "What's that?"

"It's a sweep tub. It helps keep the cows from getting anxious. When that happens, all kinda things can go wrong. "

Meredith nodded like she understood, but made a note to ask Jace later.

"Jace is probably bringing in this batch to check their tags." Willow pulled on her ear. Meredith saw some of the cows had a yellow clip in their ear.

"I'll go open the gate." Willow started forward, but Meredith grabbed her arm.

"Can I do it?"

"Sure, just open it and get out of the way."

Meredith nodded then jogged out to the apparatus. The herd was close, coming in wide, their pace steady, and Meredith laughed. She now understood the term "louder than a herd of buffalo." The sound was deafening. Unlatching the gate was easy enough, but her critical mistake was standing still and shoving it open instead of guiding it to rest against the metal sweeping tub. Her initial thought had been to avoid going toward the herd which she would have done had she taken the gate all the way open. Only now they seemed to be coming from everywhere, and thrusting the gate left Meredith exposed and in the direct line of the herd. Had she guided the gate open, she'd be by the sweep tub and could sit on the fence.

She faced the incoming cows and thought about all those videos she'd seen of people running from the bulls in Pamplona.

She turned on her heel and bolted, picking the path to run with the least amount of animals.

Willow was yelling something and pointing, but when Meredith looked in that direction, all she could see were cows. When one passed her, she braced herself to be trampled, surprised when nothing came.

Meredith ran faster, her legs burning from the exertion. If she died, at least it was at a time when she was happy. The ground shook with the pounding of stampeding cows, their hooves kicking up dirt.

Frightened, she unleashed the scream building inside her. Why hadn't those stupid cows gone into the tub? Her gaze darted around as she looked for a solution, and she realized the herd was coming in from both sides of the prairie, Tuck driving another bunch in from the direction in which she was running.

Cows were everywhere!

Like that childhood game she was the Monkey in the Middle, and wished someone would throw her a lifeline. Out of options and heaving from exhaustion, she continued scanning for options. Something, anything, like a building or fence that she could use as cover. A whistle broke through the chaotic sound, and she jerked her attention in the direction from which it came.

Jace was on a horse barreling up from behind, leaning in the saddle toward her, arm extended as if to scoop her up. She pivoted on a dime, changing her direction toward him, and hoped they could pull it off.

Only in the movies.

Thankfully, she knew about horses, and when he was close enough she reached for the back of the saddle with one hand while linking arms with him with the other. She leapt into the air when they connected and used the saddle to help pull herself around. Once seated, she wrapped both arms around his waist and buried her head into the center of his back, trying to cease her shaking and calm her frantically beating heart.

Though the pounding of the hooves continued to echo in her head, she knew they were away from the corral because the sound had faded. She lifted her head and saw the big house in front of them. Jace brought his horse to a quick halt, jumped off, and pulled her down seconds later. Her knees wobbled, and she grasped his shoulders to steady herself.

"Are you okay?" He patted her body up and down.

"Yeah, but it was a little uncertain there for a moment." She tried to laugh, but it came out shaky.

Jace stared at her, his face rigid with...anger?

Yeah, she was going with anger. The small muscle in his cheek pulsed in and out at a rapid pace. He pressed his lips together then puffed out one word. "Christ." He drew in another breath.

Silver lining? She was getting to know his moods. She'd called this one correctly right out of the gate.

"I'm sorry I messed up opening the thingy." She tested her legs for steadiness and let go of his shoulders. His hands were on her waist, his thumbs digging into her hips.

"What the fuck were you doing?" When the words exploded from him, Meredith cringed. She dare not look to see where Willow was.

"Don't yell at me." She kept her voice low.

"You could have been killed. I'll yell if I want. It's the only thing keeping me from shaking you to death." For emphasis he shook her at her hips.

"I made a mistake when I opened the corral. Live and learn." She didn't want to fight with him. What she really wanted to do was go inside and cry in the shower. She felt cold to her core, fear having driven the heat from her. Any minute now she was going to turn into a sobbing mess of a girl.

Please don't let it be in front of everyone.

"You almost didn't live and learn. Jesus, Meredith, you should stay inside or in the garden. Let us handle the cattle."

A sudden ignition of anger burst through her, removing any need for heat. Using her forearms, she broke his grip from her hips. "Oh, so that's my role. I'll just stay inside and clean the house and venture outside to collect fruits and vegetables. Are you sure that's safe? I might get stung by a bee or a thorn in my thumb." She pushed at his chest, moving him away. "Your sister can work outside with the cows, but not me. I'm too stupid." She punched his chest for good measure then stormed up the stairs.

"I never said you were stupid. Just maybe dangerous because you lack knowledge and, for the record, Willow grew up on this ranch. You didn't."

She stood at the door and faced him. "So it's too late for me to learn anything? Is that what you're saying? I'm a dangerous dumb-dumb. A moron?" She flung the door open and stormed inside to flee up the stairs.

She heard Jace pound up the outside steps then stomp across the porch, but she didn't care. She could make noise, too, and she began to stomp up the last handful of stairs toward her room, mumbling about mouth breathers and knuckle draggers.

"Meredith," Jace yelled and slammed the door.

She didn't bother to respond, continuing to stomp down the hall all while trying not to cry or apologize. She knew she should, but she felt so useless around the ranch, and now she'd disrupted the work because of her idiotic actions. He wouldn't need to point that out—she felt like every single synonym to dummy a person could list.

He thudded up the stairs behind her and, with a squeal, she bolted for their room, trying to get behind a closed door before he reached her. But he had speed, and she had Jell-O legs, and by the time she got into their room and turned for the door, he was already in the space blocking it.

She pointed a finger in his face and had every intention of telling him to get lost. Instead she said, "Don't you yell at me, Jace Shepard. I am one second from falling apart here, and I don't need you to make me feel any worse."

Instantly, his face softened. "You scared me to death. At first I didn't see you. I was watching the calves, and then I saw Willow pointing and jumping around like a crazy person. That's when I saw you running, and I froze. For one second, one second when you could have been caught under hoof, I froze and, after that, I kept thinking that I might have killed you. That one second when I did nothing might have been the one you needed."

Meredith reached out, her hand coming to rest on his chest. "I'm sorry."

He covered her hand with his.

"But how awesome was that rescue?" She needed to lighten the mood, or else she was going to say something he might not be ready to hear. Something she'd realized when she'd been running from the cattle, believing a painful death was pending. To think she had only this short time with Jace, and so much was left unsaid or...untried.

Her mind went to a wicked place. Maybe he wasn't ready to hear how she felt about him either. If she confessed her blooming love, and he did a Han Solo on her, it would wreck her, and there'd be no arranged marriage to get her out of this one.

He smiled, linking his fingers through hers. "Intense trust exercise. That's how we vet people on the ranch."

Meredith laughed and stepped closer. Jace reached out with his other arm and snagged her around the waist, tugging her toward him. He kicked the door closed with his booted foot.

"Meredith," his voice was low. "I may seem calm now, but inside I'm not. To know you're all right, I need to feel you. I want to hear those sounds of pleasure you make when I kiss you, the ones deep in your throat. That needs to replace the sound of your scream." He stepped up to her, his front pressed to hers, their hands between them. "I want to push you against the bed, strip your jeans to your ankles, and take you roughly from behind. I need this. I need you." He tugged her even closer, his fingers squeezing hers.

She met his gaze. "What's stopping you?" Then using every ounce of courage she could muster, she stretched up on her toes, let her body rest fully against his, and kissed him.

20

The whole point of taking the four days out to camp was to get away from Meredith, not be stuck with her. Not that he would be stuck, per se. Just that he wouldn't have the space to think. They'd consummated their marriage and then repeated the act over the last three nights—Willow sleeping in the cabin to "give it a test run" was an additional incentive. Then his parents had moved home, Willow had moved back into her room next door, and everything came to a screeching halt because privacy was lost with the thin walls.

Coming together for the first time had started out with all the urgency possible for a human to possess. Rough kisses, shoving her against the wall, and quick hands stripping her of her clothes. Then he'd laid her on the bed, covered her body with his, and time slowed, touch softened, and two people connected so deeply it had left him stunned.

The hell with all the potential awkwardness they might be creating. The hell with it all. He'd found a new nirvana and wanted to wallow away his time there—with her. Continuing this practice was all he could think about. He felt like a top spinning recklessly out of control, and he needed to topple over and catch his breath. When she was around, he lost the capacity to use skills that separated man from beast. Like reasoning and calculation. He became primitive and only wanted to constantly mate and promise her the world.

Now the whole damn family lived within spitting distance of each other, and this pent up whatever-it-was-called was making him crazy. Yeah, he was happy to have Pops back on the ranch, but the early mornings and late nights were becoming the highlights of his day. Something intangible had shifted. Together he and Meredith worked in harmony getting chores done, and though she occasionally would turn a perfectly good steak into unintentional beef jerky—Jace didn't care. He'd eat canned soup everyday if that was what it took to keep things just the way they were. Last night they'd gotten into bed talking about the ranch and laughing as he shared stories about growing up with the mountains outside his backdoor. He loved her endless questions about the workings of his family business. Then he had lain there for hours dreaming about exploring her body.

All the reasons why he decided to get outdoors for a few days. Clear his head.

Leave it to a meddling mother to jack up those plans.

Now they would be sharing a tent. Jeez, he'd never get anything done. All because his mother was a master manipulator.

"Someone should stay behind to help you out," Jace said.

"I have Willow."

"Wait, I thought Willow was doing summer school." He tried to focus on the distraction of his sister instead of the fantasy of Meredith naked in a sleeping bag. Good Christ, he was so easy to please. Everything she did made him hard—wear a flannel shirt, make coffee, eat a sandwich. He was a freaking lost cause.

"Her summer A class was cancelled, so she'll be home for six more weeks, then head back to campus for summer B. Let's get you packed, Meredith."

Meredith and Willow were whispering furtively. Jace strained to hear what they were saying.

"What are you two hiding over there," Marjory said, pointing to Willow and Meredith.

"Um..." Willow said.

Yep, they were up to something. Jace was certain, and by his mother's narrow gaze, she knew it, too.

"Did you say I needed to do something, Marjory?" Meredith asked.

"I said we need to get you packed." Marjory crossed her arms. "What's going on here?"

"Nothing. I was telling Meredith about some of the icky parts of rustic camping." Willow busied herself by buzzing around the kitchen, stacking items like water bottles and granola bars on the counter.

Jace would bet his sister was lying, but he had a larger pressing issue going on than whatever it was his sister was hiding.

He turned to Meredith. "When was the last time you rode?"

"Um, a few years ago maybe, but I—"

His mom shoved him in the shoulder. "Whose fault is that? From day one you should have had this woman on a horse." She turned to Meredith "You'll need some warmer clothes. It gets cool out there at night."

Jace glanced at Meredith, who looked like he felt—railroaded. "You don't have to go if you don't want to. I'm sure Willow mentioned it can be kinda grubby out there." He looked between the two. "She told you there were no flushing toilets, right?"

"It's called an alpine smear, Meredith. Once you poo outside, you take a rock and—"

"Enough, Willow! Some things should be left to the imagination," Marjory scolded.

He watched her process what that meant, a variety of expressions crossing her face. She and Willow hadn't been discussing camping. He could see that in her horrified expression, and had he been in a better state of mind, one that possessed a sense of humor, he'd have laughed. He was torn. Part of him hoped that would put her off, but another part wanted her not to be bothered by that.

"I ah...well, I don't want to be a bother, so if I'll be in the way, I'll just stay here."

Well, hell. How was he supposed to answer that? Of course she'd be a bother, just not like she was thinking.

"Jace, tell your bride she would not be a bother on this trip." His mother pushed him in the shoulder then shifted her focus to Meredith. "You at least need to try and decide if it's something you'd like to rustic camp again in the future. It's a rite of passage here. No pressure, though." She lowered her voice as if mumbling to herself. "All Shepard woman do it at least once."

Jace was curious as to how she'd react to the Shepard woman challenge. She set her jaw and pushed her shoulders back. "I'd like to go." She was quiet, but her voice was firm.

Marjory clapped her hands together with glee. "Fabulous. Let's get you packed." Marjory ushered Meredith out of the room, and just over an hour later, they had their horses saddled and loaded with the bare essentials.

Meredith in jeans, a T-shirt, and hair in a ponytail looked far different than the bride he met and married in the same day. Gone were her painted nails and polished look, replaced by a casual and appealing Meredith. Jace looked away, not wanting to make something out of nothing. So what if her nail polish was chipped off or that she wore her hair more casually.

She rode Willow's sporty mare named Fancy and, though a

bit stiff, appeared more natural in the saddle than some of the locals. "You okay? Comfortable?"

She rode past him without so much as glancing his way. "Would it make you happy if I wasn't and had to go back to the house?" She slowed Fancy and glanced back at him.

"It's not that I don't want you here. It's that I have things to do and I can't be distracted." Jeez, even that made him sound like an asshole, and there was no doubt she took it that way because she sat up straighter and swiveled in her saddle.

"So I'm a distraction?" Her mouth dropped open with indignation.

Jace couldn't help but smile. "Not a bad distraction. A good one. A real good one."

Meredith blushed and turned away.

Jace looked around to get his bearings. He'd been so preoccupied, he needed a moment to make sure they were headed in the right direction. "We'll start in the far east pasture and circle back around. I usually like to go out and work my way in, but we're getting a late start."

"You know, if you tell me what to look for, I might be some help out here. There's more to me than you think."

Jace sat back in his saddle, his reins in one hand, his other hand resting on his knee. "I know this. You've done great learning stuff around the house and pitching in, but how about you fill me in on some specifics? I know very little *about* you, and when I ask, I get silence."

She bit her lip. "I grew up around horses. We had a house next to my grandparents, and they had the horses. My grandmother used to race thoroughbreds as a business but had gotten away from that and into training, breeding, and some horse rescuing. I rode every chance I got."

"Why did you quit riding?" He moved up next to her and

pointed down into a valley, the direction they needed to go. He didn't want her to stop now that she'd started. "You know my mother died." She glanced at him, likely waiting for a nod. "My grandparents died in the same accident. My father sold off everything after their funerals. Including the horses."

"One afternoon when I'd returned from therapy, my father told me what he planned. The next day, my favorite horse, her name was Lizzy, and the others were gone. A week later, we moved away from the only home I'd known to this ugly McMansion on the outskirts of the city. Far from where I had grown up, but close enough to be just out of reach." Meredith brushed a finger under one eye then the other. "Leaving it all was like losing my mother and grandparents all over again."

She looked ahead, avoiding his gaze, and he wondered what it would be like to lose most of the people he loved in one day. And he was worried about her getting too close to her family. If ever there ever was a person who needed people, it was Meredith.

He was a top dick, thinking only about himself and getting the ranch. He shook his head, Sabrina's advice ringing in his ears. Hadn't she told him that to get something he had to give something? He was getting the ranch out of this deal. It was only fair for him to look for an opportunity to give to her.

"You were a teenager, right, when they died?" He rode next to her but didn't look at her, knowing she would be uncomfortable.

"I was sixteen." She stretched forward and rubbed her horse's neck.

"We're going to camp right at the top of that hill there." He pointed.

They rode in silence until they reached a tree that stood out from the rest. After sliding off their horses, Meredith tied them to a large branch and worked with Jace to unpack their tent.

"If you want to talk about it, I'm here. I know when we got Pop's diagnosis, I felt like the world tilted and was trying to toss me off." He paused, plucked a long blade of grass, set it between his lips, and then leaned against a tree. That day had been awful, so many unknowns, and for a man as self-sufficient as Jace, it rendered him helpless in ways he never thought possible. No matter how strong or smart or cunning he could be, it would never be enough to cure his father.

He watched her, her face changing expressions from moment to moment. Was she reliving it? Did it bring back a plethora of memories like Pops did for him? It was always a game of comparison. He'd watch Pops struggle with opening a sandwich bag and recall a time he took down a steer. Each of those were gut punches, as he would then try to envision his father paralyzed and confined to a chair. Jace pushed from the tree and scooped up the tent. After pulling it from the bag, he grasped two corners and cracked it in the air, spreading it out. Meredith took one side and staked it.

"My father was the sort who was present, but mostly in body and not spirit. So losing my mother was—is—the most painful experience I've ever had." She connected the poles and threaded them through the tent side. "It was as if my father went nuts afterwards and was determined to remove all traces of my mother." The tent was up, and Jace tossed their sleeping bags inside.

"Here, help me hang up the bear container." He tossed her a rope and carried the large cylindrical container over to a different hill upwind, several hundred feet away from their tent.

"Wow, bears keeping popping up." She looked over one shoulder, then the other.

He shimmied up a tree and tied off one end of the rope. "You should always be mindful of bears. Most are easily scared, but we got one that likes my herd. How did they die? Car accident?"

What were the possibilities of three people dying in the same accident? It had to be something transportation based unless it was something so awful and tragic he couldn't imagine.

Meredith stared up at the clear sky; she squinted at a small speck, the droning of the engine in the wind.

Jace frowned at the same spot and put the pieces together. "It was a plane crash?"

She nodded. "I read recently that there are only two places on earth left where you can go and not hear a sound made by man. Pure natural sounds. I'd like to see what that's like."

She looked forlorn, standing at the top of the hill looking into the sky. Young and beautiful was how he initially had seen her. Scared, too. But now he saw more than that. He easily recognized the loneliness, but Meredith was strong. Through her ran a deeply entrenched desire to be something other than the one left behind, the victim of so much loss. She'd been pale and thin, a bit shaky, and although she was still too thin for him, she'd thickened up some. Color stained her cheeks now, as it had done every day since she began working in the garden. She stood taller and was laughing more. Her hands were often dirty, and her desire to see more, do more, and live more was ever present. Now he understood why she had come to him.

"Your dad, he must have sold everything out of grief or something." He handed her a bottle of water, took one for himself, and sat on a small campstool he'd brought. Meredith sat on hers.

"I thought that at first, but every year he got worse, more controlling. I was accepted into Brown, where both my mother and grandmother went, and he wouldn't let me go. I went to the local college. I have a teaching degree." She glanced at him, a small smile on her lips. "Doesn't really help me here, but when I applied for my first job, my father made sure I didn't get it, or any other job for that matter."

Jace couldn't understand a father blocking his own child. "Why?"

Meredith shrugged. "I've asked him that a million times. Basically, he wanted me to do what he wanted, when he wanted, for reasons he thought were important. My father is a businessman, and knowing the political climate is essential in his business. I was his tool for getting that information."

Jace nodded and squeezed his bottle, water leaking out from beneath the lid. What kind of father did that to his child? Jace thought back to the diner and their brief reception. She'd worn a plastic smile and a vacant look, and now it all made sense. Plus, the headache.

"Hey, have you had any headaches since you've been here? Other than the first day?"

She looked at him and smiled widely. "No, unless you count the ones from your sister's chatter. Incredible right?"

Jace snorted. "She does talk a lot. We all have headaches, but Willow excluded, I take the lack of headaches as a good sign. An excellent one actually." He stroked her cheek before tucking an errant wisp of hair behind her ear. "I'm sorry I was an ass today about you coming out here. I say that a lot to you, but I promise I'm trying to outgrow it."

She laughed. "Recognizing you have a problem is the first step." She clapped her hands together in finality. "So...what do we do now?"

Okay, she needed to move away from the subject. He could understand that. Jace stood, readjusted his hat, and offered her a hand to stand. "Since we're here, we might as well take a look at the herd and see if any of the cows dropped. Grab your shotgun. Rule number one out here is to always have something for defense at hand."

She took his hand, and he pulled her up. For all the toughness she'd developed since coming to the ranch, she still needed gentle touching and tonight, after dinner, he'd try to do his part and show her how much he appreciated her.

She glanced at the weapon holstered at his flank. "Got it. Carry a weapon. Even if I don't know how to use it."

Jace swore under his breath. Yep, her carrying a gun was as useless as tits on a bull. "This is grizzly country. I'm not for the unnecessary injuring of an animal, but I'm all for my friends and family coming home alive, and that includes you. We'll get you caught up on firearms real soon. For now, grab the bear spray."

He brushed his lips to hers once, and then again, using his tongue to caress and asking her to let him in. Kissing her, touching her, required a restraint he was learning to develop. He wanted to consume her, swallow her whole like she did him, take her into the blinding world of pleasure he'd become addicted to. With his hands on her hips, he pulled her against him, her fingers grabbing onto his shoulders. Her head went back as he worked kisses down her neck. He stopped at the base of her throat to kiss her scar. He loved the pucker of skin, even more so today because it gave him a place to start kissing her wounds. He was desperate to take her aches away.

"This?" he asked and kissed the round, raised skin. He glanced at her. Her eyes fluttered open and met his gaze.

"It's from a ventilator. I was the only survivor of the plane crash." Her voice was so low he almost didn't hear it over the pounding of his heart. A tiny tear fell from her eye, others waiting for their turn.

Her words sucked the air from him. It all made sense. A girl who nearly lost her life was forced to live a caged existence. Anyone with a spirit would have run at the first chance. Meredith was no exception.

Screw the cows. There would be enough sunshine after he was done showing his wife how much she meant to him and how desperately he wanted her.

"Babe," he said and wrapped her in a hug. "I'm so sorry." He laid her down in the soft grass. Using his hands to do all the talking, he showed her a gentle love. As the sun dipped lower in the sky, he did his damnedest to make Meredith know and feel that she was cherished.

21

J ace stood beside her, his hand pressed to the small of her back, his mouth close to her ear. "Get centered."

They were close enough to home that he could see the big house, their camping technically over now that they were in sight of the ranch. Yet he was trying to extend it as long as he could by finally getting around to teaching her to shoot. He really should get back to the house and check in with Tuck. A couple more rounds, and he'd drag them home. Man, it had been a fantastic four days.

"Deep breath, narrow your concentration down the sight line of the barrel, and bring the can into focus." He knew he should keep his mind on the task. Meredith holding a gun for the first time required his undivided attention. Yet, the sight of her, the butt of the gun resting on her shoulder, her legs apart and head bent, sent heat directly to his crotch. He wanted to toss the gun aside and relive what they'd done in the tent last night out in the tall grass of the prairie.

"Okay, I'm going to do it," she whispered, leaning forward.

Jace was instantly hard. He wanted to do it, too, and with her being so willing was all it took. Heck, her getting excited over the sunrise gave him wood. Shoot, watching her clean with those long-ass kitchen gloves made him want to strip her of everything but those stupid gloves and bend her over a table.

Christ, he was a Neanderthal.

"Jace?" Her voice was hushed, like she was going to startle the old coffee can away.

"Yeah?" He was staring at her ass, daydreaming.

"Can I pull the trigger?"

He snapped his attention back to the task. "Yeah, deep breath and then pull."

A crack split the air, and Meredith staggered backward into him, her derriere pressing to his crotch.

"Holy crap, that hurt." The rifle dangled from one hand while she rolled the opposite shoulder back a few times.

He pushed her away from him before he did something in broad daylight his mother wouldn't be proud of. "You'll learn to roll with it, and after a few times—"

"I won't have any shoulder left so it won't matter." She handed him the gun then began to rub her shoulder.

"It's not that bad." He laughed at her exaggeration. "And make note—you hit the can."

She spun away to look at the fence. "I did?" she asked in wonder, then did a little dance around him before coming to stop beside him.

A giant smile broke across her face, her eyes alight with pleasure. "Give me that thing." She snatched the gun from him and moved to stand in the position he taught her. She lined up her sights on the next can, pumped the lever action, took in a steady breath, and on the exhale, pressed the trigger. The can shot off the fence. Meredith worked the lever again, moving to the next can. Of the eight they'd put on the fence, she'd taken six down. Jace was impressed.

"I think you were meant to be out in the country." He took the rifle from her and slung it over his shoulder.

She was beautiful, flushed with pride at her accomplishments. She stood taller, more relaxed. She was transforming before his eyes, and damn if his lifestyle didn't look good on her.

"Can we do some more?" Her hand was in her shirt massaging her shoulder.

"Let's give it a break until tomorrow." He pointed to Tuck's truck headed toward them. "Looks like I gotta get back to business."

Meredith's eyes widened. "I'm okay out here by myself."

He checked the gun's chamber. "You will be, but not yet. Now remember, you can't use this on a bear or mountain lion. You can try to scare them away with it, but it'll not deter an angry animal."

Meredith paled. "Mountain lion? Am I going to have problems with the wildlife?"

Jace shook his head. "Nope, it's been a while since a bear came into the yard, and I have only seen one cat out near the foothills. A drought can push them in, but we're looking at a good, wet summer."

Meredith laughed. "That's good. First bears and now mountain lions." She shook her head. "That's kinda scary. I saw this show on National Geographic about grizzlies, and I'll admit I'm scared of them."

"Rightfully so, but mostly they want nothing to do with us and vice versa."

Tuck pulled up and flung open the passenger door. "Afternoon newlyweds. I hate to be the one to break this up, but there's some head counting that needs to be done. Among other things. Oh, and your folks and sister went into town."

Jace smiled wanly at Meredith and handed her the rifle. "I keep this in my truck so will you please take it back there and put it behind the seat. You'll see some shells back there as well. In the house inside the hall closet is another rifle if you need it. Shells on the shelf."

She nodded.

"If I'm not in by sundown—"

"I'll grill some cheese or something."

"You know it goes between the bread when you grill it, right?" He brushed a strand of hair from her face.

Meredith laughed. "Is that a wise thing to say to a woman holding a gun?"

"Point taken." He stepped back, conflicted because he wanted to kiss her, but uncomfortable with Tuck watching. "You okay with these horses?" He was leaving her to get them both back to the barn. "You can leave the camping stuff in the barn. I'll get to it later."

She smiled, nodded, and swayed toward him. "Got it. See ya later."

He glanced at Tuck who was watching them like a hawk. He hesitated, couldn't bring himself to do it, so winked at her instead before jumping into the passenger seat. Tuck was driving away before he could slam the door, yammering about all they had to do and how the GPS tagging system, an expensive device they'd implemented to help with location control and herd count, was acting up.

Though he managed to stay on task, Jace frequently found his thoughts drifting back to the woman waiting at his house. Legally she was his. The last few nights under his hands, she'd given herself to him, yet he wondered what it would feel like if she committed to him mind and body. Committed to the life he had here. It was all easy and fun now because it was novel, and granted she was really taking to it, but there were hurdles and obstacles ahead of them that might make or break them. It was hard going into this backward, although if they'd dated for a few years before getting hitched, they'd be no better off. The good part of the latter scenario was that he might be able to predict obstacles. Not knowing Meredith and learning her triggers made him uncomfortable as he moved forward blind.

The day passed quickly and weary from the sun's exposure and mental fatigue, he'd finally made it home long after the sun had set. He found Meredith in the kitchen washing dishes, her movements stiff on the side of her gun arm.

"Sorry about missing dinner," he said and leaned against the island. A bowl of salad was before him, and he picked an olive off the top. "This looks good." He ate another one.

From the fridge she took a plate wrapped with plastic wrap. "There was nothing thawed so here's a ham sandwich. I thought about turning it into a Panini, but then I figured why waste the ham."

Jace chuckled and peeled away the wrap. "You eat already?" He took a large bite.

"The sandwich, yeah. I was starving. But I waited on the salad so we could eat together."

Man, that did something to him. Filled him with a flush of heat that went straight to his groin.

She reached for the plastic wrap he'd balled up and tossed on the counter but stopped and shifted arms.

"Your arm stiff?"

Meredith nodded. "I tried putting heat on it. I couldn't find a heating pad so I used a washcloth."

"Not the same, huh?"

She shook her head. "It helped a little. Better than nothing, I suppose."

Jace tossed down the sandwich and picked up her hand. "Come on, I got something upstairs that will fix it." He tugged her around the island and pushed her ahead of him toward the stairs. "In my bathroom."

He followed her into the room and pointed to the toilet. "Sit." She did as he said and chuckled.

"What's funny?"

"When you said you had something upstairs for me, I thought that was your way of trying to get me into bed..." She turned crimson.

He found the tube he was looking for and squirted a generous supply into his hand. "What makes you think it wasn't?" Kneeling before her, he said, "Undo another button so I can get my hands in there." When she did, he took her shoulder between his hands and began to massage.

Meredith winced. "That smells awful."

"But it will feel so good." He knew of a few other things that would feel good, but he wasn't sure if she was up to it or not.

After a few minutes of kneading, Meredith moaned. "You're right. That's amazing." She rolled her head to the side to give him better access.

He licked his lips.

He dipped his fingers back into the ointment. "Raise your arm," he said, embarrassed that his voice was similar to a pubescent teen's.

Meredith's gaze searched his face and then stopped at his lips. With slow and stiff movements, she raised her arm. His fingers skimmed the top of her breast, and when her eyes fluttered closed, Jace knew he wasn't going to be able to refrain. He needed to figure out how to get her from the bathroom to the bedroom without breaking the mood.

He eased his hands away, brushing his fingers along her smooth skin. "We'll let that take and do it again in twenty minutes or so."

When he looked at her, she was watching him, her lip tucked between her teeth. "Okay," she said before pouncing on him, forcing him back against the cold floor, her hands pulling up his shirt. "I have an idea of how we can spend that time." Her own shirt slid off her shoulder, exposing one breast cupped beneath a lacy, white bra.

"Hell, yeah," he said and went for the button on her jeans. They never made it to the bed, taking breaks to rub cream over achy bits. Their dinner was forgotten.

This was why only the essentials got done around the ranch.

22

Life with Jace's parents back at the ranch was better than Meredith anticipated. Overwhelmed by the transformation of the cabin and how well it suited their needs, Marjory and Pops, as he demanded to be called, slipped right into her heart, becoming part of the fibers that held together the fabric. When Marjory had wrapped Meredith into a tight hug and thanked her for Meredith's work on the cabin, kissing her forehead much like Meredith's mother had always done, something buried deep inside Meredith broke free and stretched outward with such a powerful yearning that it nearly brought Meredith to her knees.

Granted, life on the ranch would never compare to the home she'd had with her mother, nothing could replace that, but this life was darn close, and on some level just as good. Each morning she, Willow, and Marjory would cook breakfast for the men, Meredith learning at Marjory's elbow, repeating the training at dinner and burning less every day. Meredith, always an eager student, was quick to make meal suggestions and was encouraged to try new things. She wondered if she was sometimes doing too much, going overboard with being helpful, but after being stifled for so long, she couldn't help herself.

Meredith found conversation with Pops easy. Maybe because she wanted to know more about the man who helped cultivate Jace. He had a laid-back manner, a quick laugh, and would regale her with stories of mishaps on the ranch.

They were standing at the fence in a corral where the horses were eating when Pops caught her staring at a large and beautiful white horse.

"You like the look of her?" He nodded toward the horse.

"She's beautiful. Anglo-Arab, right?"

"Yup, you've got a good eye."

"I used to have one when I was younger. They look somewhat alike."

Pop's wrapped his arm around the fence post and leaned into it. "Did you ride her often?"

"Every day." In short, quick sentences, she repeated to Pops what she'd told Jace about her grandmother's horse business and growing up learning the business. "Elisa Doolittle was a rescue horse."

"That was the horse's name?"

Meredith laughed and nodded. "I called her Lizzy. We took to each other instantly. Grams said I had the touch and was hoping to convince me to take over her business when I grew up." Meredith stared at the horse and was lost back to a time similar to this one, leaning against the fence and talking to her mother and Grams. Would her life have been similar to this had they lived?

"So why didn't you?" Pops asked softly.

Meredith shifted her focus to the dirt kicked up from the horse as it trotted around the corral. "When they died, I was sixteen. Everything was sold off."

The Anglo-Arab, named Coconut, Coco for short, slowed as

she passed Meredith. When Meredith stuck out her arm, Coco stopped and let her stroke her muzzle.

"She likes you."

"Because I feed her. Sometimes I bring her apples." Meredith had taken to the horse the first time she had helped clean out the stalls. "She's very good natured."

Pops nodded. "Yes, she is. Good range horse. Used to guns, stampeding cattle, and the odd wild animal that sneaks into the yard. You want to ride her?"

Meredith jerked her attention to Pops, her breath caught in her throat. "Can I?"

"Hell ya, you can. Come on, girl. Let's get her saddled up." Pops moved slowly, pushing off the fence with a groan. She'd spent some time researching his condition so she knew he tired easily and was gradually getting weaker. Meredith looped her arm through his, and together they walked to the barn.

Pops sat on the bench and told her where to find everything she'd need. "I'd love to get on a horse myself," he said with a sad shake of his head.

"What if we could get you to where getting on wasn't as much work?" From the saddle support she had to lift the saddle up and over and nearly buckled from the weight. Instead, she staggered back and dumped the saddle on the ground. "Holy crap, that's heavy. I'm used to sliding them off the horses. Not lifting them up."

Pops laughed and slapped his knee. "Used to those English saddles? One day you'll be able to lift it." He chuckled some more.

Groaning, Meredith hoisted the saddle and put it back on the saddle support, her arms screaming from the exertion. "I don't think I can do it, Pops."

He wiped the smile from his face, though the corners of his mouth twitched every so often. "If you look in that back tack closet, there should be a few English saddles. One ought to fit Coco."

That was when the idea struck her. From what she'd seen, his weakness was in his legs and arms, and yeah, he would need that to ride a horse, but his trunk was still strong, so balance wasn't an issue. Marjory had mentioned the other night how she'd like to get out on a horse as well. "Which horse do you ride?"

"That one." Pop pointed to Moses , a large but gentle quarter horse. "But I don't think I can get on the animal."

Inside the closet, Meredith selected two saddles and lugged them to where Pop's sat on the bench. "Don't go anywhere. I'll be right back." She didn't wait for Pops to say anything but ran to the cabin and knocked.

After sharing her idea, Marjory was more than up for it. They returned to the barn, and Meredith helped Marjory shove a large set of metal stairs out into the open space of the barn.

"I'd forgotten we had these," Marjory said and attempted to shake the stairs, testing their construction. "They're in good shape."

"They're perfect as a mounting block. What are they originally from?" Once the stairs were in place, Meredith moved to saddled Coco, while Marjory set a large saddle on Moses.

"Originally we didn't have the back deck. We added it a few years ago. These were the back stairs," Pops answered.

"I hated them, but look how handy they are now," said Marjory as she led Moses to stand next to the stairs. She patted the English saddle. "It's been years since I sat on one of these."

"Hopefully it will be more comfortable than the Western saddle," Meredith said, praying she was right. There would be no big horn for Pops to hold onto.

When they were good to go, Meredith stood on the other side of Moses while Marjory offered support as Pops climbed the stairs. It took two tries but he was able to swing his leg over the horse with Meredith offering stability. After Pops was situated, the stirrups adjusted, Marjory swung onto the saddle behind Pops.

"It's like we're kids again, right lover?" Pops asked as Marjory wrapped her arms around him.

"Only this time let's not try to see how fast the horse can go and jump anything, please. These bones are getting old." Over Pops' shoulder, Marjory winked at Meredith.

Laughing while mounting, Meredith asked, "Where to?"

"What haven't you seen?" asked Marjory.

"I've only seen this part." She gestured to the house and barn. "And the far pastures by the foothills when we camped."

"You haven't had a tour yet?"

Meredith blushed. "No, there hasn't been that much time." It was a lie, and Meredith wasn't very good at lying so she looked away in an effort to hide her face. She and Jace had talked about riding out, him showing her the land, but then they'd talk and touch. One thing would lead to another, and they'd end up in bed promising to make an attempt the next day.

"Hell, that boy is slacking on the job." Pops shook his head. "Meredith, hon, go inside and grab a shotgun. We're going to ride out far."

She slid from Coco and made quick work of grabbing the shotgun, a few extra shells she stuffed in her coat pocket. She took a small backpack from the closet then filled it with bottles of water and power bars. Just in case.

Back on the horse, she followed the Shepards at a slow, easy trot. They headed away from the ranch toward the burning sun, the mountains at their back. They rode across the plains and over a small creek, the land flat and easy for riding. The scenery was stunning, from every angle. No matter which way she looked, the view only improved, and many times she was caught staring slack-jaw at the endless beauty before her. Knowing all this was within an easy ride from the house pleased Meredith. She could see herself and Jace, too, riding out to enjoy and explore.

"Look over there. There's Jace and Tuck." Marjory pointed to a tributary where several cattle were drinking and Jace's truck was parked in the flood land.

Meredith scanned the area, but didn't find him until the wading cattle shifted away from the stream. Jace and Tuck were bent over a cow that looked to be in the process of giving birth. With Pops in the lead they rode their horses down to Jace and Tuck.

"How many like this this year?" Pops called.

Jace stood, looking between his parents and Meredith, but said nothing. He walked to the large quarter horse and rubbed his neck before answering. "This is the second that we've seen."

"How many more you got out there?" Pops looked across the valley.

"We estimate five." Jace had explained to her at dinner last night that prior to birthing season, the heifers that were expecting were brought down to the lower pasture, the one closer to home, but a few always slipped through the cracks.

"That's good. The tracking system sure makes things easier." Pops took off his hat and wiped his forehead. Sweat had soaked his hair. From behind him, Marjory was making quick hand gestures to Jace who was staring at her, brows furrowed.

Pop's tried to twist in his seat to look at Marjory.

"I'm getting a tour of the land," Meredith said, shifting Jace's focus from his father to her. She hoped he wouldn't say anything about his dad being on a horse or the fatigue it was obviously causing. Picking up on Marjory's intention with her signs, Meredith said, "We're headed back now, though. I don't know about Pops or Marjory, but I'm starving."

"Tuck's headed back as well to grab a few things if anyone

wants to ride with him." He glanced at his parents, then Tuck, who looked surprised.

Pops huffed. "If you're referring to me, I think I'll pass. This might be the last time I'm able to get on and stay on a horse, and I'll be damned if I'm going to get off now. I may be tired, but I'm riding this here beast back to the house. Understand?"

Jace nodded.

Pops shifted in the saddle. "Understand Marjory? I know you're back there trying to communicate with Jace by glaring or using gestures or whatever, but I'll be the one who decides what's best for me."

Marjory snorted. "A stubborn ass like you? I don't see it. But I'm always open to find out. I love saying I told you so, and this sounds like one of those times I might get to say that."

Meredith squirmed, uncomfortable with witnessing their fight, but startled when Pops laughed.

"Damn, bossy woman. Between you and Meredith, I don't stand a chance."

Marjory hugged him. Not a fight, just familiar banter between people who loved each other.

Jace raised his brows, his attention on Meredith.

"I, ah…" Would this cause a fight between them? She was anxious for the time when she understood Jace's moods the way Marjory did Pops.

"She was the one who got Pops on the horse. Clever girl," Marjory said.

Jace crossed his arms. "Is that so?" Yep, he was not happy. His eyes narrowed. Meredith shifted in her saddle and waited for the tightening of anxiety to take over. Yes, this wouldn't be their first fight, but it would be the first one where the anger was directed at her, not coming from her.

"Looks like you have everything under control here, Jace. We'll see you at home later." Pops pulled the reins, and the horse turned and ambled away. "Come on, Meredith. I can't get off this mountain without you," Pops called over his shoulder.

"Ah..." She didn't know what to say so she tugged the reins and followed suit.

The ride back was quick, and once Pops was off the horse, he gave her a hug. "Thank you for not treating me like an invalid." He squeezed her shoulders before turning to Marjory. "I'm gonna take a nap, lover."

"You want something to eat first?"

Pops shook his head. "No, but how about you lay down with me. You ain't no spring chicken and need to rest those old bones."

Marjory smiled. "Is that so?" She took his arms and kissed his cheek. Together they ambled slowly back to the cabin.

Meredith gave the horses a good rub down and fed them extra oats before she headed to the big house to make lunch. With a sandwich and ice tea, she sat outside on the back deck and stared at the garden, wondering what Jace would say to her. A knot of apprehension sat in the center of her gut, making her food unappetizing. Willow and one of her mindless conversations would be the perfect distraction, but Willow had gone into town and Meredith had nothing but her thoughts. She hated not knowing what he might be upset about. Was it getting Pops on a horse? If it had been such a bad idea, why had Marjory gone along with it? That would be her argument.

Leaving most of her sandwich on the plate, she watered the garden, taking pride in the little seedlings popping through the ground and finding a sense of success with her hard work. Meredith wanted to stomp her foot. Yeah, Jace could be mad at her, but Pops and Marjory had been all for the ride, and his father had never stopped smiling. So there! That was what she would hold on to, and if he was angry, like she thought he was, he could just go pound sand or something. When she turned to cutoff the water, Jace was standing there. She hadn't heard him come up.

With his hand on the water spigot, he asked, "You done?" The question seemed loaded, about more than watering the garden.

She nodded, the hose going slack in her hand. She let go as he reeled it in and moved to the deck to sit at the table. She would not try to anticipate him. She'd done that with her father and hated it about herself.

When he finished with the hose, he faced her, one hand on his hip. "About my dad."

"He looked happy, didn't he?" To hide her nervousness, she peeled the crust from her sandwich.

Jace sucked in a breath, as if pulling back the words he was going to say with an inhalation, and nodded. "He did look real happy, but it's not your place—"

"Oh, Meredith," Marjory called as she stepped out from inside the house. "I've been looking for you. Pops is out like a light, exhausted."

Meredith cut her eyes to Jace and saw the thin press of his lips.

"But he's over the moon with happiness. What you did for him today, getting him on that horse, it was good for him. Good for his soul." Marjory crossed the deck. She pulled Meredith from the chair, the sandwich falling on the plate, and wrapped Meredith in a tight hug. "I cannot thank you enough. I knew he'd been wanting to do it, just didn't know how, and your solution was so simple. I feel like an idiot for not thinking of it. Thank you, child. Thank you."

Meredith hugged her back, not looking at Jace.

"I'm glad Pops was happy, Ma, but it was real dangerous of him to get up there. We might not want to do that again."

With surprising force, Marjory pushed her away and spun to

her son. "You listen here, Jace Shepard. If your father wants to do it tomorrow, he'll do it again tomorrow. Soon, he won't be able to move, and that will destroy him, so you give him what he wants. You understand me?"

Jace ducked his head. "Yes, ma'am."

She stepped up to him and put her hand on his arms. "I know you're worried. I am, too. But we have to let him live his life as scared as we may be. You understand, son?"

Jace nodded and stood like a petulant child as his mother hugged him. "I'm going to struggle with things that could put him danger," he said.

"Taking a shower puts him in danger, but your father has been very good at knowing his limits."

Meredith averted her eyes, feeling very much like a voyeur. The air was thick with emotion, so she decided to take her plate and cup inside. Unfortunately, they followed her.

"Your wife really fits in here, Jace." Marjory said from behind her.

Meredith smiled. It was a high compliment indeed.

"Why do you sound so surprised, Ma?" Jace asked.

Meredith had heard the wonder in Marjory's statement as well but had decided to let it go. She wished Jace would have too.

"I'll admit I was surprised and well...suspicious when Meredith showed up," Marjory said, coming alongside Meredith as they walked to the kitchen. "You have to admit the timing was perfect considering what Pop's had said to you, Jace."

Meredith put her dishes in the sink and began to wash them, her back to Jace and Marjory.

An excruciating moment of silence passed.

Jace sighed heavily. "Ah, well..."

Meredith longed for more dishes to wash as she finished hers. She did not want to lie to his mother, a woman who had become her friend.

"But," Marjory boomed. "You two are so well suited it doesn't matter to me how Meredith came to be here. You both are good complements to each other, and having you here, Meredith"—Marjory came to stand next to her—"is a blessing to this family. A true blessing. I am so proud you're a Shepard."

Marjory flung an arm around Meredith's shoulder and tugged her close. "You're an easy person to love," she whispered in Meredith's ear.

For the first time ever, Meredith was glad her father's demands and lifestyle choices for her had put her through an emotional gauntlet. She called upon those previously over-taxed coping skills to not burst into tears.

23

J ace and Meredith never talked about what Marjory had said that day in the kitchen. Their arrangement was easily forgotten as the day-to-day activities never allowed for downtime and wandering thoughts. Life around the ranch was fast paced, and when Willow returned to school, it meant one less hand to help out.

Pops decided it was his job to armchair quarterback and help with the new calves. He'd sit on the porch and belt out instructions while scrutinizing each step in the locate and tag process. Jace found working beside him bittersweet. Something he'd always taken for granted, Jace now wanted to press pause and enjoy. Whenever possible, he picked his father's brain about the best times to supplement feed and about the kind they should use. One day he wouldn't have his old man guiding him through the business, but Jace tried not to let that crippling pain consume him. It was hard enough watching Pops grow weaker.

While that was happening, Meredith was blossoming. She fit in among them snugly, much like the way he fit inside her. Perfectly. Her days were spent canning and freezing fruits and vegetables from the garden and then turning it over for next year's crops. As fall crept up on them, she decided to try her hand at gourds, pumpkins, and an autumn harvest with parsnips, onions, and peas. Sometimes, she brought the Farmer's Almanac to bed—having never moved out after Willow left— and would question him about frost and composting. Lord knows they had enough manure around to help with that, but each time she'd start a discussion about the ranch, they'd end up sweaty. He liked it.

All her talk of what she wanted to do around the place made him horny. Jeez, the things he found sexy. Tuck would laugh if he knew they'd made love the other night after an invigorating discussion about growing butternut squash. Then yesterday she'd found another snake in the chicken coop and had handled it herself. Instant wood. Watching her carry the shotgun had done it. Getting her target in two shots, those firing lessons paying off, had cinched it. He was falling for her.

He liked that her days revolved more around the house and with his mom and Pops than coming out into the pasture or corral. She'd invaded enough of his space that he wasn't ready to relinquish that part, too.

On the first morning of autumn, he took her out to watch the sunrise, a tradition they'd started and kept with each solstice. He could see them doing it every year, but fantasies like that were hazardous.

It was just as easy to picture them doing the barn dance every year. A family tradition that went back nearly a hundred years, the Shepard's put on an annual hoedown in their barn. Many of the locals were done with their crops or had finished at auction with their livestock. Now the resetting for next year would begin, but not before they blew off a little steam and energy.

Tonight was the night. Willow was home for the event, and the three Shepard woman had been cooking for three days solid.

Jace moved a few bales of hay to the floor to offer more seating, then looked around the space. They were ready. He watched Meredith set up a table, smoothing the tablecloth before setting the vase of flowers in the center.

This would be the first time, their brief reception aside, that they were among the town folk. They'd talked about going into town for dinner several times but never made it. If something needed to be picked up in town, Meredith and mom went in but never lingered. He got the feeling that Meredith liked to stay on the ranch. When he'd asked her about it, she'd said she'd spent enough time mingling with people to hold her over for a while and she'd let him know when the urge to start back up kicked in. If it ever did.

He had one pressing question that he couldn't hold back any longer. Only he didn't know how to ask, afraid it would rock the boat too much.

"You all sure put together a nice feast." He stood back, looking at the covered dishes on the table she'd just set out. He hoped he wasn't starting something that could ruin the evening.

"It was fun. Exhausting, but still fun." She moved to the next table and began moving covered dished from the cart they'd bought in town a few weeks back, proclaiming it would save them work. Not that he wanted to lug each dish from the house to the barn, so he wasn't about to disagree.

"Listen, Mer, I have an awkward question I need to ask." He stepped next to her, sliding an arm around her waist, hoping she would see it as a casual yet concerned question and not take offense.

She narrowed her eyes, but her smile didn't fade. "Okay. I guess I'm ready."

He dropped a kiss on the tip of her nose. "I like when you

make your 'this isn't going to be good' face. Your nose crinkles up."

"Are you stalling?"

"Yes."

"Jace." She laughed. "Just ask."

He huffed out a sigh. "It's no big deal really."

"You make it seem like one."

"A lot of people will be here tonight and in your business. They'll wonder why you haven't come to town much, and some might even speculate that you're hiding out here."

Her smile dropped. "Some or you?"

"I only want to know if that's really why you stay away from town. Are you afraid of something? I know I should have asked this earlier, but—"

"It's true that I don't want my father to find me. I want time here to know where—" She bit her lip.

"You want to be." He nodded. Some days he felt like there was no chance she'd ever leave. That their arrangement didn't make any difference because she knew she belonged here. The question "what next" was always the elephant in the room. They'd become skilled in avoiding it. Instead they'd make love, laugh like fools in the rain at target practice, and he'd slap her ass every day in the kitchen while she made dinner, but none of that meant she was going to stay.

She wrapped her arms around him. "There is always the chance my father will find me, but right now there is no place I want to be but here. There is nothing I need in town. That's why I don't go. Not because I'm scared to go into town, but because I don't want to go."

"And how will you do tonight with all the people?"

She'd told him about how her father used her to eavesdrop and report. She'd told him about how the migraines had escalated and about the night she decided to take Sabrina up on her offer.

"I'll make sure to get some fresh air if I feel the slightest one coming on. I don't see it happening. The few times I've been into town with Marjory haven't caused any, and I'm excited about tonight. It sounds fun."

No matter how hard she tried to reassure him, he couldn't help but feel like something bad was waiting in the wings.

"Stop worrying, Jace. Really." She kissed his chin. "Did I ever tell you Dirty Dancing was my favorite movie? I used to sneak watch it when I was younger. My mom said it was inappropriate for me. Maybe we can try out some of those moves later after the dance. In the privacy of our room." She wagged her brows.

"I'd like to claim that I've never seen it, but Willow's watched it a ton, and Sabrina talked about it in college so..." He rolled his hips into hers then dipped her back. Her laughter floated across the room.

When she came back up, he pulled her close and began to slow dance, humming an old country tune. She wrapped her arms around his neck and fit herself perfectly against him.

This is what Sabrina had asked him to do. Take a chance. To let himself go, and with Meredith, he found that easy enough these days. Sure, he worried about the day her father would show up, but her interest in the ranch appeared genuine, and that had to count for something.

Right?

They danced for a while, enjoying the quiet and time alone. Occasionally he'd drop a kiss on her neck or shoulder and laugh at the goose bumps that followed.

"Hey," Willow called out. "You two gonna do that all night, or can we finish setting up? Folks will be coming soon."

"Go away, Willow. I'm dancing with my wife." He liked how easily the word rolled from his tongue.

"To no music?"

"That's how we roll," Jace said, still guiding her around the room, though this time in an exaggerated waltz.

"Looks like those dance lessons mom made you do are paying off," Willow said.

He twirled Meredith before bringing her to a stop in front of his sister. "You sure know how to kill a good time, Willow."

"You're married. I thought good times were supposed to be over for you." She punched him in the shoulder then left.

Jace pointed off toward the driveway. "Looks like the party is about to start."

Meredith followed the direction of his finger and saw several cars headed their way. She sprang into action. "I have to get the rest of the food."

She dashed from the barn, her pretty, dark green skirt waving around her legs. He liked that she had chosen cowboy boots for her footwear. She wasn't polished-looking like she had been when she arrived, and he thought she was beautiful then. Seeing her now, she stole his breath; his heart stuttered in his chest then swelled with pride. Sabrina was getting an awesome Christmas gift this year.

Life with a wife had been an easier adjustment than he thought. He attributed that to Meredith. It was because of who she was at her core. She may not have known who she was when she arrived, but maybe she knew now.

Unless she was going from one imposed identity to another. This was his greatest fear, a recurring doubt that sometimes woke him from an exhausted sleep. It kept him from taking the next step, not that he was sure what that should be. Regardless, Jace believed time would tease it all out.

He stepped out of the barn and walked toward the front of the house to direct traffic. Pops leaned against a post on the porch, a big shit-eating grin on his face. Mom, Meredith, and

Willow scurried out of the house with arms full of fixings. The sun was setting over the mountains, the breeze dipping into temps that required a lined hoodie. The band, members of the volunteer fire department, struck up their first of several jaunty tunes, and dancing was quick to follow.

Meredith found herself twirled around the floor by several of the older local ranchers. Jace would manage to get in a few strolls around the hay-strewn floor before they'd get interrupted, but Meredith didn't mind. Marjory and Pops were having fun, everyone was laughing, and it was nothing liked she'd endured with her father. It was so much better, friendlier. It suited her.

She was dancing with Pops, a slow small shuffle step sort of dance when Tuck cut in. Glancing around the room, she found Jace dancing with Tuck's wife, Mandy, a nice woman Meredith wanted to get to know better. A few times she mentioned Meredith joining her book club, and that appealed to Meredith. Now that things were slowing down on the ranch, she felt comfortable taking time away. The feeling of being a guest, a newcomer, had faded, but showed up occasionally when she and Jace experienced something new together. Like tonight. Sure, she was comfortable, but acutely aware that she was a stranger to these people. They talked about someone's new baby, and she had no idea who that person was, but she was slowly putting the pieces together and looking forward to next year when she could participate in the conversation.

Meredith smiled at Tuck and thanked him for the dance when it ended.

"Aw, hell Meredith. We're all real glad you're here and I'm looking forward to getting to knowing you better." He tipped his hat and shuffled off to his wife. Wrapping herself in a hug, Meredith embraced the moment hoping to imprint it on her memory bank. It had been a gamble to trust Sabrina, but oh, so very worth it.

She scanned the room for Jace and saw him sitting on a bale of hay next to his parents, a plate balanced on his knee, his head tossed back in laughter, and Meredith knew. Her awareness of how she felt about him slammed into her like a horse kick to the chest, only it didn't hurt. It was amazing, rippling through her until it encompassed her much like being wrapped in a warm blanket. She felt lucky, happy, and... She searched for the best word to describe what she felt, but it was too new and foreign for her to quickly assign a label.

A tall man, name unknown, rushed by and jumped on a haystack next to her. He gave an ear-ringing whistle and, instantly, the band stopped playing, the dancers a second behind.

"I just got a call from the fire department. A bear mauled old man Beasley. His foreman found him. He's not sure if he'll make it. The ambulance is thirty minutes out." He pointed to Jace and Tuck. "You riding with me?"

Jace nodded once, handed his plate to his mother, then hustled out of the barn, Tuck in the rear. Others followed behind. Willow came up next to Meredith and took her hand.

"What's happening?" Meredith whispered.

"Leo is the physician's assistant. He used to be an EMT. They're going up to Beasley's place to do what they can until the ambulance gets there. Jace and Tuck are going to provide cover in case the bear is hanging around. If it was a grizzly, they like to come back for their kill."

Meredith shuddered and gripped Willow's hand. "The others? Surely, they aren't going to hunt for the bear in the dark?"

Willow shook her head. "No, but they'll go up and do a look around the property. Other's will go home and get sleep so the search can start early tomorrow."

A million questions needed to be asked.

"Let's start packing up food." Willow tugged her toward the tables where people were making quick work of cleaning up.

Unable to focus on anything but Jace, Meredith found herself drawn to the front of the barn. Jace was getting into his pickup, a shotgun over his shoulder. He glanced her way, gave a brief nod, then climbed in the truck and was gone.

Later that night, she laid in bed, alone, waiting for Jace to return, fading into sleep, only to jerk awake as she repeated the nightmare of a giant bear attacking Jace. Sometime in the deep night, exhaustion finally claimed her. It had provided a fitful rest that was later interrupted with the rooster's crow. His side of the bed was empty, the sheets tucked under his pillow and the spot cold.

24

After breakfast was made and the kitchen cleaned, Meredith sat on the porch next to Pops, who was rocking slowly in his chair, a shotgun resting against the wall beside him.

Meredith picked at her fingernails, occasionally biting one. The day was beautiful, cool with a crystal clear sky, but it was quiet. More so than Meredith liked. Maybe the ranch had always been this way during work hours, she couldn't say, but it seemed as if even the chickens weren't up to their normal clucking. All she knew was that it felt different. Unsettling, like hidden within the wind was a badness blowing across the land.

Marjory was sweeping the porch of the cabin, Willow feeding the horses in the barn. Meredith was losing her mind on the porch. She had no experience with bears. Her brief Internet search after breakfast had shown pages of information about attacks and how difficult it was to kill a grizzly. She'd walked away from the computer unable to get the images washed from her mind.

Pops sighed, slapped his hand on the arm of the chair, then let out a expletive heavy with bitterness.

"Pops?"

"I should be out there," he mumbled.

"I don't understand how they think they can find him, or if they find a bear how they'll know it's him."

Pops gave a wane smile. "They try and track the bear, but mostly wait and see if he comes back. Jace said we've been having problems with a bear, and my guess it's the same one."

"Do they hunt people?" The pages of bear attacks she'd seen flashed before her.

"Ah, grizzlies are different. Hard to say. My guess is last night old man Beasley surprised the bear, and that's why it happened."

"Have you heard if he's going to be okay?" Meredith held her breath.

"He was airlifted to the city hospital. Still waiting to hear." Pop stared out toward the road and then leaned forward. "Looks like Jace is coming home."

Meredith squinted and saw the dark fleck, Jace's truck she supposed, coming toward them. She wanted to jump from her chair, so when Pops stood, so did she, twisting her hands in anticipation as they waited for him to draw closer. He parked near the house, and when he got out, Meredith gasped. His shirt was covered in blood.

"It's old man Beasley's." He pulled the shotgun from the truck before walking slowly to the porch.

"Did it come back?" Pops stepped toward Jace and put out his hand, taking the shotgun.

"Nah, not that we saw. Lost the trail in the woods, but looks like he was headed toward the herd. Ours or Beasley's. Hard to say."

He looked exhausted, and Meredith wanted to...needed to do something more than be idle. "Are you hungry? Did you sleep?"

"I slept some in the truck. I could eat, though." When he smiled at her, she sighed with relief. He was okay. He was okay. She had to keep telling herself that. He was okay, and he was home.

"I'm going back out. I want to move the herd closer, but I'd like to shower and get fresh clothes." He stretched, his arms lifting over his head, and yawned.

Her knees wobbled. Going back out?

"Maybe you should get some sleep first." Her hope was that the bear would be found while Jace was napping. It became her prayer. She felt it was a reasonable request.

Marjory came to the porch. "Give me those clothes. I'll try and get the blood out of them. Go on inside and get cleaned up. We'll get you some food while you shower."

"Wait," Pops said. "You going back out with Tuck?"

Jace shook his head. "He split off with Beasley's foreman to start checking the herd up in the foothills. I'm gonna cover the lower pasture and work my way toward Beasley's. I'll push them all down this way."

Pops shook his head. "Not alone."

Jace put one foot on the stairs and his hand on his hips. "It's not ideal, I'll admit, but it's going to have to be on horse, Pops, and—"

"I'm not saying to take me. I know that would cause more stress than help. Take Meredith or Willow. Someone to watch your back."

When Jace glanced at her, she tried to school her face, hoping the sudden escalation of fear she felt wasn't showing. The thought of going out there with a bear terrified her, but the thought of Jace going out alone scared her more. Would she really be a help or a hindrance? Like with the cattle, would she make a mistake that could have terrible consequences? She hadn't been afraid of the herd coming in, just being caught in it.

This was different. This was a bear. A bear! What were the odds of surviving an attack?

Jace shook his head. "I dunno—"

"Come on, let's get you fed and cleaned up." Marjory gave him a push up the stairs.

After Marjory and Jace went into the house, Meredith collapsed in the chair and swallowed hard.

"You can do it," Pops said sitting beside her. "Chances of seeing a bear are slim. He needs someone to keep an eye on the area around him. He's tired—"

"We're all tired. Which is why no one should go out." She shook her head. Didn't they see this was foolish?

"Meredith, this bear is close. He's hungry, probably sick because he's hunting the herd and knows it's easy. He's trying to fatten up before hibernation. Jace needs to drive as much of the herd as he can closer to home."

"But what if we see a bear? My instincts aren't what they should be for a place like this. When the herd came in, my instincts were all wrong. I did all the wrong things. I might be more harmful than—"

"That's fear talking. To live out here means life isn't always cushy. Now go get changed." Turning away, Pops dismissed her with a flick of his hand.

There was no way she'd be able to cope if Jace went out alone. No way. Sitting on the porch worrying was far less helpful than actually watching his back. Meredith rose and went into the house.

Two hours later she was on Coco, a twelve-gauge shotgun in a saddle holster at her knee, and Jace beside her, clearly not happy she was going by the grumbling he was doing. He adjusted the pistol on his side then resituated the rope hanging from the lariat holder. Willow had saddled up as well and rode halfway with them, splitting off when they'd met up with another party who needed an extra person. Most of the town was out helping their neighbor to bring herds in and look out for the bear.

Word was old man Beasley was in critical condition, but the prognosis was optimistic.

They rode in silence along the wood line until they came to the first herd.

"Is this his or ours?" She looked at the cattle; it was a small herd with no calves.

"Ours, the tags in the ear are yellow. That's us. Beasley is green." Jace rode up next to her, took her reins, and pulled her to a stop.

"What's going on?" She looked in every direction, even rising in her seat to scan for something awful like a giant bear.

"Meredith, you need to breathe, babe. I'm not going to let anything happen to you. I'd feel better if you were safely at home but—"

"So would I. I'd love it if you were safe at home, too. I want everyone out here to be safe at home." She swallowed back the tears that threatened to fall.

Jace brushed her cheek. "Fair enough. But this bear won't stop. Even if he goes into hibernation, he'll be back in the spring."

"Pops thinks he's sick."

Jace pressed his lips together, nodded, and then answered, "That's my guess too. Not typical behavior for a bear."

Did that make the bear more dangerous? "What if we see him?" she whispered, her fingers brushing the shotgun.

"You let me handle it. Grizzlies like nice, calm talking. Don't run off. If you get knocked off the horse, play dead. That gun at your side has a slug meant to stop big-ass animals, especially if it's a grizzly, but packs serious power. It's hard to handle, and your shot has to be a precise headshot. Don't even try—go for the bear spray." He tapped the can hanging from a D-ring by her lariat holder.

Meredith nodded and bent forward, scanning the area again, silently praying this day would end soon and uneventfully. "I feel helpless. Like food, like prey. I don't like it."

"Yeah, me neither. I've come across a few before, and it's worked out. This will, too." He reached for the bell on her horse's neck and took the dong stopper off, then tucked it in his pocket. He did the same to his bell. She really hoped the noise would be enough of a deterrent.

Enough with the talk. It was time to get moving and get home. "What's the plan? We try and get these animals headed toward the ranch?"

"Yeah." Jace leaned toward her and slid an arm around her waist. "I know this is scary, but it's something we face often. You'll get used to it."

Trouble was she didn't want to get used to it. Getting used to it meant getting complacent. Like her father had gotten used to using her, manipulating her, forgetting how to see her. If they got used to bears, didn't that mean their guard was down?

Meredith pressed herself into him, pulled in by his warmth and musky scent, the shower still fresh on him. "Tell me what to do so we can hurry this up and get home."

Jace laughed, the deep rumbling sound vibrating through her. His lips pressed to the back of her neck. "We should go down a few more miles. I think Beasley has a small herd there. We can drive them toward this one and get both closer to home."

A few more miles. She could do that. Wanting something more substantial from him, like his lips on hers, she nodded and tilted her face up. Jace was quick to comply.

"If the situation weren't what it is, I'd try and talk you into a little fun in the tall grass."

Meredith punched him lightly in the chest. "Not going to happen until you get me home and in our bed."

Jace pushed her away, but righted her to keep her on the horse, and tossed her the reins. "Jesus, woman. What are you sitting around for? Let's go up and get that other herd. We got things to tend to at home." He spurred his horse on and galloped away.

Laughing, Meredith followed suit, catching up and passing him. They took turns playing follow the leader for a while, each trying to keep the lead, laughing and pretending to attempt to shove the other off their horse when one passed the other.

They made it to the herd in no time, a small collection hugging the tree line and grazing on the high grass, green tags in their ears.

"Circle around and push them that way." He pointed in the direction from which they came.

Meredith nodded and rode behind the herd.

"Come on," she called and leaned to slap the hindquarters of a brown cow.

It took coaxing, but between the two of them, they managed to get the beasts going forward at a sloth's pace.

"Switch places with me. They'll want to go back from where they came, but we have to convince them it's not a good idea."

Meredith snorted. A big ol' bear might be able to do that. Too bad a person couldn't reason with a cow. Meredith considered swearing off beef if they'd hurry, but hesitated. Her husband was a cattle rancher; it wouldn't do for the man's wife to be a vegetarian.

Meredith rode to the side of the herd, Jace taking the back, cracking his whip to get the herd moving. It was then she noticed a small calf limping along, slowing the works. She pointed the cute baby out to Jace.

"Cut them off at the top so I can get a look," he called.

Meredith rode to the front and, without doing anything other than being in their way, got the cows to stop. It was too easy, but a perk to their frustratingly slow pace.

Jace was off his mount and walking through the herd with swift purpose. Meredith scanned the area, though they'd made so much noise she doubted any bear would want anything to do with them.

"Grab the rope, will you, Mer? I'm gonna have to lug this one home on my horse. Looks like he got caught in some barbed wire."

Meredith rode to his horse, but had to get off to manage the rope. It didn't help that Moses shied or that her fingers fumbled on the knots. She considered remounting Coco, but then Jace would know she was too afraid to be off her horse. Some of the online stuff said that to outrun a grizzly, a person needed incredible speed and the capacity not to be winded. That was not her. That wasn't anyone. She hoped it was her horse, though.

"Wait here, girl," she told Coco and stroked her muzzle with one hand, the rope hanging from the other. Coco snorted, and her ears shot forward in warning.

Meredith swiveled to Jace, searching for him in the cluster of cows. Something at the corner of the herd, about thirty feet to Jace's side, caught her eye. Whereas the cows were brown, some light, some dark, this one had a rust tint to it and was far furrier. It crept slowly along the flanks of the herd along the tree line.

Coco snorted again. Meredith's heart slammed into her chest. "Jace," she croaked and dropped the rope. She reached for her horse.

Jace continued to investigate the calf.

"Jace," she said softly a second time.

From the corner of her eye, she saw him glance at her then jerk his attention to where she was staring.

She didn't need to ask if this was the bear they were looking for. It clearly was. The animal was mangy and thin, if something so large could be considered that. Two things surprised her. The first was the state of the bear, not what she expected from an animal slaughtering livestock, and the other? She was cognizant of the specifics about the bear when every part of her was screaming to run.

Jace crouched down and began to creep slowly back through the herd.

Then a cow caught wind of the bear and the herd shifted away from both Jace and the beast. The bear back peddled a few paces then began to skirt around the cattle moving parallel to Jace. The bigger cows lowed. The bear stopped, sniffed the air, then lifted on its hind legs, only to drop quickly and stomp the ground near the injured calf who scuttled away.

Meredith sucked in a breath. "Easy girl," she whispered to Coco who was shifting nervously beside her. "Stay nice and still." She made small strokes down Coco's neck, her attention on Jace and the bear. "Atta girl, I'm going to give you a special treat when we get back."

If we get back.

She stroked down Coco's wither until she felt the hard leather of the saddle. Using touch to guide her, she continued searching until she bumped the cold metal of the twelve gauge. With a flick of her thumb, she undid the strap that kept it contained, then slid the shotgun from its holster, her attention on the giant beast. Jace's horse shied nervously beside her, turning in a circle. Meredith continued talking to the horses to calm them, keeping her voice steady while her mind screamed hysterically.

The herd shifted again, splitting open and exposing Jace. The bear lifted his nose and sniffed, turning in Jace's direction. Meredith slowly slid the shotgun out of the holster and brought it to rest against her shoulder. Bless Coco for her loyalty.

With one eye on Jace, the other on the bear, she fumbled to find the safety. She sighed with relief at the audible click of its release, though she barely heard it over the pounding in her ears. She pumped the gun, chambering a round, and stared down the barrel to line up the bead sight. A tear ran down her cheek.

"Easy," she said, to both her and the horses. "Steady."

The bear stalked toward Jace, stopped feet from him, and rose on its back legs. Meredith's hands began to shake.

In a flash, the bear lunged into Jace's space, and simultaneously Meredith pulled the trigger, aiming for the head.

The boom from the shot leaving the gun was deafening, making her head fuzzy. When the kickback slammed the butt of the gun into her shoulder, blinding pain seared through the right side of her body and brought her to her knees.

The bear's claws were up and out, raking down as he fell toward the earth.

Through streaming tears and scorching pain, Meredith pumped the gun a second time then tried to bring it up, but the muscles in her shoulder refused. Gritting her teeth and screaming through the pain, she forced her arm up. The gun against her shoulder, she took aim, but the bear was on the ground, not moving.

And so was Jace.

25

Dizzy, Meredith dropped the gun and fell forward onto her hands. She closed her eyes and tried to clear her head, but the ringing was deafening. She called on the yoga breathing she'd done with her migraines to help her garner some control.

A spray of water hitting her face brought Meredith back to the moment. She snapped her eyes open. Coco was snorting on her! The horse whinnied and, using her muzzle, nudged Meredith out of her fog,

Jace!

In the twenty or so seconds it took for the ginormous bear's central nervous system to cease working, it had raked its large paws down Jace's back and left side. Maybe it was more that the bear was in motion when he was shot than a last ditch attack but, nonetheless, Jace had caught the business end of the bear's claws. Fortunately, if that word could be used, Jace had done what he was supposed to, balled up as tightly as he could and covered his neck with his hands,.

Jace lay next to the bear on his side, a bright crimson stain spreading across his jacket, the acrid odor of blood filling the air.

Meredith scurried to him as fast as her weak legs could manage, still clutching the shotgun.

"Jace, Jace," she cried, though it sounded distant and muffled to her, her ears ringing loudly. Tears poured down her face. A large gaping wound ran the length of his forearm. Matching wounds were at his shoulder, ribs, and hip area. It was unsightly, his flesh flayed open. Meredith dropped the shotgun and pulled off her jacket. The worst of the wounds looked to be at his ribs. She jerked off her top layer, a flannel shirt, and balled it up so the cleaner side was against the wound, then she ripped her T-shirt down the front to make long strips to wrap around him, leaving her in nothing but her bra and a coat to cover her.

"Jace?" She touched his face. A beady pulse throbbing in his neck gave her the courage to not freak the hell out.

She felt a vibration rumble through his chest and recognized it as a moan.

She pushed back a lock of hair from his forehead and kissed his temple. "Babe, come on. We have to get you back home. I need to wrap these wounds." She sniffed and wiped her nose on her shoulder.

He moaned again, and his eyelids fluttered opened. His eyes were cloudy with confusion and pain.

"Hey, can you sit up?" She tried to modulate her voice, afraid she was yelling, since it felt like she was speaking into a tin can. She held his arm, cradling it against her legs, and wrapped one last strip around the wound. Her own shoulder screamed with each move, making her work sloppy and difficult as she was forced to use her non-dominant hand.

"The bear?" she thought he said. At least it looked like it and sorta sounded like it.

She looked over his shoulder at the bear, but had to look away; even in death, it was terrifying. She glanced at Jace and shook her head. "We need to get you home."

Jace pushed up on his good arm and roared in pain. The stains grew larger. Meredith put a hand to his chest to stop him. She pressed her shirt to his side with her injured arm then began to wrap the area.

Jace closed his eyes and sat still. When she was done, she stood and offered him her hand. Slowly, he joined her, leaning heavily against her and her injured shoulder. She walked with him to his horse and helped boost him up. It took three attempts, and after Jace was on, she could see what the task had cost him, his face pale, sweat across his forehead.

"Go," she yelled and slapped the horse's rump. It sprang into action. On the way to her mount, she stopped to pick up the gun and her coat. She was able to get the coat on one side but left it hanging over her injured shoulder.

When she looked up, she found Jace had circled back and was watching her. "I think you've dislocated your shoulder," he yelled and rode to her. She slid the gun into her saddle holster and hoisted herself up. She needed to sit down. She needed a drink. She needed to pass out.

They were a pair, both injured, but Jace was losing blood, and she wasn't. Clenching her teeth, she kicked at Coco's flanks and shot off. Jace would follow, that she knew. Tucking the reins under her legs, she opened the saddlebag with one hand and took out the radio; they were miles from cell service. She made her mayday call. She didn't know what protocol was required so instead blubbered into the small handheld piece about a bear and their situation. Jace was slumped in the saddle, and she feared he'd fall out at any time.

About a half mile from the ranch, Willow broke through the forest, her horse racing toward them. When she saw Jace, she blanched and gasped, then rode up alongside him and took the reins, letting him fall further forward on his horse. Meredith rode on his other side, hoping she could catch him if he fell. When they come within range of the house, a truck was waiting for them, but Willow waved them off.

"It will take too long," she called and kept up the breakneck pace. She didn't stop until she was at the steps of the house.

Meredith fell more than dismounted and rushed to Jace. She didn't care that she was in her half hung coat and bra or that her arm had gone numb as it swung loosely from her shoulder.

Leo, the EMT from the other night rushed out, and following behind him was Tuck. They caught Jace as he slid from the saddle and quickly carried Jace inside. She tried to follow, but Marjory stopped her.

"Meredith, we have to take care of that arm." She led her into the kitchen and peeled the coat from her. "I want you to take a deep breath and focus on that." Marjory forced her into a chair and started moving her arm, tucking it into to her side and then slowly sliding it out. It was agonizing. Following a loud pop, Meredith's pain was immediately diminished, and she started to weep.

She jumped from the chair. "I need to see if he's all right!"

Marjory pulled her close. "Honey, Leo is just getting started—"

"I tried Marjory. I really tried. I did everything I could think of." Meredith clung to Marjory.

"I have no doubt. Meredith, look at your shoulder. I know you fired the gun. That's all anyone can do. Now, let's get you cleaned up."

Meredith shook her head.

"At least put some clean clothes on. At least a shirt." Marjory tucked a strand of hair behind Meredith's ear.

"Here," Willow said as she came into the room and handed

Meredith a tumbler with amber liquid in it and another flannel shirt. "You need this. Do one quick swallow."

Meredith took it from her, her fingers numb and stiff, likely from shock. She tossed back the drink. The burning sensation as it ran through her from head to toe felt good. Made her feel alive.

"Leo says that some of the wounds are deep, but the one on his side didn't puncture a lung, just bruised it. He's cracked some ribs, too. Leo's putting Jace's pieces back together as we speak."

"Won't he need to go to the hospital?" Meredith asked. She set the tumbler down, and with Marjory's help, put on the shirt.

Willow shrugged. "He needs to try and stop the bleeding first. The ambulance is on the way."

Meredith nodded and swayed on her feet.

"Let's get you cleaned up."

She slumped against Marjory. "I need to see Jace. I'm sorry I couldn't stop the bear, Marjory. I'm sorry. Tell Pops I'm sorry." Once she started crying and apologizing, she couldn't stop.

Marjory took Meredith's face between her hands. "Hush, darling. You did amazing. You saved his life. Pops and I will be forever thankful. We're so proud of you keeping a cool head under those conditions. But Meredith, you are covered in my son's blood, and it makes my heart ache to see it."

Meredith nodded, gulping in large pockets of air, hoping to gain control.

"Take a shower, then we'll drive together to the clinic when you get out. I hear someone coming now."

There was no siren, but the sound of a car speeding toward the house.

Meredith nodded and stepped into the bathroom. She waited for an indication that Marjory had moved away before she came out to stand in the hallway by the stairs. If they were going to take him to town, she was going to get one last look at him before they left. When the doctor ran up the stairs, the house seemed to be placed on pause. Not a sound as people waited for word.

Finally, a door creaked open, and a shuffle told Meredith that Pops was coming down the hall. His frame filled the space at the top of the stairs. Marjory and Willow came to stand next to Meredith.

"He's going to be fine. Might need some physical therapy, but most of the wounds are superficial enough not to cause worry," said Pops.

"Most?" asked Marjory.

"The ones on his torso are the worst, but Doc Jensen doesn't see the point of going into town when he can do everything here. We'll have to go get a prescription tomorrow." Pops started down the stairs. "Take me home, lover. All this drama wore me clean out."

Marjory waited at the landing, then tucked her arm into his. "I need you to hold me, Wes. I don't think my heart's stopped racing." He patted her hand, leaving Meredith and Willow behind.

"I could use another stiff drink since I have no one to hold me. You?" she asked Meredith.

Meredith shook her head. "Maybe after I get this off." She touched the rough, dried blood on her chest then went into the bathroom to scrub it off. It felt like an eternity before the doctor came downstairs and handed her a prescription and listed several things she should watch for, fever top of the list. After she saw out the doctor, Leo, and Tuck, she bounded up the stairs. Willow was sitting next to the bed, having pulled the rocking chair up so she could sit by her brother.

"He might be waking. I thought I'd keep him company until you got up here," she said.

"Thanks," Meredith mumbled as she stared at Jace. He was frighteningly pale.

"Here"—she jumped up and then pushed Meredith into the rocker—"rest. We'll split shifts watching over him. I'll give you some time with him then come back in an hour so you can get some sleep."

Meredith began to protest, but Willow hushed her and then quickly left the room.

With no one else around but Jace, Meredith let her tears fall again. She'd almost lost him. As it was, he could still get really sick with an infection or have complications. Meredith would not borrow trouble. Those potential problems would have to get in line if they wanted a chance at Jace.

She leaned toward him and brushed a lock of his hair back and whispered his name, the words "I love you" ready to spill out. She'd known she had these feelings yesterday at the barn dance, but today they needed to be said. She'd held her tongue with her father for years, and it had gotten her nowhere. Holding it in with Jace was not going to be a habit.

"I love you," she whispered. "Please wake up. I need you to tell me you're okay."

He stayed motionless, his breathing barely visible.

She whispered the words again. This time he mumbled, and Meredith sat up straight.

"Jace?"

His eyelids fluttered opened, then he blinked heavily a few times as if he was fighting the pull of unconsciousness.

"Hey babe," he croaked.

A relieved giggle escaped her. "Hey, want me to get you some water?" Without waiting for his response, she jumped up and dashed to the bathroom where she retrieved a small cup of water. Back at his side, she helped him raise his head to take a drink.

The work of it was obviously taxing as he was sweating when they were done.

"You're going to live," she told him. "A few cracked ribs and a bruised lung is the worst and you have all these stitches down your arm. Leo said the sum was in the sixties."

"I'm sorry." He winced as he shifted to free his uninjured hand from out beneath the covers, then took her hand.

His apology nearly broke her. He was likely in some serious pain and was thinking of her first.

"I'm so glad you're going to be okay." She squeezed and considered telling him again her feelings. This time while he was alert—ish.

Jace gave her a wolfish grin. "I'm sorry you're going to have to do all the work."

She stroked his hand with her thumb. "It's okay. It's what family does for one another."

He looked puzzled. "What? Family? More like wives. But some wives really like it and prefer it, actually." He yawned and then followed it up with a grin.

"Wives? What are you talking about?" She was beginning to think they were talking about two different things.

"I'm talking how you said we could fool around when we got home, but if you're wanting to get your goods from me, you're gonna have to climb on top and do all the work. I won't complain, though." He yawned again.

Meredith pulled her hand from his and crossed her arms. "You're talking about sex?"

"Yeah, you wanna give it a try?" He reached for her, but she slapped his hand away then stood up in anger.

"You're lying there with stitches holding you together because a bear clawed you. *A BEAR!* And you're propositioning me? That's the first thing to come to your mind? Sex?" She didn't bother to see his reaction instead she stormed out of the room.

The stupid man didn't deserve to hear what she had to say. She slammed the door to the guest room with as much force as she could muster.

26

Jace felt like a million bucks if that million bucks had been crapped all over and then lit on fire, only to be stomped out. Yet, he'd be damned if he was going to spend another full day in bed, much as his body would like. Seven days was his limit. He moved cautiously, stretching in slow motion so not to pull anything or pop stitches. His entire right side still felt like he'd rammed it repeatedly against a steel wall. Forget about taking a deep breath, the bandage around his ribs wasn't the only restriction. His stitches felt as if stretched to the breaking point even when he exhaled.

Getting out of bed was the hardest. Using his stomach muscles to come to sit, from any position, ached like a son of a bitch. Today, he considered waking Meredith, but she'd waited on him hand and foot for the last week and was exhausted. He looked to his side; Meredith was deep in sleep on the edge of the bed, one arm over her eyes, her breathing slow and steady.

Biting back a groan, he rolled to his non-injured side and pushed up slowly since that was the speed he was resigned to —sloth.

When he checked her again, she hadn't moved. The large blackish-purple bruise from the shotgun was beginning to fade, and he would be glad when it was gone. Every time he saw it, he was both angry and scared. That day could have gone so many different ways with horrifying outcomes. Because of Meredith, they were both alive.

She'd kicked off the covers. One quick skim down her long legs, her silky boxer shorts riding up her thigh, and he contemplated three different ways he could show her his appreciation. He'd easily come up with more except he was fighting a splitting headache, and last time he'd brought up sex, she'd slept in the guest room. It had taken lots of pleading and confessing he needed help to get her back in his bed.

Aspirin first, love the wife into oblivion second. She'd probably fight him some, concerned it might cause him discomfort, but he'd bring her around. He had to. He needed to be close to her, to feel her in ways that were deeper than holding her hand or kissing her lips. He swung his legs out of bed, then slowly eased to a stand.

Christ, he ached from head to toe. Twenty-six stitches had been required where the bear's claw had sliced into his shoulder and arm, but they'd been child's play since he'd passed out on the third stitch they'd put into his side.

"Where are you going?" she mumbled.

"Headache, and I'm hungry." Jace pulled on jeans, taking pleasure in knowing moving while upright was getting easier, fatiguing still, but easier a little bit every day.

"I'll get stuff for you. You should rest." She rolled from bed and stretched, her T-shirt rising slightly.

"You want me to stay in bed, then you'll have to get back in there with me and make it worth my while."

She narrowed her eyes. "Is there nothing else you think about other than sex?"

"The ranch." He loved to get her ire up.

She stuck one hand on her hip. "I'll have you know that your ranch is running perfectly well with me stepping in. In fact, Tuck and I have to check some fences today so I need to get moving."

"Great, but its time I get back to it. Can't stay in bed forever."

She rolled her eyes. "But you can stay in bed a bit longer to heal."

"If I stay up in this room another day, I might burn the house down just so I can get out of here." He was getting real squirrely and feeling caged in.

"Okay, but take it slow. Rest. Please." She waited for him to promise he would pace himself before disappearing into the bathroom. "Do you need me to help you downstairs?" she called through the door.

Jace tugged on a button down shirt. "I think I can manage." And even if he couldn't, he'd never tell her that.

Two aspirin and a full breakfast cooked by his sister's skilled hands, and Jace felt like he'd joined the living. Desperate to be of some use, he even did the dishes so that Willow could get to other chores. After he was done, he decided to sit outside and watch Tuck and Meredith with the horses and catch his breath. He snagged his Stetson from the closet, thankful Tuck had brought it home after he'd retrieved the bear and taken it into town to the vet for an autopsy.

Outside, he sucked in the biggest breath of air he could stand—which was pitifully small—and felt better instantly. He's missed the feel of the sun and the taste of fresh air, the smell of livestock caught on the edge of the breeze.

Forgoing the chair, he leaned against the rail instead.

Meredith waved. "You should be resting," she called across the yard.

"What do you call this?"

"Pure laziness," Tuck answered. "Real cowboys get back in the saddle."

"Man, you don't like your job?" Harassing each other was a longtime favorite past time for him and Tuck.

Feeling like he could just as easily lean against the corral as he could the porch railing, Jace decided to make his way to Tuck and Meredith. He was halfway there when the sound of glass shattering came from his parents' cabin.

Seconds later, his mom screamed, "Oh my God, Wes!" in a voice so frightened his heart skipped a beat. Without care or consideration for his wounds, Jace ran to the cabin, though the heartbreak in her shriek told him he was already too late.

27

For Pop's funeral, the city shut down as the good folks of Bison's Prairie said goodbye to one of their own. Jace watched the grave diggers—one of whom he went to high school with—lower his father's casket into the ground.

For the preceding three days before the funeral, an endless line of well-meaning locals cycled through their house bringing food, flowers, and stories of Pop's that were so inflated they could be called tall tales. Listening to them only made the painful throbbing in his chest ache more. This was a wound that would never heal, no matter what they said about time's potency. The open space in his heart created when Pops died could not be stitched closed.

Meredith slid her arms through his and leaned her head on his shoulder. "Do you want to be alone?"

Wasn't he already on some level? It was now up to him to make all the decisions on the ranch. To carry out the ideas of his father and to do so without said visionary to guide him. Jace looked over at the big house. His mother and sister were on the porch talking with others. They put up a good front, but he could tell they were holding it together with duct tape and spit. Much like he was. Of course, he had Meredith, too.

"I'm okay. Let's go help out Mom and Willow." Following one final look, he nodded to his father's casket then walked with Meredith to the house.

They fed what seemed like hundreds of people, and by early evening Jace could no longer ignore the pounding in his head. In the kitchen, he found the aspirin and choked down dry two pills. Then he leaned against the island to catch his breath, wishing coffee would magically appear. Or a large tumbler of whisky.

A tall, older, balding man came into the room. He was dressed in dark dress pants and a polo. Jace knew his type. Corporate. Right down to his suede shoes. He'd dealt with them during auctions. This guy looked like he enjoyed playing hardball. He also looked out of his element.

"I'm sorry for your loss," the man said and pointed to two glasses drying by the sink. "May I?"

"Be my guest." Jace sunk into a stool. "I don't mean to be rude, but who are you?"

The man pulled from his pocket a flask and poured two fingers of gold-colored liquid into each glass. He handed one to Jace. "I'm Marcus Hanover, Meredith's father." He extended his hand.

Jace straightened and stuck his hand into the older man's. He didn't see any resemblance to Meredith. So this was the guy Meredith was running from. She had thought life with a stranger was better than staying with her own blood.

He should kick him out. Trouble was, Jace was in no shape to do that.

"Does Meredith know you're here?" He wondered what she thought of her two worlds colliding.

"Not yet." Hanover gestured to the stool next to him. "May I?"

"Sure." Using the tip of his boot, Jace pushed the second stool to him.

When Hanover sat, he did so with a weary sigh. "I'm sure you don't have a good impression of me. If I were to go by Meredith's perception, I wouldn't have one of me as well."

Jace waited. He wasn't about to make him feel good or bad about what had transpired between him and Meredith.

Hanover nodded. "I'd like to explain my actions from my perspective."

"Your side of the story." Jace sipped the whisky, a rich and smooth full-bodied spirit that spoke of money.

Hanover sighed. "When I met Meredith's mother, she was the same age Meredith is now. I was older, established, and set in my ways. I will never understand what she saw in me." He smiled sadly. "I grew up with demanding, cold parents so being the same was all I knew. Until Rebecca. She showed me it could be different. It sounds stupid, but I'm an old man whose daughter wants nothing to do with him, so I'll just say it—Rebecca added color to my life. When she died…" He shook his head, his thumb running the rim of his glass. "When she died, everything went dark again. And Meredith paid for that."

"You should tell this to Meredith."

Hanover shook his head. "She won't hear it. Why should she?" He swiveled to Jace, intensity winging his brows. "You have to understand something. Meredith is all I have left. When she disappeared, it was like losing her mother all over again. I can't lose her. I won't survive it. Did she tell you how her mother died?"

Jace nodded.

"I almost lost Meredith then, as well. For weeks I watched her struggle on a ventilator, and I promised that, should she live, I would do everything in my power to protect her. I was the luckiest dad alive when I got that second chance, and then one day she disappears. I was relieved beyond measure when the private investigator found her. Thought I'd keep my eyes on things until I heard about your bear attack."

"Your daughter saved my life."

Hanover pressed his lips and shook his head as if trying to erase the image. "I try to imagine her being in that situation and..." He tossed back the remainder of his drink. "Please understand that I can't lose her. You want to protect her as well, don't you? Help me protect her. Tell her to come home with me. I can keep her safe there." His words were urgent and pleading.

Jace was weary and standing at the crossroads. His father was dead, the deal he and Meredith had struck was now null and void, yet the last thing he wanted was for Meredith to leave. She fit in here. "She's my wife. Do you think I can't protect her?"

Hanover looked at his chest as if he could see through the suit Jace was wearing to the wounds underneath.

"That's not something that happens all the time. Hell, it doesn't even happen every year. Just a random occurrence."

Hanover shook his head. "Yes, and planes crashes are random occurrences, too."

Fuck. Who was he to take a man's child from him or to want Meredith to have her past unresolved. It was one thing to choose not to go home but something completely different when one couldn't. From the moment his family was given Pop's diagnosis, Jace had tried to make the most of the days with his dad. He would never want to be the reason she never had that with her own father. Ideally, he'd like to see Hanover and Meredith find some middle ground.

He stood quickly, unable to hide the wince that followed the sharp pain in his ribs. He was ready to leave this conversation, desperate to get outside and clear his head. He needed to know one thing, and that was what Meredith would do now that her father had come.

"Why don't you talk to your daughter first? Let's see what she has to say." Would she be able to forgive a repentant man?

Hanover nodded. "But I think she'll listen to you. She's hiding here from me. If you could tell her to come home and just see how it's changed—"

Jace shook his head.

"Do you really want her here knowing she might still be running from her old life? Wouldn't you want her here because she wants to be? You're her first real boyfriend." Hanover plunged the metaphorical knife.

"I'm her husband."

Then Hanover twisted said knife, not once but twice. "You're a novelty. Do you have what it takes to sustain it? Like what your parents had?"

"Don't talk about my parents. You know nothing about them and what they had." Jace shook with anger. He didn't want to deal with this. He wanted to grieve for his father.

"I've been listening to stories for the last few hours about your father. He sounds like a remarkable man, one who would raise a remarkable son. Ask yourself if you are happy with the way things are right now."

Jace shifted. Nothing would give him more peace of mind than knowing where Meredith's heart and intentions lay. Especially after the last week. She was probably scared, shaken to the core. Life on the ranch was more than her garden and a snake in the coop, and he wasn't sure she was ready to embrace that anymore.

He stared Hanover down. "I'll talk to her, but I'm not making any promises."

Hanover jumped up. "That's all I can ask for." He extended his hand.

"Promise to do what," Meredith said, standing in the doorway. She stared at her father, her expression...angry?

"Meredith," Hanover said, dropping his hand to his side.

"Why are you here?" She crossed her arms over her chest and moved to stand next to Jace.

"Why did you leave?" He stepped toward them, but Meredith put her hand up, stopping him.

"I should leave you two alone." Jace stepped away.

"You can stay. There's nothing he can say that is worth hearing." She stood ramrod straight.

Hanover took a seat on the stool, his shoulders slumped in defeat. "Hear me out, please."

Jace gave her arm a squeeze and left her alone with her father.

F or a man who'd spent the last eight years speaking only to her with words heavy in irritation, derision, or intolerance, he was unnervingly calm and...well, the look on his face was off. On anyone else, she would think he was sad. Marcus Hanover the Third didn't do sad. Not since his wife had died, and certainly not when he found his runaway daughter.

"Are you going to start talking soon? Because you are crashing a funeral, if you haven't noticed, and the last thing I want for these people is to make their day worse by causing a scene. So say what you want and leave."

"I want to know why you ran away. I have my ideas, but I need to hear it from you."

"Why would I stay, Father? What was there for me?" She was no longer afraid to speak her mind. This was her home, and she was surrounded by people who cared about her and wanted the best for her. It was the Shepards who had filled the emptiness in her life.

"Meredith, I will not tolerate that tone—"

Meredith tossed her head back with a derisive laugh. "You

won't tolerate that tone? You want to know why I left? That's one reason right there. You're a cold, unloving man, and I'd rather live with complete strangers than another day being your patsy. Not once did you ask me what I wanted. Not once did you show concern for me and my well-being." She pointed to the door. "You need to leave. Now. You need to leave and never come back."

Briefly, her father looked away, and when he looked back, tears glistened in his eyes. For the first time since her mother had died, she saw the man who'd taught her to ride a bike. She saw the softness in his expression, a look she remembered from her childhood.

"I'm sorry Meredith. Everything I did was because I—"

"Don't say it was because you love me." She shook her head. "Love doesn't look like that."

"But fear does." Father wiped a tear from under his eye and stood. "You were all I had left. That alone frightened me. I wanted to protect you while protecting myself in case I lost you."

"That doesn't explain why you used me for your business purposes."

"Initially, I thought I was giving you a purpose, too, a job of sorts. Then having you work the crowd simply became my modus apparatus. It was easier to be that type of guy than a worrying father." His gaze never wavered from hers.

Meredith was lost for words. In the beginning, this conversation was all she wanted from her father, to understand why. Now? It would take more. Something big. He'd broken her trust, and getting that back would take work and time.

"Father—"

"Just think about coming home with me. Talk with that—your—your husband." He stepped up to her and, catching her off guard, pulled her into a hug. "I'm so relieved you are all right," he said before letting her go. After a final squeeze to the shoulders, he kissed her forehead and left.

Shocked to her core, Meredith didn't know what to do next, at least as far as her father was concerned. Hopefully she and Jace would get a chance to talk about it tonight. If he was up for it.

After all the guests had left and Willow had gone back to the cabin with her mom, Meredith found Jace sitting in the dark in his office, a bottle of whisky beside him.

"Hey," she said softly.

He nodded.

"Want me to start a fire?" There was a chill in the room, and she wrapped her arms around herself while moving toward the fireplace.

"Leave it," he said and set his tumbler on his desk.

"Can I get you anything?" She wanted to take his pain away.

He shook his head. "What's the deal with your dad?"

"There is no deal. He left." Maybe talking about him right now wasn't a good idea. There was a weird vibe in the room. She expected grief, but anger seemed to be present as well. She supposed that was how men dealt with their emotions.

"He'll be back." Jace sat forward and grabbed her hand, then pulled her before him.

"Yes, I'm sure he will." She looked down, trying to read his expression, but he was staring at her chest. "Why don't we go to bed," she suggested.

He shook his head, then slid his other hand under her skirt, up her thigh, and then skimmed his fingers across the seam of her panties.

"Jace," she whispered, her knees wobbly.

He tugged her closer, her legs bumping the chair as she came to stand between his legs. He tugged again, and she nearly fell into his lap. Sensing what he wanted, she leaned forward and climbed onto his lap, straddling him, her skirt rising to her hips. Clothes weren't removed, only shoved aside. Lips brushed across bodies, and his hand tangled in her hair, clutching tightly. He took her there with such fierceness and urgency she felt as if they were racing against something. Being caught? Time? She wasn't sure, but the frenzied need called out the loudest so she ignored everything else but that. When it was over, he led her to bed where they repeated it, only this time with less urgency and more sadness. No words, only touch with Jace running his hands over her body as if he was memorizing every curve.

They fell asleep in each other's arms.

29

Watching Meredith sleep was amazing and painful at the same time. Painful because he'd forgotten that she might not always be there and this might, in fact, be the last time he would be able to enjoy this voyeuristic activity. Jace was an honorable man who was compelled to do the right thing. Too bad he didn't know what that was. Pops would know what to tell him, and not being able to ask made the ache in Jace's chest throb harder. At least his old man had died happy and, hell, Jace was thankful Pop's heart attack had been quick, his death instantaneous. There would be no wheelchairs or ventilators, which Jace tried to see as a silver lining. Pops would have hated that. Jace hated the whole damned situation. He simply wanted his dad back.

Brushing a hand down his face, then wiping his eyes, Jace decided coffee might help him swallow the lump in his throat. He knew what needed to be done.

Downstairs he made a large pot of coffee and stuffed a dinner roll from last night's wake in his mouth. He would check the herd and feed the chickens, but not before he spent a few minutes sitting on the fence. Tuck would be in soon, but Jace needed some time to clear his mind, come to terms with his decision. Maybe he'd talk to Pops out there. After filling a Thermos, he pulled on his jacket. His boots—still speckled with blood—were by the door and reminded him that his mom could have been burying her son and husband within a two-week period. He could understand Hanover's angst about Meredith. Following a quick glance at the empty stairs, he quietly left the house. His mom's cabin was dark, and he hesitated, wondering if he should check on her.

He'd let the sun rise fully first. He sat on the fence—no small feat getting up with his aching ribs and bruised lungs—and weighed the options of Meredith staying, leaving, the ranch, Willow, and all the responsibility that was now his. With the sun high in the sky and the roosters crowing, Jace couldn't linger any longer and got about starting the daily chores. His mother sat on the porch of her cabin with a mug of something hot—likely coffee—and gave him a sad wave before looking away. He left her to her thoughts.

He was coming out of the barn when a small limo came down the lane. It stopped by the porch stairs, and Hanover stepped out. Meredith was on the porch in a flash, arms crossed, and a scowl on her face. He couldn't hear what they were saying, but Jace could read her body language. Whatever Hanover was saying was working. Meredith's arms dropped to her hips as she faced her father. When he pulled her into a hug, Meredith didn't resist. When they separated, she caught sight of Jace and bee-lined for him, Hanover waiting on the porch.

"Hey, did you get any sleep?" She stepped close and searched his face. She was stunning with the morning sun behind her, no makeup on her face, and how he loved her ponytail. She looked every bit suited for the ranch, but hadn't that been her role with her father? To blend in? He didn't want to question the past months, but the lack of sleep, the onslaught of grief, and the easy-found doubt were prominent in his mind.

"Enough." He glanced at her father. "What's he want?" Though he could take a stab at it and likely hit the mark.

"He wants to stay for a bit. I know the timing isn't the best but..."

Well, Christ on the cross. He was about to do something stupid, except he needed to know. If she stayed, he would always wonder if it was because she was too afraid of what was waiting for her on the other side. He wanted to be the greener grass for her. He wanted to be where her heart and soul craved to be. Like his heart and soul did. He didn't want to be her hideout. Yes, he craved her, too, but letting her go now would hurt far less than her leaving unexpectedly. Especially knowing he'd been too chicken shit to set her free.

What was that stupid ass saying? If you love someone set them free?

He leaned against the fence and touched her shoulder. "How does this feel?"

"Awful, but the ringing in my ears is getting softer. That's a good thing." She smiled.

"It could have gone horribly wrong," Jace said. His body ached as he imagined what today would be like had the bear attacked her or killed either or both of them.

"I am well aware of that. For a while, I think I'll stay close to home."

"And you want your father to be here?"

"I think this is a safe place to face him, don't you?"

Jace looked at her father's limo, so out of place, and he decided to make a clean cut. "I think you should go home with your father."

Meredith laughed nervously. "What did he say to you yesterday in the kitchen, because you know how he is."

He would not let her hide out here. He was no better than hen shit on a pump handle if he did that. He stared at the splatter of blood across his boot. "He's missed you."

She snorted. "He missed controlling me. He missed using me. He missed—"

"He talked about losing your mother and then losing you, Meredith. He's scared and hurt."

"Bullshit." She shook her head.

"Do you really believe it's bullshit? What if he were to die tomorrow? Would you be okay with how things are right now?" Jace glanced at the cabin where Pops had lived. "He's all the family you have left."

Meredith's hesitation was all the indication Jace needed; he was doing the right thing. If she went with her father and wasn't able to find a middle ground with him, then so be it. At least she'd tried. He wanted that for her. He wanted her to have that peace, and he would spend the rest of his days trying to fill that void in her if that were to be the case. If she came back.

"Are you telling me to leave?" She stepped away, searching his face.

"I'm saying you should have some answers."

"I have all the answers I need. I—" She pointed to her father.

"Your answers are based on limited information." Over her shoulder, he noticed his mother was watching them from her porch.

"Do you want me to leave?" Her eyes were wide, her face pale. "That's it, right. You want me to leave. We struck a deal, and now that Pops is—" She looked away, tears filling her eyes. "It really was only a deal and nothing more."

"I want you to be sure of the choices you make. I spoke with your father—"

"And the two of you know me better than anyone and went

ahead and decided everything without so much as asking me what I wanted." She gave a curt nod and crossed her arms.

"Meredith—"

"You know what's crazy?" She waited for him to shake his head. "I love you," she whispered. "There is nowhere—"

"I'm sure you think you do love me. I've given you a safe place to hide and a chance to have a life. But it was a limited one, here on the ranch. Now you have a chance to do whatever, go wherever, and be whoever you want to be. You need to know what it is you want. You need to be sure about who you are."

They stood facing each other, though neither looking the other in the eye. The air around them seemed to still, as did the animals. Yesterday, they'd made love in the sweetest way. They'd embraced their life, mourned the loss of Pops, and rejoiced in the breaths they took since surviving the bear. Today they were talking about living those lives apart. Well, Jace was. But who were either of them to decide something for the other?

Meredith closed her eyes and tried to think beyond the heartache she was feeling. She'd just told Jace she loved him, and he'd basically Han Solo'd her. Like she'd feared he would. Who was she, he wanted to know? Today of all days, she'd woken more clear about who she was and what she wanted.

"I know who I want to be. I'm already that person. I like who I am." She wrapped her arms around her chest, hoping to hold her body together and hide the trembling that was about to overtake her and break her into a thousand pieces.

"I think—"

"You think? What about what I think? I suppose that doesn't matter now that you have your ranch. Goal achieved."

"You haven't had enough of living your life to say that, Meredith. You should go." He kicked the dirt with his toe while pulling his hat lower on his face. "In fact, I should go, too. Lots of cattle to round up, and your father is waiting." He looked over her shoulder to the waiting limo.

Meredith searched his face and found nothing of the Jace she'd come to know and love. This stranger was cold and distant. She stepped back and noticed his mother. He'd even had the gall to say her father was the only family she had. Didn't Marjory and Willow count? She was grieving Pops as much as the rest of them. The world seemed to close in around her, colors muted. Everything to the side of her faded away as the world before her narrowed and began to disappear.

She swallowed and gave a small wave to Marjory. Her throat tightened. When Jace bent to pick up the lasso, groaning from the stiffness, she didn't feel sorry for him. She'd saved his fool neck, and this was his life revelation? Normal people wanted to do more, see more, and be more. He just wanted her to go away so he could get back to work.

She narrowed her gaze, his backside facing her. Something inside her snapped. It was so loud she jumped, and she could hear it echo on the wind. The colors of her world were tinged with the red of anger. She lifted her booted foot and, with all her might, planted it against his butt and shoved. He went sprawling into the ground face first.

"You're a stupid, stupid man, Jace Shepard. And you don't deserve me." She spun on her heel and stomped toward her father's car.

"What about your stuff?" he called.

"There's nothing here I want," she yelled back.

Meredith waited until the car was off Shepard property before she broke down.

30

Sabrina stared at him like she wanted to do to him what they did to the turkey at thanksgiving—break his neck.

She'd come a few days after Pop's funeral, having been out of the country, and until now he'd done a good job of avoiding her, knowing if she got him alone she'd chew his ass.

He'd been right. His urge to sit on the fence and mope had gotten the best of him and, risking the chance, he'd come out to watch the sunrise and lick his wounds. Sabrina had found him moments later.

"I can't believe you let her go." She held up one finger. "I'm going to ask this next question even though I'm confident I already know the answer. Before you told her to leave, did you by chance tell her how you felt?" She stepped close and looked at him, shoving his hat up and away from his face.

"Ah, well..."

"I'll take that as a no. I'm going to also guess that part of why you didn't was because you wanted to test her. To see if she'd come back on her own. Am I wrong?"

Jace sighed and rubbed his hand along the wound on his

side. It ached something fierce. The pain actually radiated from the center of his chest and moved outward and left him breathless all the long damn day.

"You're a moron. A big gigantic stupid ass imbecile." She crossed her arms, her foot tapping madly, causing the grass to swish slightly.

He nodded. "Yeah, I reckoned you'd see it that way." Frankly, he saw it that way, too. Every night he thought of at least a handful of different, better ways he could have handled that last day with Meredith.

"How do you see it, Jace? Another relationship that didn't work? You expected her to go so you made sure she did?"

"Well, Rina, it was a little like playing house, to be honest." He'd been telling himself that for the four days she'd been gone. Even though her clothes were in the closet, her dog-eared Farmer's Almanac on the bedside table, her toothbrush in the holder. Knowing she was alive and okay was what kept him from destroying the house with his grief. Because what if she did come back? Having her stuff ready for her would say that she was welcome. Or so he hoped.

Rina stepped close and slapped him upside the head. "If you weren't wounded, I'd punch you in the gut for that stupid remark."

"Come on, tell me it wasn't." Please. He needed to know she hadn't been buying time with him and his family.

Sabrina blinked at him, owlish. "Oh, sure. Okay. How about I find you another bride, and you can start over? Maybe a blonde this time? Here, I might have some pictures." She fumbled her phone out of her pocket.

Jace couldn't even imagine another woman. Each fantasy in his head starred Meredith.

"Shit, Rina. What should I have done?" He pounded his fist into the wood rail he was sitting on.

"Let me tell you what Meredith heard, and then you can tell me what you think you should do. Because you've already done the damage. Whether you fix it or not is up to you."

Jace nodded and waited.

"You never told her that this was her home."

"Yeah, but then she would've stayed from guilt or comfort or whatever."

"Are you really that stupid? You have to stop expecting women to leave you, Jace, just because three women who weren't right for you to begin with did."

Begrudgingly, Jace admitted he'd fucked up. He left them too open-ended, allowing too much room for interpretation. She didn't know how he felt any more than he knew how she felt. Sure, he had told her with his hands and body, but that just made the feelings all the more confusing. Basically, he'd deserted her. Jace repeatedly tapped his hand against the post, struggling with the emotions that came with acknowledging he was indeed an imbecile and he alone was responsible for pushing her out the door. She'd be a fool to want a horse's ass like him. She was right. He didn't deserve her. Though he desperately wanted her.

"What are you going to do?" Sabrina came to rest against the post, her voice softer and, dare he hope, offering help?

"I dunno." Honesty was the way to go forward with this. That, at least, he knew.

"I suppose you should ask yourself—do you want to wait to see if she comes back, or do you want to go after her and find out how she feels? Which works better for you?"

Jace hopped off the fence, his side screaming with the sudden movement. "Where do I find her?" He was ready to go now. Without a doubt. He'd rather her turn him away and know for sure than always wonder what could have been.

"Funny you should ask that. I happen to know where she'll

be tonight." Sabrina started walking to the house, but he quickly outpaced her.

One flight and six hours later, he was dressed in his best suit, the one he'd worn when he married Meredith, and stood outside an art gallery in Dallas. Sabrina slapped him on the back and wished him luck, then disappeared into the building, leaving him to figure the rest out on his own. Inside, a low buzz of chatter filled the space, and an attendant handed him a program. A quick glance at the paper told him he was at a silent auction for a veteran's home. Jace spotted a bar in the center of the room and figured there was a good place to start. He was out of his element and needed to get his bearings before he spoke with Meredith. He had one shot and wanted it to be perfect.

The ambience was cold, the glass structure of the building and angled lines partly to blame for the unfriendliness and insincerity of the place. The people only exemplified it. The men were in tuxedos, the women in whatever sexy gown they could pull off and sporting jewels that glistened brighter than the chandeliers.

31

Meredith tossed back a brandy and fought back the headache, stepping closer to the shade of the fake potted plant she was using for cover.

She and her father had come to mutually agreeable terms and were beginning their new relationship like Jace had wanted, and to be honest, she did as well. Not without some reservation, her father was giving her the freedom to fly, even offered to buy her a house, in his neighborhood, of course. All-in-all, it was a good start. Her act of good faith was to attend this one event. Though, knowing it had been her mother's favorite charity fundraiser hadn't helped to stave off her anger at the excessive-ness of it all. Why couldn't people just give money to the veter-ans? Why did they need to get a material object in exchange? Shouldn't the selfless act of giving be enough? She wholly regretted coming. The chitchat was inane, the auction items excessive, and the food over processed.

Meredith snorted. She'd become a new sort of snob, the kind that knew there was more out there, better living, and it had nothing to do with socioeconomic status symbols. She was spoiled from eating fresh from her garden, a reward from her hard work. From witnessing Mother Nature's glory as the seasons changed, and experiencing the touch of a man who found her breathtaking. The ass! He'd ruined everything. Thanksgiving was coming. Thoughts of the holiday made her wonder how it would be spent on the ranch, a holiday she'd been looking forward to. Would it be like one of those in a Hallmark movie? Fun and full of family love and cheer?

Darn that Jace Shepard and his stubborn ways! She wanted to clock him for his stupidity. She wanted to give him a piece of her mind, but in reality was too scared to go to him. A second rejection would devastate her. She wanted him back desperately.

"You look like you lost your best friend."

Meredith jumped and slowly faced Sabrina. "I'm sure you have a whole lot of things to say to me, but I don't want to hear them." For emphasis, Meredith waved her hand as if pushing away the impending conversation. "If you're here for your money since I didn't stay a year, ask your friend. He's the one who told me to leave."

"You'll be surprised because I actually have nothing to say." Sabrina handed her a champagne glass.

"Nothing? Really?" Meredith scanned the crowd. She had to keep her eye on Lyle Brady. He'd already tried to get close to her earlier, and she feared his wandering hands would result in her slapping his face. A scene she did not want. She spotted him a few clusters of people away.

"Well, not really. I mean, I might ask you what you plan on doing once you figure out what it is you want. But I'm guessing you haven't gotten there yet."

Meredith snorted and honed her focus on Sabrina. "I'm there. It's your fool friend who's clueless."

Sabrina raised a brow. "Oh, is that so? Are you doing something about it then?"

Anger shot through Meredith. "What can I do? He asked me to leave. He basically said he didn't want me anymore."

Sabrina grimaced. "Did he really, or did you think that's what he was implying? I'm sure you've figured out that men really suck at communication."

Meredith rubbed her temple. "I don't know Sabrina. It's all so confusing."

"You could try going for what you want." Sabrina tapped her glass to Meredith's. Then said, "Just a thought," before walking away in a swoosh of her skirt.

Meredith sighed and chugged back her champagne. Sabrina was right. She did need to go for what she wanted instead of hiding behind a plant feeling sorry for herself. Hell, she'd killed a grizzly bear. Conquering Jace Shepard had to be easier.

Someone ran their hand down Meredith's backside, causing her to gasp with surprise. She swung around and found Mr. Brady leering at her.

"I brought you another champagne, dear," he said and forced the glass into her chest, his knuckles brushing her breast.

"Get your hands off my chest, Mr. Brady. You should be ashamed of yourself." She didn't step back, afraid it would look like weakness to him.

"Because I enjoy touching a beautiful woman?" He snorted, his hand staying against her.

"Because you have no right." She bit out the words, "Remove your hand."

His eyes widened, and then he laughed. "What happened to sweet, compliant Meredith?" He stepped closer, his hand going up and down the outside of her dress, curving around her boob.

"She killed a bear and therefore is no longer intimidated by you. This is my last warning." She stepped aside and thrust his hand away, champagne splashing over the rim.

"Look what you've done." He leaned close to her face,

pinching her chin between his thumb and index finger. "I might have to spank you for that."

A shiver of repulsion ran through her. Nothing about that sounded sexy. Every bit of it was meant to be controlling and demeaning.

Meredith stared him in the eyes "I warned you." She lifted her skirt. Lyle's brows shot into his hairline, excited pleasure rippling over his face. Once her leg had enough room to move, she swung it back and kneed him in the groin, dropping him.

"I asked you to stop touching me. If you ever do it again, I will put more force into my swing. You understand me? And as for compliant Meredith? She got tired of being pushed around by people like you." She didn't wait for a response, but floated away, riding a magic carpet of pleasure and self-pride.

She felt good. Damn good. Next battle, Jace Shepard. She'd already told her father she wouldn't live with him, but they could continue to talk and work on their relationship. She now needed to tell him that would have to happen in Wyoming. She was going home. She would tackle her fear of Jace not wanting her later.

She was halfway to the exit when she heard her name echo across the art gallery's large, open room. She turned toward it, expecting to find her father and his anger. Jace stood by the bar dressed like he had the first day she met him. She blinked to clear her eyes, thinking it was a mirage.

Nope, it was him.

How crazy had she been to think this man wouldn't suit her? To believe he might have been harsh without knowing anything about him. He walked toward her, his Stetson on his head, his face shadowed, but she didn't need to see him in full light to know what he looked like. He was etched on her heart. She saw him everywhere she looked.

Now here he was. She met him halfway, swallowing the large

lump of fear that had gripped her throat. It had to be good that he was here, right? He wouldn't come all this way to give her a toothbrush, would he?

When they stood before each other, the chatter around them halted. Meredith crossed her arms over her chest and stood straight. "I have something to say to you, Jace Shepard."

"I'm sure you do, but may I go first?" He took off his hat and brushed back his hair.

She fairly swooned, the stupid man, playing with her like that.

"Be my guest," she said, hoping she sounded terse and not weak. She might throw herself on him at any moment.

"The other day, when you left, I meant to say something, but I neglected to." He ducked his head then looked up at her.

Her heart slammed into her chest. The look of regret on his face was sending a signal she wasn't sure she was reading correctly. It felt a lot like another break up.

"Well, get on with it." She clenched her teeth so she wouldn't cry.

"I meant to say I thought you should go and try to make amends with your father. Life is too short to have bad blood between you."

She opened her mouth to tell him off. She already knew this, but he put his hand over her mouth to shush her.

"I also meant to say I would go with you if you wanted, but if it was something you needed to do alone, I understood. I want you to know that I'll be waiting for you should you decide to come home." He nodded once, kissed her cheek, and then stepped back. He turned on his heel and walked away.

Meredith's mouth fell open as she processed his words. Was that a declaration of something?

"That's it?" she called to his back.

He turned. "Pretty much." He set his Stetson on his head. "You need something more?"

Time to go for broke. "Yes, actually."

Jace nodded as if in thought. "I see."

She threw her hands up in disgust. "You see? You are the daftest man I have ever met, and I have met a ton. Look around you. This room is filled with them, but right now you're leading the pack."

Jace laughed. "I love you, Meredith, and I want you to come home. I want to have babies with you, talk about the garden every year, but we can skip killing large wildlife if you don't mind. I've had my fill with that."

Instantly, she burst into tears, covering her face. She felt his arms slip around her.

"Babe, don't cry. Be happy."

"I am happy. Now," she said between her hands.

"Me, too," he said, peeling her hands from her face. He cupped her cheeks and delivered a soft, yet desperate kiss to her lips.

EPILOGUE

Two Years later

Meredith walked across the prairie, each step sinking slightly into the freshly fallen snow. The sun would be setting soon, and she wanted to get to the fence before it did.

"Here," she huffed and handed Jace the thermos of coffee. He jumped off the fence, took the thermos, and set it aside. He offered his hand to help her up.

"You sure this thing can hold me?" she asked, one foot resting on the rail and pressing down.

"Yeah, even with that fat baby in your belly, I still weigh more than you. Here, let me help." Groaning, he pushed at her ass to pretend to lift her.

"You aren't funny," she said and situated herself on the top rail.

"I know, but you're overly worried, and it's my poor attempt to take your mind off it." He picked up the thermos and sat next to her.

"Wouldn't you be worried about squeezing this ginormous thing out? Especially after all that talk about how big a head you had and—"

"I promise, it's going to be okay." He draped an arm around her.

"You can't promise that." She relieved him of the thermos and poured them both coffee.

"Mer, we'll have Thanksgiving with our family tomorrow, and on Friday head into the big city to wait for this bruiser. We can go to book stores or chocolate stores or whatever you want."

Even though she was a week out from her due date, she was apprehensive and ready to get close to the hospital. Sure, she could have the baby in town at the clinic, but she wanted more than a family doc. She wanted a practiced baby doctor who was ready to give out meds.

To distract herself from her worry, she went through her list of dishes she needed to make tomorrow. It was their second Thanksgiving together.

"Listen, I know we sorta talked about names, but I'd really like to name him after my dad," said Jace.

Meredith nodded. "If it's a boy, I'm in full agreement with that. If it's a girl, I'd like to go with my mom's name, Rebecca."

Jace nodded. "I like the sound of both of those." He leaned across and brushed a kiss on her temple.

"I think my dad is lonely. He comes out here a lot, but even here he seems sad or maybe...I don't know. I want to do something for him."

"Besides giving him a grandchild?" Jace chuckled.

"Yeah, besides that. I have a crazy idea. How about we ask Sabrina to, you know, match him?" She cut her eyes to Jace, curious to see his reaction.

He sipped his coffee before answering. "Find your dad a wife? I'm not sure even Sabrina can manage that."

Meredith laughed. "True. Maybe we should build another cabin on the property and let my dad live there?"

Jace choked on his coffee. "I'll call Sabrina in the morning."

Meredith sat up straight and sucked in a breath.

Jace laughed and nudged her shoulder. "That desperate, are you? I'll call her now if you want."

Meredith shook her head.

"What's the matter then?" He searched her face, before realization dawned. "Christ, now?" He jumped from the fence, tossing the thermos into the snow, spilling coffee everywhere.

"I think we have a little time. It's just my water." She let him lift her off the fence. "We can stay and watch the sunset."

"You're crazy woman," Jace said, swinging her up in his arms and trotting off.

"I can walk," she said between laughs. "Put me down. You're going to shake this kid out of me."

Jace stopped short and eased her to her feet. "Are you sure you're okay to walk?"

"No, but it's way more comfortable than having you jostle me home." She grabbed her belly and grimaced.

"Stay here. I'll get the truck and come get you." He jogged off.

Meredith continued to walk. She was not about to be left in a field to birth her child like a cow. No matter how much a cowboy her husband was. She was a hundred yards from the house when he brought the truck to a screeching halt beside her. He ran around the truck and opened the passenger door, ushering her in.

"We'll make it to town in no time," he assured her and peeled out.

"Let's hope so," she said, and between contractions called the doctor then his mother.

The thirty-minute ride to town took fifteen, and three hours later Wesley Jace Shepard was born. Mother and baby were doing well. Wesley's father passed out immediately after he cut the cord.

It was another tradition they would add to their family.

———

Enjoyed Jace and Meredith's story? Well, come hang out with Cori and Fort. They used to be childhood enemies and now she's been hired to pretend to be his fiancee. Sparks are guaranteed to fly.

Open your phone's camera
to scan the QR code and
SAVE

Link will take you to
KristiRoseBooks.com
Buying from me means a
deal for you.

MEET KRISTI ROSE

Hey! I'm Kristi. I'm the mom of 2 and a milspouse (retired). We live in the Pacific Northwest and are under-prepared if one of the volcanoes erupts.

I grew up in Central Florida and have skied in lakes with gators.

I'd love to get to know you better. Join my Read & Relax community and then fire off an email and tell me 3 things about you!

Not ready to join? Email me below or follow me at one of the links below. Thanks for popping by!

You can connect with Kristi at any of the following:
www.kristirose.net
kristi@kristirose.net

BOOKS BY KRISTI ROSE

The Wyoming Matchmaker Series Whether marriage of convenience or star crossed lovers, everyone earns their happily ever after in this series.

The Cowboy Takes A Bride

The Cowboy's Make Believe Bride

The Cowboy's Runaway Bride

Book 4 Coming 2024

————

The No Strings Attached Series- A flirty, fun chick lit romance series

The Girl He Knows

The Girl He Wants

The Girl He Loves

Beach Town Love- boxset

————

Samantha True Mysteries- These laugh out loud, action pack books take place in the Pacific Northwest. Join Samantha, an adult with dyslexia who's hid behind photography, on her adventures in her new life as a Private Investigator. A job she inherited when her new husband died unexpectedly and left behind a mess and another wife.

One Hit Wonder

All Bets Are Off

Best Laid Plans

Caught Off Guard

Two Time Loser

Dodged A Bullet

Audiobooks

———

The Cold Case Mystery Series:

Bone of Contention

———

PERFECT PLACE: A Liars Island Suspense

Perfect Place

Campus Murder Club (YA Thriller)

Campus Murder Club

.

Milton Keynes UK
Ingram Content Group UK Ltd.
UKHW020945120424
440994UK00014B/380

9 781088 263778